BETWEEN SONG AND SEA

EVELYN GRIMALD

TARNEY BRAE CREATIVE ENDEAVOURS

For my Wild Willow

CONTENTS

AUTHOR'S NOTE

This book is the second book in the Forgotten Magics series. While each book can be read as a standalone, there are some characters and interconnected arcs that may appear in more than one book.

Also, this book contains a story about sirens, selkies and druids. Be aware that only the bare bones of these creatures are taken from actual myth. Most of the information you will find is completely and totally made up for the sake of story.

I hope you enjoy this magical adventure and don't mind the few liberties I've taken.

~ Evelyn

PROLOGUE

He carried his child in his teeth and swam for the sake of every scrap of magic in her tiny body. He prayed to long forgotten deities that the currents would carry him fast enough to escape the things that were sure to follow after. He prayed that he could keep his daughter safe until he reached land. After that, well…there was very little that was safe on land for his kind, but right now the sea was far more perilous for the precious creature in his teeth.

The sky was dark and starless by the time he flopped out of the water, his seal's body ungainly in the shallows between land and sea, especially with his pup in his teeth. Finally, shoving himself onto the beach with his front flippers, he was far enough away from the pull of the ocean to shed his skin. Still, he took the time to tuck his daughter into the shadow of a rock before changing.

It had been ages since he'd come to land, far longer than the seven years required between changes by his people. He'd never had an interest in it before, instead fascinated by the sea and all it had to offer. The change was worse than he remembered, his seal skin sloughing off of his form like an urchin scraping its poisonous spines against his flesh. He grunted and barked until that was no longer possible, then he let out a low moan with his human vocal chords.

Panting, he crawled on his hands and knees to where his daughter lay, waving her tiny fists in the air in protest at being taken from the water.

"It will be well, my little pearl," he said, stroking her face. She sucked in a deep breath, preparing to let out a wail as the gills slipped away from her neck. He put his finger to her lips, and she quieted. "Don't cry," he begged. "If you cry, you will draw them to us. I need you to be silent until we get to safety."

She puckered her face in displeasure, all four limbs waving now, furious at this new development.

Swiftly, he rose, wrapping his seal skin around his nethers and holding his daughter in his arms. He tripped on human legs, the form so clumsy and strange after such disuse, but never once did he drop her. And never once did she cry.

There was a human settlement at the top of the cliffs, he remembered. He followed the fresh water creek that flowed into the estuary inland, its call tantalising, even if it were not so seductive as the song of the sea. The song he'd been foolish enough to heed. Now, his daughter would pay the price.

"Please," he murmured, pressing his nose into the

bald head, inhaling her salty, sweet ocean scent. "Please let me be doing the right thing."

It was better, surely, than the alternative. He and the girl's mother had agreed on that much. Then, he had taken the child, barely a few minutes old, from her mother's arms and fled. He hadn't been able to bear looking back to see if she was watching. He would never see her again, that much was certain. He didn't want his last memory to be of her despair.

The land rose gently until he was surrounded by low hills of windswept grasses, mosses, lichens, even flowers, all leading into the trees in the distance that surrounded the lake. It was foreign and unfamiliar to him, like a tale of legend told by his grandmam when he was only a pup himself. He tried to remember those tales now about the humans that lived in this place, so close to the sea. They lived in strange caves made of dead plants and stone, he remembered. They had mastered fire, a pointless substance to one born of the water. They were suspicious and dangerous and strange in their beauty.

And they would save his daughter.

The scent of magic in the air caught him by surprise. He had not thought to find such things here, in this desolate place. Hadn't he been told that humans were the least of the magical beings? Still, there it was, that scent, sharp and fragrant. It was so unlike the scent of the magic that permeated the ocean, instead closer to the overwhelming smells of the plant life around him. But it was assuredly magic.

He turned towards the scent. His daughter blinked

her large, luminescent eyes at him and he smiled down at her. She frowned, her expression serious. She shivered.

He cursed, silently. He didn't know a thing about the needs of babes, certainly not ones without seal skins. Her own magic and her blood had sustained her in the water, but here on land, she was more human than anything, and he knew nothing of what humans required. He held her closer, trying not to squeeze her. She was so fragile.

So precious.

There, on a slight rise, far enough away from the stream that any floodwaters would never reach the entrance, was one of the human stone caves, surrounded by growing things and the scent of magic. A stick stood outside the garden with feathers and twine and stones tied to it. He tried to pass and was immediately struck back.

He let out a gasp and fell, his balance not good enough to prevent the fall. His arms were full of his child, so he could not steady himself, and he collapsed in a heap of dirt, his seal skin loosening around his hips enough that he feared it would fall off and he would lose it. A ridiculous fear, but hardly irrational.

Finally fed up with all that had happened to her on this, the day of her birth, his daughter let out a furious shriek and settled into a desperate wail.

"No, no, please be quiet," he begged, brushing his hands over her face, her hands, her head, trying to soothe her. It was too late; she was well and truly upset and was going to let the world know. Behind him, the creek responded to her mood and its babbling waters swelled and rushed over the rocks beneath its surface. He tried rocking her, tried putting his finger in her wide, screaming mouth, but nothing helped.

The door to the cave opened and a human woman stood there. She was old, her hair grey, her form stooped, but that did not change the power in her gaze. It was not strong, but it was precise, focused. And it was focused on him.

"Please," he said, holding out his child. "Help her!"

The woman stepped forwards, her step sure and smooth as his was not. She stopped a few paces from him and studied him and his child for a moment. "The world has a few more tricks up its sleeves yet, I would think."

He didn't know what that meant. What sleeves were, what she was talking about. He only knew that she was his last hope and his daughter's only chance. The woman stepped closer. He could barely contain his involuntary flinch at being in such proximity to a human. He held himself very still, though it was difficult with a wailing infant in his arms.

"Come, selkie, stand. I mean you and your child no harm," the woman said, her words like a promise. One he—perhaps foolishly—believed. She held out her hands, and he gratefully placed his daughter in them. As soon as he was no longer holding her, it was like some part of his heart had been wrenched out, worse than losing his seal skin would ever feel. He stood and wrapped his skin more tightly around himself.

"Please," he cried, "I cannot keep her in the sea with

me. She is hunted, in danger. I need you to take her, watch her."

"In danger?" the woman asked, her gaze piercing. "In so much danger that a master of the seas cannot protect her?"

He winced, but nodded. His inability to protect what was his was a deep wound, one that would not swiftly heal. He knew that, and yet he had to do what he could to see his child safe. Even if that meant leaving her with humans.

"She is a half-breed," he breathed. He reached out to touch his daughter's face, pulling back at the last moment. Prolonging the moment would only hurt more. "Her mother is a siren. Our union was forbidden because of the child we would create. The others will hunt her."

The woman looked down at the child, her eyes softening. "I know a little of what it means to be hunted, selkie. Magic is a dangerous thing, but it should not be forsaken."

He didn't understand those words, either. Magic was hardly forsaken here, not if her scent was any indication. It did not matter. This human would take his child. Keep her safe. It would have to be enough. "You will protect her?"

"I will raise her as if she were my own," the woman promised. She studied the child, still screaming into the night. She ran a finger touched with magic over the girl's cheek. The child quieted and stilled, her mouth forming a perfect circle of surprise. Then, a miracle: she smiled.

His heart dropped.

"Thank you," he said, turning away. He could bear no more.

"Wait," the woman said. He turned back and saw her gaze harden. What she must think of him, abandoning his child. He had known humans who did the same, leaving their children to the mercy of the sea. Many were taken by the sirens, whose domains were the souls of the drowned. Others were adopted by the selkies, given skins so they might live beneath the waves. Never did either bloodline give up a child of their own. It was unthinkable. His throat tightened.

"There will be a price for this. The giving of a child is an ancient magic even I cannot control," the woman said. "She is powerful, and I will need every advantage to keep her from being found."

"I have no gifts," he said, spreading his arms. He had only his seal skin and he would not give that up. Not even for his daughter.

"Then return and bring one," the woman snapped. He flinched.

"It will be seven years before I can walk on land again." Would she care for his daughter in that time? He needed her to be safe while he was away.

"Magic is patient. I will see you in seven years," the woman said. She shifted her grip slightly so that his daughter could look at him while still being cradled gently. Carefully. He nearly sagged with relief. He would see her again, in seven years' time.

"Goodbye, my little one," he said, reaching out to touch her head one last time, unable to resist, though it tore at his very being. He turned away again and his daughter began to wail again behind him.

"Wait!"

He turned back, frowning. What more could this human want of him? How much more painful could she make this?

"What is her name?" The woman's eyes were wide, sad.

"Mara," he whispered. "Her name is Mara."

It was the only connection to the sea he could give her, for she would never set foot in its waters until the magic in her veins took form, some many years from now. She was a creature born of the sea twice over, and all he could give her was a name that captured the waves. It was not enough.

It would have to be enough.

He turned and slipped away from that human woman who cradled his daughter, not looking back once. He followed the creek back to the tantalising call of the sea and slipped into his seal skin with greater ease than he had slipped out of it. As he swam into the oncoming waves, he thought he heard an infant's cry, the sound carrying through the air like the waves crashing against the cliffs. The sound of the sea.

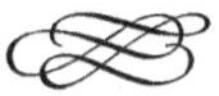

"**R**idiculous." Kyle Livingston scowled at the back of his horse's neck, hardly seeing the vast landscape around him. "Absurd."

He stood out in the hills of this northern country, surrounded by green and purple heather, grasses, ferns, sporadically interspersed with trees clustered together against the wind that came off the sea and roared through the divots in the towering hills. This was a place of hardiness, of natural beauty that was as unassuming as it was dangerous. It was a pleasant early summer's day, but the wind still bit sharply and the sun was blinding. Kyle Livingston, on the other hand, with his black hair, grey eyes and clothes reminiscent of the best tailors, was obviously a creature who did not belong in this wild place.

His scowl was one of two things marring his aristocratic features and neat appearance. The other was a scar running across his left cheek.

He scoffed again and pitched his voice to match the

tone of one of the professors at his old university. "A waste of time, gallivanting off after children's stories."

His horse tossed her head at her master's inattention, then leaped over the creek, running through the path before them. Livingston grunted and wobbled in the saddle, but managed to keep his seat. He knew better than to scold his horse; she alone had stuck with him through this unforgiving and unimaginative country.

"Unscientific! Chasing after something better left in the bowels of history. A waste of a good career. The laughingstock of the entire university." He clenched his hands on the reins again and tried not to let the fury blind him.

"So what if I want to pursue a study of magic?" he grumbled, swatting ineffectively at a midge that buzzed around his face. "It's not as if it doesn't exist!"

He knew without a doubt that magic existed, had seen it with his own eyes. It was responsible for the scar across his face, though Livingston did not blame Briony for the injury. She was his friend, Sir Aidan Rouelle's wife, and one of the last Keepers of the Wild in the world. Her magic was strong and when she was in distress, the wild came to her call. It had resulted in an accident the year before and left Livingston with his scar. It had been during that same adventure that he had met the witch, Alyssia Wisteria, who told him of a druid in his very distant ancestry.

Oh, no, Livingston *knew* that magic was real. It was the rest of the world that seemed to want to forget. After the incident with Briony, Livingston had sworn that he would study magic and put together a volume of all its many facets so that when it did return, when the world was forced to acknowledge magic again, people wouldn't be ignorant. They would have somewhere to turn in the midst of uncertainty, and it would be his work that guided them. What would the university academics say then?

He was self-aware enough to recognise that a good portion of this dream was his own arrogance in wanting to carve out a niche for himself in the world of academia that was unsullied by the idiocy of the other academics, a subject that was his own. The rest of that dream was a desperate curiosity, one he had never been able to quench.

He swatted at another midge, possibly the first one returning with friends, and snarled obscenities in a language lost to time. His curiosity was to blame for bringing him to this unforgiving land that laughed in the face of the pathetic humans who wandered here, and his pride was to blame for making him stay.

He'd heard rumours of a creature that lived in a lake up this way, some short distance from the sea. It was said to appear and disappear in an instant, so elusive that many said it did not exist at all. Maybe that would make up a decent chapter in his manuscript. Maybe it would not.

He had learned, in the months of his travel, that most of these stories were, indeed, nothing more than rumour. But where there was one story, there was bound to be another that was not rumour. Already, he had talked with three hedgewitches of different lineages, caught half a sighting of a creature that was described to him as a tree spirit, and mapped several ruins that were meant to be druidic in nature. It was proof that magic still roamed this world.

Unfortunately, it was hardly the scientific proof that he needed to lay claim to his legacy in the vaunted halls of academia.

"Tallmadge." Livingston saw the marker on the side of the path, an abbreviated name carved into a stone that had nearly been overtaken by lichen. At least he was on the right path to somewhere and not completely lost amongst these hills.

He urged his horse faster, but she just twitched an ear and kept on at her usual steady pace. "Useless creature," he grumbled, though he knew otherwise. She had been a gift from Aidan and Briony for his journey, trained by the Keeper herself, though Briony rarely bothered with domesticated creatures.

The horse had been a blessing, keeping him out of trouble on multiple occasions. There was a wildness about her, though, and he had never got her to respond to any name he tried. Surely, he thought, she must be magical in her own right, though again he had seen no evidence to the fact.

Livingston tilted his head back and studied the slopes of the hills, gradually declining to a sort of flatness that led to the cliffs and then the sea. What if they were right, those ridiculous stuffy academics? What if magic was not merely another facet of the universe, but dead, except for Briony and those few witches that remained? What if they were the last of their kind and after them would be no more? What if he truly was being a fool? He used to be an advocate for the rigid methods of academics, the logic and the sureness of something that was tangible and could be proven. Was he chasing fancies now? Wasting his time?

Livingston shivered. He reached up to touch the scar on his cheek. That was all the evidence he needed. He would keep searching for that definitive proof that would show the world how right he truly was.

Tallmadge came into view, a few cottages on the sides of the hills that became more numerous buildings the closer he drew to the cliffs and the few spots where the land sloped gently into the sea. It was nothing like the bustling business of town, with every sort of business and person that you could imagine. Frankly, Livingston wondered if he would be able to get a decent meal here that didn't include fish. This journey was his dream, but he did miss proper cuisine.

"This is going to be a good thing," he said to the horse. She tossed her head. "It will! I am going to find a lake monster and write a whole chapter on northern magical creatures. I am going to gather definitive evidence about such things. I am going to be a respected scholar."

The horse snorted and kept walking into town. Livingston sighed. Everybody was a critic.

THE HOUSE he was letting for his time in Tallmadge was surprisingly comfortable, given his country surroundings. He had not had much trouble with the leasing agent when he wrote a month back, despite it being nearly summer. Apparently, Tallmadge wasn't much of a holiday destination, so the house selection was relatively large. He had chosen something middle of the line, with only one drawing room, three bedrooms, all the various serving rooms and a dining room that could seat an even dozen, should he be required to host a dinner to gather information.

Upon arrival in town, however, he had realised that he had taken one of the nicer houses in town by accident, immediately setting himself aside as a wealthy individual. Things that were commonplace in town were noteworthy here. It was a foolish mistake, one that he should have foreseen. It was too late now, for he was here and in possession of the key and the house.

"Welcome to Tallmadge, sir," the housekeeper said, her accent thick and her attitude deferential. "Would you be wanting a tour of the town? My brother's son, my nephew, delivers the post and knows everybody around. As you're here on business, that is, it might be useful."

"Thank you, Mrs. Cusper," Livingston said, wondering just how the woman knew he was in town on business. Though his business was odd enough that he doubted the wonder would last long. He had been treated with enough suspicion in other, far larger towns that he had no doubt Tallmadge would close ranks on him. If he could get enough information before then, it would be enough. But he didn't trust small towns to trust him. "For the moment, I need only a map of the town and its surrounding areas. I will worry about establishing myself socially later."

Mrs. Cusper, thoroughly starched and pressed, blinked her owlish eyes in amazement. "Oh, there's no need for dithering, sir. The best event of the year—saving the Yuletide ball, that is—is tomorrow night. Mrs. Rushworth is hosting a summer gala over at Rushworth Manor. Everyone who is anyone attends and when Mr. Garvin—the letting agent, that is—knew you were to arrive today, he made sure to mention it to Mr. Long, whose wife is cousin to Miss Mardew, who is a dear friend of Mrs. Rushworth. I heard tell from my nephew that an invitation was sent to arrive by evening post by Mrs. Rushworth herself!"

Livingston sat in the large overstuffed chair in the drawing room, upholstered in a pleasant blue fabric, unable to find a single thing to say to that list of people and events. His housekeeper must know everybody in this town. Either that, or truly everyone in these small towns must be a close friend or a relation of everyone else. What a terrifying thought.

"I see," he managed. A ball. He had not attended one since the impromptu affair at Blackwell Downs over a year ago, and that had even been far more pleasant than some he had attended in town. Generally considered handsome, though he did not understand why that mattered, he was implored to dance with all the young, eligible ladies by various parties. He much preferred a quiet evening spent in with a book. Not a commonly held opinion and not one often voiced. Socialising was a useful matter when searching out information held outside of books, but it was not always an enjoyable one.

"Oh, yes, sir, it's a wondrous event, the talk of the whole county. And it will be so nice to have someone new to attend, I think. It would so some of those young fools to have a bit of competition for the young ladies, indeed it would." Mrs. Cusper nodded firmly, eyeing Livingston as one would a prize horse.

"I'm not here looking for a wife," he protested, nearly rising out of the chair. "I'm here on business. Research!"

"Research?" The housekeeper seemed frankly puzzled by the idea.

"Yes," he said, trying not to be exasperated. "I am doing research for a book I'm writing."

He wasn't sure how many details to give his house-keeper. It was better if he told the people hereabouts what he was researching, or everything was likely to get misconstrued by the wheels of gossip. Even with the lack of information on his research topic, Mrs. Cusper nodded with another gleam in her eyes. This woman was quite dangerous with her nods and her knowledge of everybody and everything in the town.

"Oh, of course," she said, brushing at her skirt. "Research for a book you're writing. You gentlemen must have something to occupy your time, and not everyone feels called to hunting or horse racing like others. An intellectual, yes, that will be *quite* the thing. Why, Tallmadge even has a travelling library!"

Stars and stones, a travelling library, Livingston thought dismally. Likely distributing novels of the most absurd sort to all the giggling families about. He would not get a single lick of sense from the books from this library. For once, couldn't he be required to do research in an established town with a long history of magical sightings?

"Now, I imagine you'll be busy these next few days, settling in and everything. Just you leave the details to me. I've already sent for some fish from the fishmonger's, and there'll be a nice steak and kidney pie for tea. You just tell me your favourite meals and I'll see to it that Cook has all the ingredients. And if there's anything wrong with the house, just tell me and I'll fix it. The furniture is—"

"Mrs. Cusper," Livingston said, trying not to sound too harsh. He hated interrupting people; it was generally better for his research if they talked without hesitation, but there was such a thing as too much conversation. "I am feeling a bit fatigued from my journey. I think I'll just go up and rest for a while. There's no need to prepare supper for tonight. I think I'll go find the local public house and eat there. Get the lay of the land, as it were."

"Oh, but my nephew—"

"It won't be necessary." Livingston held up a placating hand and smiled gently, a look that generally went over well with the older female population. "I do better if I can explore around on my own. Ask directions, talk with people casually, that sort of thing."

Mrs. Cusper nodded, her cheeks flushed slightly. "Then, ah, I'll keep an eye out for the evening post," she murmured.

"Thank you, Mrs. Cusper. I'm sure you will prove to be invaluable during my tenure here," Livingston said. Then, without waiting for the woman to blush again or delve into further conversation, he swept from the drawing room and went up the stairs as quickly as he could. He would make a tour of the house on his own, when everyone else was asleep. For now, he picked one of the several bedrooms at random and tossed his bags onto the chair by the window. Then, he settled himself onto the bed and tried not to think too much.

It felt as though he'd been doing nothing but think for the past six months, and frankly, he was beginning to grow weary. How long was he going to wander around the country, hoping to find something that—except for a few weak examples and a dying line of magic—did not appear to exist except as a memory?

He might have druid blood in his veins, but it apparently counted for very little in these modern times.

Refusing to dwell further on the disappointments of his research trip, he shucked off his boots and lay back, falling asleep within minutes. The headache persisted, even in his dreams.

CHAPTER 2

Mara knelt in the dirt near the creek and pulled up a stalk of skullcap, checking the roots as she went. "The harvest is going to be late this year," she muttered, putting the specimen aside. Her grandmother would have to do what she could with the meagre dried supplies from last year. Satisfied with the bed of skullcap, Mara reached her hand towards the water and called up a few droplets of water to wash the dirt from her fingers. The water nymph that lived in the creek gave her a look before splashing water at her.

"I only needed to wash my hands!" Mara protested with a slight laugh. The nymph lifted her head out of the water and rested her arms on a large boulder.

Compared to Mara, with her light brown hair streaked with strands of gold, eyes the colour of the sea at dawn, and sun burnished complexion, the nymph was an oddity. She was old for her kind, with wrinkles at her eyes and mouth, and her skin was pale, blues and greens showing through. Her hair looked like seaweed, though none grew this far into fresh water. She was a strange creature, and yet Mara loved her all the same. It was natural, after all, when the nymph who lived in the creek and her grandmother were her only friends.

"Your birthday draws near," the nymph said, wide eyes studying Mara as if she expected her to change then and there. "Your power will manifest soon."

"Oh, you mean as something more useful than a minor water talent and a singing voice that prevents me from being expelled from house parties?" Mara asked. She tried to keep the bitterness from her voice and failed. Disregarding the dirt that clung to her roughly woven green skirt, she sat on the rocks by the creek and dangled her hand in the water. It was cold, as it should be despite the heat of summer, and if she listened hard enough, she could hear the murmur of voices in the water.

She wasn't meant to be listening at all.

"I would not jest at such things," the nymph warned, watching the ripples in the water around Mara's fingers. She pulled them back with a sigh. Prolonged contact with the water was not allowed. The nymph continued. "You are a mix of two powerful bloodlines, Mara Del Sol. When your power finally manifests, it will not do so quietly. I would not tempt fate into granting more than that when the time comes."

"I don't *care* about that," Mara grumbled. She swiped an unruly curl back from her face. "I am nearly twenty-eight years of age. I live on the edge of town with my grandmother. I love her, and I do not care that she is a hedgewitch and herbwoman. I only wish…"

The nymph blew bubbles at Mara, a sign of sympathy this time rather than the laughter that usually accompanied that action. "The humans are dangerous. They don't like anything associated with magic. Perhaps their shunning of you is safer than their attention?"

It was an argument Mara had heard nearly her entire life, from the time she could understand that not every girl could pull shapes out of the water or sing to entrance any audience. She had been a day away from her seventh birthday when her grandmother finally explained it to her. That she wasn't even human, but a half-siren, half-selkie abomination sent to live amongst the humans to keep her from danger. Her grandmother had hardly used the word abomination, but Mara felt the sting, nonetheless. She almost preferred the story about her being a foundling child that was spread around to the citizens of Tallmadge. It was easier pretending to be the unwanted child of a prostitute than a being people did not even believe existed.

And if they did believe, they would exploit her. Or worse. Mara had heard enough tales of Grandmother Cait's hedgewitch ancestors and their persecution to keep her mouth well and truly shut.

"It would be nice to have a few friends," Mara said. "If I am to spend my life amongst the humans, at least I could have a few human friends. You are wonderful, but other creatures of the water would not understand our friendship, and you know it."

The nymph shrugged, a gesture Mara had taught her when she was twelve, then stiffened. Her eyes widened and she dived beneath the shallow waters of the creek, vanishing entirely before Mara could so much as blink.

"Hello, Grandmother," Mara said, not looking up from the water. No one else was wandering about the open hills at this hour. Their cottage was a few hundred feet away, high enough on a hill to be away from any potential flooding during the spring melt, surrounded by a garden of flowers and herbs both medicinal and beautiful. It was Mara's home and her sanctuary. Some days, it felt like a prison.

"How is the harvest going to be?" Cait asked, leaning over to pick up the skullcap and examining the roots. Before Mara could answer, she clicked her tongue in disappointment. "Another few weeks at the least. Spring was so late this year, I'm surprised I have any herbs left!"

"I think your garden will do just fine. It's the envy of all others in Tallmadge," Mara said. She stood and dusted herself off, not even sparing the creek a backwards glance. Her grandmother beamed and wrapped a strong arm around Mara's waist. They could not be any more different, Mara mused, with her height and lean figure and Cait's shorter, stockier frame. But they were still family.

"Now, I hear the Rushworths are throwing their annual summer ball," Cait said, examining Mara with a twinkle in her eye. "Did they invite you to sing again?"

Mara nodded. "I refused, though."

"Why? I thought you loved being able to sing for people." Was that actual despair in Cait's eyes, or was she just confused? "It's the only gift you have that you can share openly."

Mara sighed and shrugged. "I know, and I do enjoy it, but…I am twenty-seven, have no female friends, and have had no suitors. Those few people with whom I *can* be friendly care only about my singing at various house parties. Or are our patients, desperate for the help that your herbs provide. I'm tired of being stared at by those who deign to invite me to sing at their parties, who expect me to remain and be talked about as if I were just a pretty bauble for entertainment. I'd rather just be your granddaughter and assistant."

"And a fine herbwoman you make, too," Cait said, giving her another squeeze. "Speaking of, I need you to make up another set of poultices for infected wounds. I've had more complaints of fishermen sticking themselves with hooks this year than ever before, and you know how bad rusty metal is for cuts. Not to mention they never seem to take proper care to keep their injuries clean. Pah!"

Mara nodded and disengaged her grandmother's arm from around her waist before stooping over the herb garden and expertly plucking a few plants. She was careful not to bruise any leaves or damage the remaining stalks. It was something she had done a thousand times before and could do it in her sleep, identifying herbs by scent as well as touch and feel.

"When we go into town today, I need you to come with me for little Hettie Cartwright's ankle. She is always so much calmer when you sing to her," Cait continued, gathering the herbs Mara handed to her in the apron she wore.

"Has her mother had more trouble with her?" Mara asked, her thoughts still with the nymph and the stream. Going into town meant she was closer to the ocean, too, and if she played her cards right, she could stand at the edge of the cliffs and listen to the beating of the waves on the rocks far below. Or, maybe, she could go down to the docks and help tend to some of the sailors and fishermen, though Cait only allowed that if she were truly overwhelmed. The ocean was just out of reach, yet the longing was always there.

"You know what young children are like; they have too much energy for their own good and have no idea how to rest and nurse an injury. And with Mrs. Cartwright busy all day with the laundry, she can hardly be expected to keep a close eye on Hettie."

Mara hummed a sound of acknowledgement and sympathy as they entered the cottage. Inside was just as tidy as the outside, with herbs hung from the rafters in the stillroom, the kitchen divided into a spot for making poultices and mixing herbs and actually cooking food. The house often smelled of pungent concoctions, but it was a happy, beautiful scent more than it was overwhelming.

Mara ground up those herbs which needed grinding while Cait murmured her spells over the boiling cauldron, adding just enough of a spark of magic to make the mixture's effects last longer. Some hedgewitches, Mara had been taught, were better at wards, others at charms. Cait specialised in healing and herblore, making her the perfect herbwoman. Especially since the local doctor charged an absurd amount of money for his services, and was a boor besides.

"Well, if you're not going to sing at the Rushworth's ball, then you won't be able to tell me all the ridiculous antics of the attendees. I hear this year's unmarried girls newly out in society are particularly silly." Mara's grandmother snatched the mortar and pestle from her hands, dumping the contents into the cauldron. It fizzled for a moment before settling once more into a steady boil.

"When were they ever not particularly silly?" Mara asked. Her grandmother was quite fond of gossip, despite not tolerating any about Mara herself. She said gossip was the best way of finding out news. In a town such as Tallmadge, Mara had to agree. Nothing was done but several wagging tongues knew of it within the first ten minutes of it happening. To keep up with anything of societal import, one had to listen to gossip. It also meant one could become the subject of gossip in an instant due to a careless word or action.

"The year you were first among them, there were some good eggs," Cait sniffed in response. Mara smiled indulgently.

"The year I was first among them, they were so appalled that a supposed foundling child was not only attending the ball, but singing at it, that they would have snubbed the event altogether. Mrs. Rushworth was the only reason it still went on, and I was made to be certain I knew my place was only the entertainment," Mara said. Her voice was devoid of bitterness, but she had felt its sting several times over. Now, though, she lived her life the way it was and despite wishing for a few human friends, considered it very unlikely such things would happen. That was just the way of things in this world, and she did understand. Mostly.

"Pah!" Cait slammed the mortar onto the counter. "Fools, all of them!"

"Products of society, Grandmother," Mara replied. She leaned over and kissed Cait's hair. "You'll just have to forgive them for being what they are. Not all of us can shed our skins and become something else."

Not that Mara had ever done that. She'd been forbidden from swimming at all, even in the distant loch, for fear that something undeniably magical would happen. Like, for instance, becoming a seal. Or drawing the attention of the ocean's spies. The irony of a child of the ocean not knowing how to swim was not lost on her.

Cait eyed Mara suspiciously. Then her shoulders slumped. "You are a good girl, child. Life has not treated you as well as it should, yet somehow you keep smiling. I certainly am not as kindhearted as you."

Mara laughed. "I can hold a grudge quite well, dear Grandmother. Or have you forgotten how many of Tallmadge's upper-crust I would prefer to sing into oblivion?"

There, now her grandmother was smiling again. She gave a wry chuckle and waved her hands over the cauldron once more, giving a last spell to the poultice before tipping the whole thing into a bowl with cheesecloth over top, which drained out the excess liquid. The two of them packaged the poultices in linen and in small sachets. Mara added dried herbs to make it smell better and packed other jars and boxes for delivery to their customers.

By the time the pair had finished the preparations, the sun was high in the sky and town was sure to be bustling with people. Mara hefted two baskets over her arms and followed her grandmother down the hills and into Tallmadge itself.

This town had hardly changed in all the years Mara had been running its streets. There, on the corner, was the bookseller and provider of fine stationary, opposite the dressmaker's and next to the haberdashery. The stall selling fish was up all year, despite being made from old wooden boards salvaged from shipwrecks on the beach. Beside it were the purveyors of produce and livestock. Then, the town square, surrounding a large statue of the founders of the town, the crew of the *Tallmadge* who had been wrecked here some two hundred years before. Or, at least, that was how the story went. If you actually looked at the town records, it showed quite clearly that Tallmadge was founded by Sir Rupert Tallmadge, gifted the land by the king some generations ago for services rendered. The wrecked ship was always the more romantic story.

Most of the people that she and her grandmother visited couldn't afford the services of the local doctor, and were generally on the outskirts of town, in the houses that were well kempt, though in need of some larger repairs. Still, these people were generally good and gracious and always treated Mara and Cait well.

Their first stop of the day was the Cartwright family. The mother was a laundress and spent her days up to her elbows in water and lye, sometimes leaving the skin raw and blistered. They gave her creams and poultices more frequently than many others. But little Hettie Cartwright was Mara's patient for the day.

She crouched by Hettie's bedside and admired the rag doll wrapped in the girl's arms. "She's beautiful," Mara said, infusing her voice with just a touch of soothing magic. "Does she have a name?"

"Elizabeth," Hettie whispered, clutching the doll closer.

"A beautiful name. Now, I've heard that you need some special magical potion for your ankle, so that it can be healed. Is that right?" Mara asked. The parents cared naught for magic, but the children still believed in miracles and wonders. She envied them, sometimes.

Hettie gave a hesitant nod, her lower lip wobbling. Mara reached out and brushed her hand over the girl's blonde hair. "Oh, there's no need to cry, your majesty," Mara said with a gentle smile. While she was distracting the girl, her grandmother sat at the end of the cot and started unwrapping the poultice and some linen strips with which to wrap the ankle.

"Elizabeth is scared," Hettie murmured.

"Well," Mara said, "there's nothing to be scared of. But just to be sure, I'll sing a song that will keep all the bad things away. Would you like that?"

Hettie nodded silently, her big eyes welling with

tears. Mara smoothed her hair once more, and just as Cait started unwrapping the old bindings on the girl's ankle, Mara began to sing.

When she had learned the truth of her magic, something deep inside her had clicked in understanding. She knew now that the joy that rose with each note, the truth of feeling and that burst of energy that poured just a little of her own soul into the song, that was magic. And with that magic, she could instil emotions into listeners. She could make them cry, or laugh, or beam with joy. She could make lovers blush and children giggle. Or, as in this instance, she could soothe.

Her voice was steady and sure as she sang, and slowly, Hettie's breathing smoothed into an even rhythm and she remained calm as the healing poultice was put on. Turmeric to reduce inflammation, dandelions for healing, a touch of honey to encourage the process along, and several others for a pleasant scent. The child took a deep breath as the bindings were re-wrapped tightly, but she did not flinch as Mara's voice climbed and fell over the strains of a familiar lullaby. The words did not matter so much as the intent, and even before Cait had finished her wrappings, Hettie had fallen asleep.

Mara closed her eyes as she finished her song and let out a shaky breath. She loved singing. She felt so invigorated by it. By the magic in her veins, that spark touching her soul. But, as she opened her eyes again, she knew that she was the only one who could truly understand what it was for her to sing. That magic she possessed came straight from the sea and those tempting waves. Singing awoke her longings for things that could never be, just as dipping her fingers in the creek did.

She longed for the sea. The world she belonged to did not want her, and the one she wanted would happily tear her to pieces for the magic she possessed and feel no regret for it.

Mara lay Hettie back on the bed and followed her grandmother out, on to their next stop. She told herself she would be content with her life, lonely and isolated, because it was good. And if she could not be content? Well, she knew the consequences would be dire.

CHAPTER 3

_L_ivingston was already determined to leave, and he had hardly been at the Rushworths' for an hour. After fending off the interminable conversation of his housekeeper over her joy at the invitation and the people who would be attending, he had managed to dress in his fine attire and make it to the summer gala with only a small delay.

Upon introducing himself to his hosts, who were decked out in their finest jewels and clothing, as if this were the event of the season, they had immediately introduced him to several other couples, all—as far as he could determine—with unmarried daughters.

The giggling behind fans while the girls batted their eyes at him was enough to make him cringe. The not-so-subtle questions of their parents as to his income, his standing in society, even his interest in academia, was even more infuriating.

Would it be too much to ask to spend a quiet night home with his research?

"So, Mr. Livingston," a woman spoke, considerably shorter than he with her grey hair inexpertly dyed black and piled on her head. Given his height advantage, he was able to see the strands of silver that had escaped her dye, twined through with pearls and feathers. He thought her name was something like Feston or Fenton or Farley, but he had hardly been able to keep up with the string of introductions that evening and his head was beginning to pound. "What brings you to Tallmadge? I'm sure it's nothing like what you're used to in town."

"I'm here on research," he said, giving the vague answer he always used. Eventually, he was going to have to be more precise if he wanted to find out anything of value for his book, but he was already being stared at enough with his dark hair and scar across his cheek. He'd heard more than one girl proclaim him "dashing" and preferred to avoid more scrutiny.

"Research?" The poor Mrs. Fenton or Farley's husband blinked at Livingston through owlish spectacles. He seemed somewhat sensible, but was prevented from entering into any reasonable conversation by means of his wife interrupting him every few seconds to comment on the party. "Nothing to do with weather sciences, I hope? We had one of those chaps out some five years ago. He was hopeless at predicting storms, but seemed quite keen on eating at every fine party he could."

Livingston winced. It wasn't unheard of for

younger sons who had no chance of inheriting a majority to enter into the realm of academia and then attempt to marry as well as possible while out on research trips. The true academics loathed that set.

"No, I don't study weather," Livingston said. Maybe it was time to speak honestly. People might be less inclined to invite him to these parties if they knew the truth, and he certainly didn't want to be bombarded with questions about his intentions. "I work through the university, but I fund everything myself. They don't support my particular area of interest except as a sideline in history."

Mr. Farley—was that his name?—looked very interested. His wife blinked a few times then waved her fan at someone across the room. It was too much to ask that she scurry away, but at least she was distracted.

Livingston continued. "I'm researching magic. All its forms, what it was like in ancient times, how it still exists today. Hopefully it will be quite a comprehensive volume."

Farley or Fenton or whatever peered closer at Livingston. He cleared his throat. "Magic you say? Hmmm." If he'd had a pipe, the man would have been smoking up a chimney.

"Oh, how *interesting*," Mrs. Farley preened. "To be able to investigate such an uncommon topic, you must be given a great deal of freedom by the university! Why, did you know that there are rumours of an honest to goodness monster in the loch just ten miles from town?"

He didn't know how, given that he was usually quite good at saying the right thing to cause people to lose interest in him, but Livingston had miscalculated grossly. Instead of being put off by his researching what would in such polite society be considered an eccentric topic, his very eccentricity meant that he was wealthy enough to afford it. And he was, but that wasn't something he wanted bandied about. He may have just signed his freedom away. He would be soundly pursued until he left Tallmadge.

"I'd heard something to that effect," Livingston said, trying not to grit his teeth. He needed these people to tell him things for his research. He did not want to alienate them. He tried to remind himself of this before he went and did something ridiculously rude, like walk away without a second glance.

"Oh, look, here is our Sophia. Sophie, darling, come meet Mr. Livingston. He's writing a book on magic!" Mrs. Farley waved her fan again, this time at a young woman of about eighteen or nineteen, walking arm in arm with another young woman. Livingston assumed that Sophia was the dark haired waif, her curls the truth to Mrs. Farley's poor imitation. She regarded her mother with a cool, polite look, and curtseyed to Livingston.

"Mr. Livingston," she said, inclining her head. "I hope my mother is not regaling you of tales of our lake monster. We haven't had a confirmed sighting in four generations."

Livingston felt his mouth twitch and tried to hide

his amusement at the girl's wry humour. She did not seem to be phased at all by her family's overeagerness. "If the lake monster is not a worthwhile target of my research, then perhaps you know of better magic hereabouts?"

Sophia considered, ignoring the spluttering of her mother and the contemplative humming of her father. Then, she nodded. "The local herbwoman is rumoured to be a witch. If anyone about the area knows of magic in Tallmadge, it would be she."

Livingston's heart beat faster. He had interviewed several hedgewitches during the last six months, all of whom had nearly no magical power. But a witch? A true witch like the one who had told him of his druid ancestry? That would be someone worth speaking with.

"Oh, her?" Mrs. Farley waved her hand dismissively. She gave a nervous giggle and looked about to see how many people were watching. Four, by Livingston's count, though he was trying very hard not to pay attention. "She just peddles herbs and homespun remedies. People grant her too much skill. Certainly Doctor Thompson believes her to be a fraud, just selling useless things to cheat people out of their money."

"Doctor Thompson merely doesn't care for the fact that Cait Del Sol can treat people as well as he does, and for half the price." Sophia turned to look at her friend, who was gesturing to her. "If you'll excuse me, Mr. Livingston, Father, Mother."

With a curtsey, she was gone. It was refreshing to be

treated as a normal person, Livingston mused. He wished the young woman well and looked about to see about extricating himself from the conversation. He'd even consider dancing if it got him away from the desperate mamas.

"Well! She really is a good girl, Mr. Livingston," Mrs. Farley said, batting her eyes. "Just a bit headstrong. Fond of books."

"Nothing wrong with that," Livingston said. "Now, where can I find this herbwoman?"

"Truly, sir, you do not wish to seek her out. She won't be any help to you unless you want to know what herbs grow in the hills! She and her granddaughter are better off staying there."

Mr. Farley finally decided to speak up. "Granddaughter? I don't remember that Del Sol woman having a granddaughter."

"You remember her, dear. The woman who sings at some parties? You won't believe this, Mr. Livingston, but I hear that the woman adopted the child from a foundling organisation! It is so untoward, raising a child alone in the hills, and a foundling one at that."

He was done with this conversation. He had no interest in where a person came from, only who they were. And these people may have been from the world of high society, but they were insipid and judgemental, and certainly of no help to his research.

"If you'll excuse me," Livingston said, bowing slightly. "I find myself in need of some air."

He heard only the polite murmurs before striding off, ignoring the waves of his hosts and the smiles of the girls who would try to trap him in marriage. Young, relatively pretty, and of no interest to him. If he were ever to marry—a fate he had not yet decided upon—he wanted an intellectual partner, not a giggling child. He wanted company that matched his interests and did not drain his spirit as these events did.

He went to the doors leading out into the garden, ignoring the wandering couples or gaggles of people, instead heading to the dark and secluded corners where he might have a moment of peace to think and to breathe. This was a cultivated garden, but the edges beyond the neat and trim beds lead up into the hills with their scraggly trees and their dark crags. There was wildness up there, and that was the only magic Livingston knew.

Someone's distant step on a twig rent the air with a *crack*, eliminating all other sounds for him. The murmur of conversation, the pleasant warmth of the lights, it all fell away and suddenly he was back in that moment when magic surrounded at him. He had lain on the ground in a tempest wrought by Briony Marsh, the Keeper who had unleashed her wild magic and let storms brew. Livingston had been there, had seen how powerful she was. He knew how unprepared the world was for magic's return, and he did not once doubt it would return.

He pressed his hands to his head, the scar on his cheek throbbing. He was here, in Tallmadge, at a ridiculous party, not there. Not amidst a storm that would not care if it tore him limb from limb. Not amongst the power that could grant life to plants and birds and wolves just as well as it could take it. The wild magic was just as it should be. It cared naught for the woes of others, only that it defend itself. No matter who had been in the way.

Aidan, Livingston's great friend, had stepped in and saved him, but he couldn't help think that something had come between the two of them that night. Ever since, Livingston had tried to be supportive. He even liked Briony quite a lot. But the memory of that night haunted him in a way that these people could never understand.

That was why he had to do something. And researching magic, writing a book that all could read so that they could prepare, that was what he could do.

"Are you quite well, Mr. Livingston?"

He turned and found Sophia and her friend walking down the path towards him. He forced a smile and bowed. "I found it a bit close in there, and yet I come out here to find that I am unaccustomed to all this open space."

Sophia nodded, though her eyes said she didn't fully believe him. "The highlands are a wild place, indeed. If ever you wish to find magic, it will be there."

Her friend murmured agreement. Livingston did not doubt that they spoke the truth. There was something slightly unsettling about the black abyss of these hills at night. He turned his back on the feeling and the hills. "Perhaps you can tell me more about where to find this herbwoman who may be a witch. Or, if you prefer, a tale about the lake monster would suffice."

Both girls chuckled, not quite a giggle, smiles dancing. Sophia started walking back towards the house at a measured pace and Livingston obligingly walked beside her. "Well, the lake monster is supposed to be a being so ancient that its kind was here long before humans even walked the world. They say that it lives deep within the waters, rising only at certain times to mate or to birth its young. Its monstrous form is reminiscent of dragons and—"

"Oh, a dragon, is that all?" Livingston interrupted. The girls once more broke into laughter. Sophia smiled brightly.

"It's what we tell all those who come here in search of it. Mostly people on tours through the highlands. Truly, though, the only evidence we have of such a being even existing is a collection of a few sketches of wobbly monsters and stories handed down through families. The herbwoman, Cait Del Sol, is a far more realistic target if you are searching for signs of magic in these hills."

Sophia's reticent friend finally spoke up, her voice high and bell toned. "My aunt uses her tinctures almost exclusively. She says that they are spelled to work against any intensity of headache, unlike Doctor Thompson's, which are nearly ineffective unless used in high doses."

Tinctures? Was that all? That was the specialty of such people. Hardly proof of magic.

"No one's ever seen her perform a spell, mind you," Sophia added thoughtfully. "She lives at the base of the hills and is too far outside of Tallmadge for people to go spying on her. But her products and services are very good. Better than others. And she wears this pearl at her throat, about the size of a robin's egg. It's streaked, not pure white, but is said to amplify her magic. Plenty of people have offered for the pearl. Even streaked, it is of remarkable size. She won't part with it, though."

Tinctures and large pearl that was more than likely a family heirloom. Livingston made the appropriate noises of interest, but it sounded to him like this was another dead end. Perhaps a hedgewitch, if that, but hardly anything more. No, all he would find in Tallmadge were legends of the Faeries that were in every village, and tales of the lake monster. Well, he was here. He might as well go about and conduct interviews to take some of the stories down. If he were lucky, he might get a whole chapter on the monster.

He doubted that he would be so lucky.

After escorting the two young women back into the ballroom, Livingston sought out his hosts and told them he was taking their leave. He made some excuses about still being tired from travelling, and having an early morning for research, then left. He did not care if he was being impolite by leaving early; there was only so much of this society he could take.

No desperate girls or their equally desperate parents had got their claws into him, he was not obligated to any dinner parties in the next few days though he knew invitations would arise, and he had learned at least a little about the withered magic of the area. It should have been a successful evening, but all he felt was drained. Weary. Exhausted.

He would see the research through, at the very least. Then, perhaps after he was done with this town, it would be good to go back to the university and spend some time there. Time away from the futility of this journey. Time to rethink his plans.

CHAPTER 4

*D*rizzle filled the air as Mara took her basket across the creek to where some wild St. John's wort grew in a sheltered lee between two hills. It was closer to Tallmadge, but few people ever went there unless they were lost because it was more difficult to access. As such, it was a haven for plants of all sort. Cait had once tried seeding the field with seeds from her own garden, but the native herbs and plants had quickly overtaken the intruders. Now, only a few of the original planting remained, their stock strong enough to make any tinctures or mixtures more potent.

Mara loved days like this, when the sky was grey and endless and water filled the air. It wasn't an oppressive rain, nor a deluge, just a drizzle that settled on her skin and her hair and kept her cool, despite the summer warmth. If she had been near to the ocean, she knew that the waves would be almost lazy and the water would reflect the infinity of the sky. But it was just as lovely in this field, skin kissed by water that still remembered the sea.

Her hands buried deep in the dirt, brushing away other plants and insects from her precious harvest, Mara began to sing. Around her, a few bees buzzed closer, as if drawn by her voice. She directed her energies outward, a song of industry and joy at the rain, and the field seemed even more lively in the drizzle than on a bright day. A courageous bee settled on Mara's hand, her wings fanning and buzzing, her legs yellow with pollen. Mara crooned a few notes to the bee, then smiled as the creature took flight to her next flower.

She lived for days like this, full of water and song and joy and little else. No troubles, no woes, no fears about her future or doubts about her past. Just the music and the open air.

She filled her basket, taking a few wildflowers as well to brighten a windowsill, then began her journey back home, still humming. Maybe she would accept an invitation to sing at a party in town soon. Her music should be shared with the world, even if the world did not appreciate its instrument. Or perhaps she just preferred an audience. She chuckled at that thought, shaking her head and wondering at her folly, then left the field and its treasures for rockier terrain.

The ground at the edge of the lee was craggy and filled with small rivulets where the rain had, over hundreds of years, burrowed its way into the ground. Her steps were as sure as her voice, the path one taken over and over again.

Then, she spotted the creek and stopped singing in the middle of a phrase. The disjointed magic fell away, as startled as she was to see a human there in the middle of her wild home. Someone—a man, it looked like—was crossing the creek with uncaring strides, and if he wasn't careful, the water nymph was going to pull him in for intruding without asking permission.

"Stop!" Mara cried. There was a reason why few people ever visited the cottage. Some claimed it was the distance from town, but invariably, all those who found themselves crossing the creek met with some sort of watery accident. The nymph was Mara's friend, but not so with other humans. They might not see her, but she could make herself known in many ways: mud on the bank that held a shoe, a surge of water over a bridge, slick surfaces on which to walk. She was precocious and temperamental and rarely appreciated company.

Unfortunately, this man heeded Mara's cry right in the middle of the water, his foot balanced precariously on one of the large stones people used to cross. The nymph's hand shot out from the water before Mara could do anything to stop her. Her long fingers wrapped around the man's shoe and ankle and pulled. The man, completely oblivious of the creature in the water, just wheeled his arms and slipped. He fell headlong into the crisp hill-fed waters.

Mara ran the last distance to the creek and leaped over the rocks, glaring at the nymph as she did. The man was already spluttering indignantly as he slid up the bank a ways. He was soaking wet from the waist down, his sleeves likewise drenched. His shoes would surely be ruined.

"Are you alright?" Mara asked. She knelt beside him and set her basket aside. A cursory glance told her that he seemed to be in order—at least, there was no obvious bleeding—and that he was new to Tallmadge. At least, she'd never noticed a man with his dark looks and intense expression before, and she'd lived there her entire life.

"You distracted me," the man said, voice deep and earthy with a definite grumble present. "I was crossing fine, but you distracted me and I slipped."

Mara managed, barely, not to snort her amusement at his words. People without magic were so blind, sometimes. "I apologise," she said, soothing and calm. "Are you hurt?"

"No," he snapped, wringing out some of the water from his jacket. "I came out here looking for the herb-woman. I was told she might be able to help me."

Ah, yes. A man not from these parts who had come to seek out her grandmother. That meant he was probably a man looking for anyone to cure an incurable disease—either his or someone he knew well—and had heard of Cait's likely magic. It was a sad tale, but it happened from time to time, and the seekers invariably went away furious or weeping.

"For what sort of remedy?" Mara asked. Perhaps she could head him off, send him away before he even got around to bothering Cait. A man of his age, it might be something so simple as impotence, which she could handle herself. Not that he would ever speak to her about such things, given her age was likely close to his. No, they preferred her older, comelier grandmother for that.

"I'll ask the herbwoman, thank you." He was beginning to push himself to his feet, now glaring at the sky as it added to the offense of his wet clothes. Mara rose and considered helping him before taking a pointed step back. He had already accused her of causing him to slip. She might as well let him stand on his own. Especially if his pride was already wounded by the reason for his seeking her grandmother out.

He did quite well in his efforts, too, until he put weight on his left ankle and the joint buckled. He nearly fell again, this time muttering darkly. Mara leaped in and grabbed his arm, supporting his weight. He frowned, studied her for a moment, then shook her off. She raised her brows, but took another pointed step away from him. "Thank you," he said, barely polite enough for common courtesy. "I think...I must have twisted it when I fell."

"I can have a look, if you like," Mara offered. She supposed she should feel a little badly for this man, given that it was her friend that had tripped him. But he was being a little too standoffish and Mara wasn't one to tolerate rudeness. Still, he was hurt, and she was her grandmother's apprentice.

"I'll be fine," he grumbled. "I just need to find the herbwoman."

"For your ankle, or this mysterious remedy that brought you all the way up from Tallmadge?" Mara asked, barely restraining her amusement. The man studied her again and his appraisal seemed to shift slightly. He now actively frowned at her instead of just incidentally.

"I'd prefer to discuss that with her. If you could direct me to her house, I would be most obliged." He even went so far as to give a half-bow, though it was surely mocking. Mara flicked her eyes to the cottage, a mere few hundred feet away, and donned her best smile.

"I shall improve upon your request and take you to her myself," Mara said. Then, gathering up her basket and pointedly walking two steps in front of the man, she started towards the house. If he was so attached to his pride that he could not even accept help for his ankle from her, then he could very well suffer for it. She'd put an extra dose of willow bark in the poultice she made up later to soothe the ache, but it was worth it.

Finally, after Mara turned twice to make sure the man was keeping up, they reached the front gate that kept the garden mostly contained. "Grandmother!" Mara called. "Company!"

She saw the moment the man realised his error. His eyes—a grey almost the same colour as the sky—widened. His mouth, finely shaped and smooth, twisted wryly. He let out a soft chuckle and shook his head. Mara couldn't help her own returning smirk. She led the way to the door and pushed it open.

Cait was waiting in the stillroom doorway, drying her hands on her apron. She blinked in astonishment as Mara led the stranger into the house. Then, a frown of admonition. "Mara, child, why is this man limping?"

"Ah, I beg your pardon. I was crossing the stream and became distracted. I slipped. Your, ah, granddaughter came to my rescue." The man gave another of those half-bows, though this was far less mocking than the one he had given Mara. "I am Kyle Livingston."

"Cait Del Sol, and my granddaughter, Mara. Well, at least you crossed the stream close to the cottage and not farther downstream. It's a pain to walk up the hill on a sprained ankle." She gave him an appraising once over, noting the wet clothes and the disgruntled expression. She spared enough time to exchange a glance with Mara, quietly exasperated, then Cait immediately bustled their unexpected guest into the drawing room, which had long since been converted to a patient visiting area. "Off with your shoe and sock. And your jacket is soaked; give it to Mara and she'll hang it by the fire in the stillroom. At least it will be slightly dry before you leave."

Mara did as she was asked and returned to the room just as this Livingston fellow peeled off his sock to reveal his swollen and red ankle. "That will bruise up by tomorrow," she said. Cait shot her a frustrated glance and Mara shrugged.

"I assume it's not fatal." Livingston's voice was dry and flat, but he looked less cantankerous than before, likely a result of being seated rather than standing on the offending limb.

"Not unless you're stupid and try to walk back to town. I'll brew a poultice and wrap it, then I'll get Mara to hitch up Old Wallace to the cart and take you back to town." Cait ran her hands over the ankle and Mara saw the tiny sparks of magic that indicated a more thorough examination. Cait muttered something and bustled off to the kitchen to grab her ingredients.

"It won't take long," Mara said. She sat in one of the other chairs. "Though we have time to discuss why you wanted to see my grandmother, in the first place. If you are so inclined, of course. Not that I know anything of herblore."

Livingston sighed through his nose. "You're as well versed in the craft as she is, aren't you?"

"Except for the cultivation of a few plants that seem to prefer her care to mine, yes." And the magic, of course. Though Cait did often say that Mara could likely sing a spell into a brew just as well as any hedge-witch. She was a little afraid to try; mesmerising people during her performances was one thing, trying to infuse magic into a brew was an entirely different matter.

"I apologise for my behaviour earlier," Livingston, now the picture of the polite gentleman, though there was no hiding the slight undertone of irritation. Mara wondered what he was doing in Tallmadge. She hoped it wasn't a search for a remedy that could not be found, nor nothing so mundane as a cure for impotence. She liked this man, in spite of his rudeness. "I was not expecting the distance to the cottage from town to be so far. And to have it end in the creek, well..."

"Why have you come out this far? Surely you could have waited to find myself or my grandmother when we came into town. We're there nearly every day." Maybe he hadn't known that. Mara knew full well that some of the townspeople could be a little reticent to outsiders, no matter how well proportioned physically or financially.

"I thought it would be more polite to come to you," he said. He chuckled again, the sound just a touch dark, and ran his hands through his hair. "Instead, it seems I've put you out even more."

"It's an easy poultice," Mara said, putting just a tiny amount of magical reassurance into her voice. Livingston nodded and seemed to relax. It wasn't quite the same as singing, but it was sometimes effective in those who were receptive to magic. Not everyone was, especially these days. "Was the matter you wished to consult my grandmother on private? Should I leave?"

Really, she didn't want to leave, not now. But she didn't know of any other way to ask what he wanted with Cait without being painfully blunt in her questioning. Livingston seemed to realise this, because he was fiddling with the buttons on his shirt cuffs and starting to scowl again. Perhaps she could have phrased that better. Having a patient upset, even if it was only a sprained ankle, was detrimental to healing. Living away from other people had not served her well in the intricacies of socially acceptable communication. She was more blunt than many a woman, and had been told as much several times, though never by her grandmother who was just as blunt as she.

"I came to Tallmadge to do some research, and was informed that your grandmother might be able to help me with the matter. Of course, that was before I was distracted and sprained my ankle."

"I didn't distract you," Mara said. At least he was here for something other than a medical ailment. Research was certainly an unusual request, though occasionally they did get botanists who were interested in particular highland varieties of certain herbs, or their medicinal properties. It would be a simple matter of escorting him on a herb gathering mission, with a few discussions of the properties of certain plants, if that were the case. Yet her ire was starting to rise. She was trying not to feel frustrated by this constant allusion to her fault in his fall, but her temper was like the sea: calm and placid, even lively, until the pressure changed, then she was as changeable and furious as the waves.

"You did. You called out—"

"It wasn't to you," she snapped. "I was talking to…"

Fool. If he didn't think her crazy before, he surely would now.

"To whom? Your grandmother? She was inside."

"Very well, if you wish to know, I was talking to the water nymph who pulled you into the water. She doesn't tend to listen to me on the best days, but I have tried to teach her some manners. Obviously, I'm not very good at it. Though, I must say, if this is how you treat perfect strangers who do nothing but offer to help, then I can hardly be sorry at her lack of decorum." Then, Mara pushed herself out of the chair and stalked to the kitchen to see what was taking so long with that poultice. She didn't care whether this Livingston character thought her as crazy as the moon. She was tired of being forced to hold her tongue about magic. She was tired of being so separate from the world of humans. She was tired of lying that she didn't feel her own magic changing as the cycles of the moon changed.

And she was tired of being treated as nothing by people—handsome men included—who cared only for her relationship to the herbwoman. There was, after all, no reason to be rude to someone who was just trying to help!

So she bottled her fear into anger at this gruff, intrusive, impolite guest and happily took the mortar and pestle from her grandmother. She ground the herbs to dust.

CHAPTER 5

Rarely had Livingston felt such the fool. He was an intellect, a scholar, and while he was not particularly adept at the various subtle rules of society, he rarely made such blunders as he had made today. His mother had taught him that much, at least. He could try and blame his mistakes on the ball the night before; he had been thoroughly annoyed at the attention and wanted nothing more than to do his research. He had woken in a bad mood that morning, still reliving the indignities of the gala. The walk up to this cottage had calmed him somewhat, and he'd even felt mildly charitable towards the people who gave him directions as we went. Then, he'd slipped crossing the stream and all his cheer had vanished.

He was *certain* that this Mara Del Sol woman was laughing at him. She'd been smug when he clawed his way out of the creek, though he acknowledged a mild sense of humour there as well. Her grandmother was brusque, but at least that was expected—all the other herbwomen he'd met had been of a similar bent, their days too full to spend hours on niceties. Mara, though she was beautiful and vivacious, seemed more inclined to taunt him.

News of his research must have reached this remote place. She'd just snubbed him, made a mockery of his interests, telling him a nymph had pulled him into the water. Livingston was hardly a simpleton, and he knew when to retreat. This place was no good for him or his research and he preferred to leave with at least some semblance of his dignity intact. He would not be laughed at. Not even for magic.

He'd have to cancel his lease of the house, he decided. That would be an annoyance, but a mild one. And Aidan was probably in residence at Blackwell Downs. Maybe Livingston could spend some time there and figure out his next move. He could bury himself in his books until this humiliation was well and truly forgotten. There were many ways to do research. Or perhaps this was a sign that he should move onto a more favourable topic. Either way, there would be no help in this cottage or in Tallmadge.

He was just about to leave, pushing himself out of the chair, when Cait bustled back into the room with a bowl in hand, Mara behind her with steps that were strong and graceful. Immediately, the older woman shot him a glare that had him sitting quickly back into the chair. He coughed nervously.

"Thought about leaving, did you?" Cait asked, her voice harsh. "Too proud to take medical help from a lowly herbwoman?"

Mara frowned at him, her glare cutting. But when she addressed her grandmother, her voice was soft, soothing, almost entrancing. "I think it more likely he is embarrassed to be associating with me, since I told him about the nymph in the creek."

Cait's eyes widened in surprise and the look she gave her granddaughter was nothing short of astonished. She looked between Mara and Livingston and made a sound in her throat that was somewhere between a laugh and a question. Her chin lifted. "Did she, now? And is that what had you so eager to leave, Mr. Livingston? Are you so set in the ways of this modern world that you can't even accept what little magic remains in it?"

"No, I—" he started, but the look that Cait turned on him was nothing short of ferocious and he swallowed his words back.

"I'll have you know, sir, that I'm a hedgewitch, and I did use a spell on this poultice of yours. I've been using spells in my mixtures and potions and tinctures my whole life, and not once have I had any complaints about my work not being good enough. My granddaughter is not a fool, sir, nor does she tolerate them. So if you wish to disdain her and me because of our magic, then you can very well hobble your way back down the hill towards Tallmadge and let Doctor Thompson, that bumbling idiot, treat you instead."

Mara lay a hand on Cait's shoulder. "I believe, Grandmother," she said, the corners of her mouth twitching upwards, "that you are meant to allow him space to rebut your arguments. Or politely take his leave, if that is his preference."

Cait sniffed. "Very well. What is your response, Mr. Livingston?"

He was struck dumb, his stomach twisting uncomfortably. Could he have mistaken everything? He thought he was being snubbed for his research, as he would have been the evening before if not for his money. Instead, he had been praised for being a bit eccentric because it meant he could afford a great deal. This, though, was something entirely different.

This was likely truth.

Now he felt double the fool.

"I, ah," he tried to say. Then, clearing his throat, he offered a weak smile. "I am actually in Tallmadge to, ah, do research on that very subject. Magic, I mean. I'm writing a book on the topic and have spent the last six months trying to gather anecdotes and tales and evidence to bolster my research. It all started when I met a Keeper of the Wild and…and…is there truly a nymph in the creek?"

He was desperate, and babbling, and he knew it. But this could be his chance. This could be the proof that he was looking for. This was something more than just tales of old. He didn't even care that Cait was a hedge-witch and not a fully fledged witch. He cared about this more than he could say, no matter how many times he thought about giving up. He'd gladly fall over his feet apologising if it meant that these two would talk with him.

Mara and Cait exchanged some silent conversation

in the space of a glance and Livingston felt his face grow hot. What if they thought he was, in turn, making light of them, laughing at them? He didn't know how to reassure him that he was telling the truth, except to show his research which was, except for a few notes in the small notebook in his pocket, all back at the house.

"Research?" Mara asked, eyes wary. She drew up a footstool and steadied her grandmother's elbow while the woman sat. Then, without any ceremony at all, Cait started putting a poultice on his ankle. He yelped. It was *cold*.

"Oh, don't be such a ninny. It'll keep the swelling down." Cait was abrupt, but he didn't mind. It meant they weren't laughing at him. Right?

"Yes," Livingston said, looking at Mara. Her gaze was sharp enough to cut. His mouth went dry. "I, ah, I've been to several villages like yours, interviewing people about local legends and folklore, sometimes about druidic ruins. I've interviewed three other hedgewitches. It's a good start, but I would love to see the nymph, maybe get a sketch of…her?"

"Her," Mara confirmed, handing over a cloth so Cait could wipe her hands. "Though you won't be able to see her."

"Why not?" He was devastated. "I promise I'll not startle her. Do I need to bring a gift? I know some of the Fae are rumoured to appreciate that."

"It's not that. Only people with a water affinity can see her. If you didn't see her when she pulled you into the creek, then you don't have a water affinity." Her words were so simple, but they felt like a blow to him.

And she just sat there, apparently uncaring at the cut she'd delivered.

He knew of his own druid bloodline, though he'd been told that any magic he might have was many generations removed. But to be so completely mundane was more than a little disappointing. And for this woman to say so without a hint of remorse stung. He had hoped—what had he hoped, exactly? That he was special? That he had at least a trace of magic in him, not just the forgotten memories of an age lost to time? Had he been trying to place himself above the common crowd just because of his heritage? Surely there were thousands of people with druidic blood-lines. Yet there were no druids. They were all as normal as he was. Some bright, hopeful light dimmed inside him and he set his mouth. He still needed to do his research, though. That much he would not give up.

"Perhaps you can describe her to me. Draw a picture. Tell me what she's like," Livingston practically begged Mara. A line appeared between her brows and her polite smile fell a little. He quickly turned his atten-tions to Cait, not wanting to push too hard. "And if it's not too much trouble, Mrs. Del—"

"Miss," Cait put in. "I never married. Or mistress, if you must."

"Forgive me," Livingston put a hand to his chest. "Mistress Del Sol, I would like very much to interview you. About your magic. About the spells you use on your potions and remedies."

"I thought you had already spoken with a few hedgewitches," she said, quirking a brow. Her hands were deft at wrapping the linen bandage around his ankle and a moment later she was done. It would be a little awkward to get his shoe on; he would probably have to forgo the item until tomorrow. And his sock was still wet, so he just left his foot bare, resting on the stone of the floor, warm in the summer weather.

Cait watched him with intense eyes. "What more could you possibly need from me if you've already met my kind?"

"None were well-versed in herblore, as you are. I would like very much to know how you use your magic in your preparations." He looked between the two women who were cleaning up after tending to him. "Please. I am desperate. The university already thinks me the fool for pursuing such a topic. They would rather pursue science or mathematics, or even history that suits their particular intent than magic, than stories they believe should be left to children. The world is unprepared for the return of magic, and I believe that it *is* returning."

Mara and Cait shared another of their wordless glances, this one tight with worry. He could tell that they were putting up walls, closing ranks on him, and it was like another thing, another dream, was being taken from him. He could not allow that, not now. It was all he had left of his own life, his own goals and passions. He had money, sure. Some relative standing in society. Even a smattering of a reputation as a scholar, though he was apparently tearing that to shreds with his own two hands. But none of that mattered at all to him compared with the tantalising promise of magic.

"I have to let people know," Livingston said. "I have to prepare them. I can pay you for your time if—"

"Absolutely not!" Cait snapped. Mara bristled beside her. "We do not require your money, sir."

"I apologise," Livingston said. He tried to smile, tried to look contrite and respectable. He was probably failing miserably. "I just…I would really love to discuss magic with you."

Cait took a deep breath, handing her supplies off to Mara, who darted out of the room. The older woman put her hands on her hips and glared down at Livingston. "I am the only hedgewitch around for three counties. So long as you don't disrupt our work with your talking and your questions, then I will answer what I can."

He sagged with relief. "Thank you, Mistress, thank you. I cannot tell you how much this means to me. If there is anything I can do to repay you, please do let me—"

Cait held up a hand, expression hard. "If I wanted to put up with simpering, I could just as easily go deal with sailors who get fishhooks stuck in their hands. You will be discreet in your questions if we are around other people. Say something about how you want to learn about the botany hereabouts. Not everyone is so fond of magic as you, Mr. Livingston, especially not so near the sea."

Especially not so near the sea? What did the sea have to do with anything, he wondered. Still, he could tell that she was serious, and he did not want to alienate his new source of information. So he bowed his head in agreement. "I can do that. What of your granddaughter?"

"Mara?" Cait reared her head back, the pearl at her neck catching in a beam of sunlight. It was of remarkable size, as Sophia had said the night before, and Livingston wondered if it was indeed meant to enhance her magic. He mentally added that to his list of questions. "She's not a hedgewitch."

No magic, then. "I merely meant to ask if she would be involved in the questions, if she knew as much as you." Livingston dismissed the woman from his mind, though, for she held no interest to him if she had no magic. No matter her striking gaze.

"She's as well-versed in herblore as I am," Cait said, still looking wary.

Livingston nodded, but said nothing. He pulled out his notebook and a pencil. "May I…may I begin now?"

"It will take the girl a minute to hitch up the horse," Cait admitted, albeit reluctantly. She settled herself in another chair and lifted her chin. "You may ask your questions."

He wasted no time. "The nymph, how long has she lived in the creek? I admit to not knowing much about the creatures, only that they are beings of water."

"Spirits of water," Cait corrected, tone harsh. "Used to be they were as well known as the Fae around these parts. They are spirits tied to bodies of water. Protective of their territory. They protest when people dump rubbish into the water, do their best to keep their lands clean. Around here, even those who do not believe in magic are smart enough to declare their intent when crossing bodies of water without a bridge. They believe it nothing more than a Northern superstition, one of many, no matter how necessary it truly is."

Livingston scribbled down the information before he realised he was being quietly chastised for his unintentional treatment of the nymph. He winced.

Mara reentered the room, and looked to be in slightly better spirits than before, for her smile was easy and she did not hold herself as if worried. Good. He needed her to at least be civil towards him, for the sake of his questions to her grandmother.

"The wagon's ready," Mara said. Cait nodded and straightened, though she did not rise from her chair.

"Good. You need to get back to town and rest that ankle," Cait said firmly.

"I have more questions!" Livingston protested. Mara made a delicate sound that would have been a snort if coming from a different woman, then went to the door.

"Your questions can wait," she said. "The horse cannot. Come. I have things to fetch from town and do not want to be late. You may return another time."

Livingston was smart enough to recognise that he was being put in his place. His money and influence counted for nothing here. He was at the mercy of their good will, and he would have to work hard to earn that since he started off so badly. He stood, keeping his weight off his bad ankle, and hobbled after Mara.

"Thank you, Mistress Del Sol," he said, bowing as he supported his weight on the door. "I cannot convey how much this means to me."

"Hmph," was the haughty reply, but there was a hint of a smile behind those wise eyes.

Livingston left the cottage for the bright, warm day, finding an ancient-looking draft horse hitched to an open wagon. Mara waited in the driver's seat, the long bench the only reasonable perch unless one wished to be tossed about the back. She quirked a brow at Livingston and he bit back a sharp reply, instead heaving himself onto the bench beside her and ignoring the slight throb in his ankle. He was about to say something—perhaps a compliment would put her in a better frame of mind towards him—when she clicked her tongue and flapped the reins. The horse tossed his head and started moving, and Livingston knew, without a doubt, that winning over Mara Del Sol was going to be his most trying challenge yet.

He wasn't sure he wanted to bother.

CHAPTER 6

The researcher's reticence only lasted about half of the trip into Tallmadge, which was a little disappointing to Mara. She had hoped that this Livingston character would keep silent for the entire journey, thus making it easier to dismiss him and his questions about magic as something meant purely for her grandmother, meant for this mysterious book he was writing. But when he began asking questions of her, Mara felt her throat tighten and her knuckles became white as they gripped the reins.

"What was it like, watching your grandmother practise magic your whole life?" Livingston asked. He was reaching into his pocket for that notebook and pencil. Mara wanted to throw both over the side of the wagon. What was her grandmother thinking, agreeing to answer his questions? She should have just sent him on his way!

"I imagine it was very like any child watching their elders ply their trade. Mysterious until you have seen it done a thousand times." Mara kept her voice cool and devoid of her own magic. She did not want to rouse this man's suspicions. She did not want to draw his attention in any way.

Because this book that he was supposedly writing? It would be an excellent story to bandy about while he asked questions about those who might have magic. About those sought out by the sea. He was just a little too desperate for information, his attitude straddling the line between gruff and deferential. His act was perfect, for he seemed exactly the sort to be a scholar out on a research mission. But there had been others' whose acts were perfect, too, and every one of them had been a spy for the beings who lurked beneath the waves. Her grandmother knew that, and yet she still agreed to answer his questions. Mara wanted to yell, but now was certainly not the time.

Beside her, Livingston frowned, eyes glowering at his notebook. "I, ah…that was not precisely what I meant."

"Then you should learn to be more precise with your questions," Mara returned. She clicked her tongue at the horse and directed him down the track to Tallmadge, which was stony and rough thanks to the spring melt depositing all sorts of debris along the way, making it nearly invisible even to those who knew it was there. It usually cleared out by the end of summer, but they were hardly there yet. "I suggest you hold on; there's a hole in the road."

Her warning was given just a second too late, because the wagon jostled and Livingston bounced about in a most undignified manner, nearly losing his seat entirely. Mara tried not to smirk.

The man muttered something about proper road care, then straightened and readjusted his grip on his notebook. He hadn't dropped it, then. A shame.

"Let me rephrase my question," he said, the tone just shy of being a demand. "What does her magic look like?"

Mara blinked. "Look like?"

"I have talked with three different hedgewitches and spent time with a Keeper of the Wild. Not one of their magic looked the same to me. The Keeper—Briony—was possessed of magic that whispered until it became a storm. One of the hedgewitches fairly glowed with power when she brewed her tea. Another grew dim as shadows when she talked with the birds. What does your grandmother's magic look like?"

Mara considered for a moment, both on the question and whether she should answer this man. Yet her grandmother had promised him to provide answers to his questions. Was it meant as a distraction from Mara, drawing attention to her own magic? Or had she sensed some kernel of truth in his desperation? Magic *was* returning to the world. Mara could hear it in the tides and the trickling of the creek and even the song in her own bones. But the world of humans had forgotten their heritage long ago. They no longer remembered the forces that could shape worlds. If someone could remind them, then they could perhaps be saved when the tide of magic washed in. But if

Livingston were false, would this information prove dangerous?

Mara did not know.

But she answered anyways, a sort of quiet compulsion to speak her truth borne of years of silence. "Sometimes, she puts a spell on a potion to increase its efficacy. A cold remedy made better for sore throats. And when she does, there's this sort of…arc of light that shimmers over the cauldron. Barely there, but strong enough to make you remember things you've forgotten. It's beautiful."

Livingston took down her words dutifully, but there was something in his expression that Mara caught out of the corner of her eye that made her think of a smile. She had not realised this man could smile genuinely. She focused her attention on the road ahead. They were approaching the town and would soon be on its paths and amongst its people. Talking of magic there would do no one any good.

"Beautiful," Livingston echoed her. He frowned and shook his head. "Perhaps I can convince your grandmother to perform magic where I can observe."

And then what? Mara wondered. Learn to do magic himself?

"Here we are," she said, nodding her head to the buildings that made up Tallmadge. "Where are you staying? I don't want to have to explain to my grandmother that I let you walk home on that ankle after bringing you all this way."

To her surprise, Livingston made a sound in his

throat almost like he was embarrassed. He pointed to a turn. "Two streets over. Number 17."

Unable to contain it, Mara threw her head back and laughed. "You took Alder House? What could possibly have possessed you to take the nicest house available? Are you travelling with family, perhaps? A wife who demands such luxury?"

Livingston growled something under his breath and tucked his head in such a way that his dark hair covered his eyes. "I was unaware of the magnitude of the house when I took it. The leasing agent was hardly effusive on its size."

Mara swallowed her snort of laughter. She'd obviously struck a nerve, and while he might very well be a spy, she did not want to turn away any potential business from Cait. If he were truly that wealthy, and circulated in the right circles, a word or two from him could do wonders for business. Whereas a word in the opposite direction could easily do damage. Was that why her grandmother had pandered to this man?

"I apologise," Mara said. "I did not mean to berate you for your choice in house. It merely seems impractical for a research trip."

Now Livingston sighed, which was rarely a good sign in a conversation. "It was a mistake," he said, that growl beginning to creep back into his voice. "One I apparently will be paying for eternally."

Mara remained silent for the rest of the way to the house, thankfully only a few hundred feet away. She pulled up the horse with a click of her tongue and clambered off the seat before Livingston could do something foolish like try to be polite and offer to help. Instead, she helped him and delivered him to the door. "Keep off of that for at least a day, if you can, and replace the wrappings this evening. Wash the poultice off then; it will have done its work. The joint will be tender for a while, but my grandmother knows what she's doing. That poultice should reduce the swelling immensely."

Her instructions delivered, Mara turned with a swirl of her skirts and climbed back on the wagon.

"Wait!"

She looked at Livingston, leaning against the frame of the door. He licked his lips as if nervous and closed his eyes. "Thank you," he said. Mara was astonished. But she just inclined her head and drove away.

All through her errands in town, she felt as though she were moving in a daze, her thoughts torn between worry over this new stranger and the proximity of the water. She nearly dropped the cuts of meat for their supper and leaned against the cart. She was only one street over from the cliffs that looked over the sea. It wasn't the docks—a place she was not to venture on her own—but it was close enough to those tantalising waves that she could not resist their call. All thoughts of the stranger and his light, gleaming eyes disappeared.

Leaving the horse and wagon tethered to the post outside the butcher's, she wandered to the cliffs as if in a dream. Once there, she looked out over the expanse of water, forcing her eyes to stay focused on the sky— bright and blue, teeming with birds wheeling over the clouds and the boats bringing in the day's catch—before they inevitably slipped to the water below.

It was placid and deep today, the water closer to the colour of slate than of blue. The boats on the water barely made a ripple against the ocean's mighty surface and the waves beating on the cliffs had the sound of routine and rhythm rather than fury. It was majestic and immense and full of so many hidden dangers that Mara could not even dream of walking along the shore without fear.

But she loved it with every fibre of her being.

She wrapped her arms around herself and bit her lip to keep from crying out. A single tear fell down her cheek, and she dashed it away before any townspeople could see and comment.

"You, who hate and desire me so much," Mara breathed, voice shaking with fury, "can you not even let me live my life in peace? I am deprived of your touch and your song and must live my days amongst the earth and the trees, and not once do I receive your sympathy, only your ire. You send *spies* after me so that you might know me and claim my power for your own. I am your *daughter*! Yet you care nothing for me."

She missed her father just then. The one being whose connection to the ocean could not be doubted. He could only visit once every seven years, but occasionally he left gifts by the estuary that the nymph carried up the creek to her. Mara had a box full of shells and dried bits of seaweed and driftwood that her father had given her to show that he thought of her, that he loved her. She had never met her mother, but on those too-brief visits, her father assured her that her mother's songs were full of sorrow for her lost child.

It was one thing to know that you are loved, and quite another to be standing impossibly far from those who hold your heart, never able to join them, to be with them.

Mara was always drawn to the ocean, to its waves and its depths. And she loved it, truly, but she also wished—not for the first time—that she could be just the simple foundling child that her grandmother claimed.

Human. Normal.

At least then, this agony she carried would be for something within reach.

Maybe then she could trust people like the researcher, instead of instinctively keeping herself closed off.

She dashed away another tear and turned her back on the ocean, all but running to the wagon. She hoped beyond hope that this Livingston character was not another spy that the ocean sent to all the coastal towns, forever searching for her. She could not bear one more hurt from those waters.

Mara drove the wagon back through town, cutting through the marketplace. It was the fastest way back to the hills, though there were more people about than some of the quieter, side streets. It was a mistake.

"Mara Del Sol!" A woman wearing bright blue and purple bustled forward, a parasol waving above her head like some peacock's plumage. She was a good friend of the Rushworths and every year, after the summer gala, tried to put together a garden party that would outdo her friends. It never did, but she always tried.

"Mrs. Bunting," Mara said, nodding her head though she did not climb off the wagon. "I hope you are having a pleasant day?"

"Oh, yes, indeed I am! I was just organising some food for my annual summer garden party. The flowers are so beautiful this year!" The lady leaned forward as if conspiratorially, though her voice carried across the street. "I even ordered some pineapple from a hothouse in town, can you imagine!"

"Sounds lovely," Mara said, trying to keep any waspishness out of her voice. She didn't want to alienate these people because of her own pain. It was unfair to them, when they were hardly cruel, just wrapped up in their own existence.

"Doesn't it?" Mrs. Bunting giggled, pressing a gloved hand to her lips. "I heard you weren't at the Rushworth's ball this year. Was your voice not in good health?"

That was the excuse Mara had given, and now she wished she could claim the same thing once again. "It was not," she said. "Some allergies, you understand."

"Of course I do!" Mrs. Bunting flapped her hand. She beamed up at Mara. "I'm so pleased that you're feeling better. Surely you can come to my little gathering? I know it's nothing so formal as a ball, but I have no doubt the guests would be glad of some entertainment. Oh, do say you'll be there!"

Mara opened her mouth to refuse. She didn't want

to go and be paraded about before all these people. But she loved singing. It was as much a part of her as the ocean and she so rarely got to practise her gifts. They had become stronger, more insistent, in the last few months. And it was the only real connection with these people that she had. Was she not just crying about her loneliness? Her lack of connection to the waters that had birthed her?

Maybe this would have to be good enough, living in this world amongst these people.

"I'll be there," Mara said at last, trying to smile. A part of her wondered if she were making a mistake at this, doing something foolish—especially with this Livingston character wandering about—but the rest of her was smiling. Her horse tossed his head, a good enough indication to move on. Mara clicked her tongue and waved to Mrs. Bunting, feeling happy for the first time in weeks.

She'd dealt with spies in the past, and if this Livingston was a spy, he was just another of many sent to all the coastal towns. She would deal with him as she had the others. And then, she would continue to live her life, not the life of an ocean-bound fugitive.

CHAPTER 7

*L*ivingston decided that having a sprained ankle was not the worst thing in the world. It did cause an unfortunate amount of fussing from his housekeeper, but she then left him alone to his work instead of insisting that he take a tour offered by her nephew or son or whoever it was, or offering him up for more social invitations. Likely, she got bored with fussing over someone who either ignored her attempts or blatantly refused them.

He then had two whole days of relative peace. He wrote up his notes about the nymph and about Cait, adding her to the section on hedgewitches, and the nymph in the creatures of the north section, which was woefully underwhelming. None of the information he'd gathered from Cait or Mara was enough to fill those two days, but he had a chance to make up a list of questions to ask, requests to fulfil, and managed to organise the unstructured mess of his manuscript into something more befitting a proper academic work.

He'd even got a chance to read a short volume on fables, jotting down information as he could.

In short, it was wonderful.

Until, that is, word got out about his injury and the hopeful families looking to create a connection with him came to visit. He blamed the helpful Mrs. Cusper for the leak in information.

Livingston settled into the chair in his drawing room—it had the best light for the morning—and opened his notebook to start rereading some of the pieces he'd written out, when the bell for the door sounded. He perked up. Perhaps Mara or Cait had come to check on his ankle, or answer more of his questions. A moment later and he dismissed the notion; while willing to answer his questions, neither had seemed particularly thrilled about it. He doubted they would seek him out. Why none of the magical people he'd interviewed seemed eager to speak with him, he did not know. Was he that odious?

Mrs. Cusper bustled into the room, wiping her hands on her apron and looking absolutely delighted with herself. Livingston immediately put his notebook and pencil away and silently grieved for the remainder of the morning. Indeed, no sooner had the housekeeper entered the room than the Fulton, Farley, whatever their name was, family shuffled into the room.

"Mr. Livingston, the Farleys," Mrs. Cusper said, grinning widely. Mr. Farley looked about the room as if appraising its architectural attributes. Mrs. Farley bounced in wearing what appeared to be a massive amount of flounces, looking keenly at the furniture and dressings of the room before settling her gaze on Livingston himself. And their daughter, Sophia, elegant in white trimmed in lavender, just looked mildly amused. There was a fourth member of their family, a gentleman grown, his features taking more after the mother than the father, well dressed and holding himself with an air that was just a shade shy of pompous. A mysterious brother, Livingston imagined. And a dandy at that.

"Mr. Livingston, we were so distressed to hear of your injury!" Mrs. Farley said, sitting on the settee almost before he indicated to her it was acceptable. Sophia sat beside her and the brother beside his sister. Mr. Farley went to stare at the clock on the wall.

"It is but a mild sprain," Livingston said. "I was foolish enough to cross a creek without permission."

Testing the water, perhaps, this mention of supposed northern superstition. All he received was a giggle from the mother and a knowing smile from the young Sophia.

"Oh, indeed!" Mrs. Farley said. "I don't believe you met my son, Bartholomew. He wasn't at the Rushworth's ball, the other night, being away in town on business."

Bartholomew lifted his nose with a dainty sniff, as if being in town were far preferred to being at some ball. Given that Livingston would, too, rather be at his house in town than socialising needlessly, he was inclined to agree, though for very likely different reasons.

"I hear you came from town recently yourself,"

Bartholomew said, his voice decidedly superior and with an unfortunate nasal tone. "A marvellous collection of people. Wouldn't you agree?"

"I have lately been travelling about the countryside on research," Livingston deflected. Then, he added, "And I much prefer the quiet of the university to the noise of town. Far easier to ignore those who pander to anyone they see as maybe providing a useful connection. Then, I try not to bother with such people, preferring books to balls."

Sophia snorted a laugh, which she covered by coughing into her hand. Mrs. Farley blinked, but only simpered at Livingston. Bartholomew tightened his mouth but said nothing.

"And how goes your research here, Mr. Livingston?" Mrs. Farley pressed on. "Sophia told me that you were hardly interested in the lake monster. Everyone seems to come here to catch a glimpse of the monster, but it's nice to explore around, I'm sure!"

"I have spoken with your local herbwoman," Livingston said. He didn't want to bandy about the fact that she was a hedgewitch; not everyone was so accepting of magic as he, as the woman herself had pointed out. "She seems to know a great deal about local legends and creatures and tales of magic."

"Do you mean Cait Del Sol?" Mr. Farley asked, interrupting for the first time, his attention finally on the conversation. "A good woman. Smart. Capable. She did well for Bartholomew when he was a boy. Sickly child."

Bartholomew stiffened, cheeks flushing. "It was

nothing more than normal childhood sickness, I'm sure."

His father made a noncommittal sound. Mrs. Farley seemed to have lost the thread of the conversation and cast about to see if she could regain control. "Are you attending Mrs. Bunting's garden party in three weeks' time? It should be a lovely event. Rumours have it she's trying to make it more like a village fair than anything."

Livingston made a noise in his throat. He was horrified that this was what his life had come to. He was a respected scholar! He should not have to be contending with garden parties and socialising. He should be arguing papers and credentials with fellow scholars. He should be researching. He should be doing many things, and all of them had been given up in pursuit of magic.

His mother and father had both warned him that society was something he would have to endure in the pursuit of his scholarly ambitions, but he'd never believed them. Oh, he'd learned the role to appease his mother and earn the pride of his father, but he'd always assumed that he would be spending his time in the library or debating with other scholars. Not trying to wheedle tidbits of information out of people who didn't even care about his research. He blinked and realised he wasn't sure if he meant the Del Sols or the Farleys, then wondered if it mattered.

It did, he thought. *It did matter.*

The visit with the Farleys extended another half hour before they made their excuses about having to go visit other people. His flat expression and lacklustre answers likely contributed to their early departure. Twenty minutes after they left, another family stopped by, this time just a husband and wife—the Sandhams—expressing their welcome to him and asking about his intentions regarding attendance of the garden party.

By the time lunch came and the visiting hours were over, Livingston was fairly itching in his skin. He felt trapped, ensnared, exactly where he never wished to be. The endless parade of people suited some, like Aidan and even Reggie Townsend, but Livingston had never cared for it. Unfortunately for him, he was possessed of his father's entire fortune and that made him prey to certain responsibilities, even of the social variety.

After lunch, he found no relief in planning out his book, so instead called for his horse to be saddled and gave up all pretence of trying to heal his ankle. It throbbed slightly as the mare started out through the streets, hooves clattering on the cobbles, but he ignored the pain. A few people nodded their heads respectfully. Thankfully, no one stopped him for conversation, something in his expression warning them off.

When he reached a reasonable distance from the centre of town, he urged his mare into a trot, then a gallop, and took to the hills with alacrity and the sort of desperation that drove men to the heights of folly. Thankfully, his horse was surefooted and wiser than he. She took him through the heather and grasses without argument or question. She even leaped the stream where the nymph had grabbed at Livingston with a snort and he would have sworn that she flicked her ears with self-satisfaction at the spot where the nymph had supposedly been.

The cottage was quiet, the only activity the buzzing of bees and a lazy cat stretching in the sun. The sun was beginning to set, and it was possible that there were herbs which could only be collected at night. Or the women were out visiting other patients. All he knew was that a lump in his stomach fairly stank of disappointment when no one answered his knock, and that was hardly acceptable.

He wanted to research magic. He wanted to keep pursuing this topic despite the warnings of the other scholars. He wanted to *know*. But he had to acknowledge that he was being foolish. According to every rule of society, drilled into him since a young age and further discussed when he became a scholar up until the day his father died, he was being more than a fool. He was heading into the depths of lunacy. To risk everything on something so…intangible. And here he was, staring at the door to an empty cottage, hoping beyond hope that someone would answer the door so he might be saved from his impossible questions.

No one did.

He went back to his horse and directed her farther into the highlands. It was too early to go back and listen to another night of Mrs. Cusper's conversation over his supper. He didn't want to go to the pub, either, for fear that he would be drawn into conversation that way. He wanted to be alone, but he also wanted company. No, he realised a moment later, he wanted a challenge. A puzzle. Something to think on so that he wouldn't be stuck with his own ideas.

The horse went where she chose, turning into a tuck between two hills that smelled greatly of wild-flowers. Another turn and they were following a tribu-tary to the creek that ran by the herbwoman's cottage. This, they followed for a while. Livingston wondered whether there was a nymph in these water, too.

Then, voices.

They were hushed, harsh, and coming from a glen surrounded by trees hardened and twisted in the wind. It almost sounded like an argument, though he was unable to discern the actual words. He was only able to tell that Cait and Mara were the ones arguing.

Almost without thinking about it, he dismounted from his horse and crept towards the trees, making sure to keep his head down and his steps quiet. He peered between the leaves and his breath caught.

Cait was walking around a circle etched into the dirt and lined with stone. She had a bowl with what looked like water in one hand, and the other held the pearl at her throat. She was saying something in a language that Livingston did not know, her voice rhythmic and severe. Inside the circle was Mara, kneel-ing, her hair unbound and her expression just a touch wild. She had her hands pressed into the earth and tears were in her eyes. Every few steps, Cait would dip her fingers into the bowl of water and fling a few drops at Mara. And every time one of those drops hit her skin, Mara winced as though she'd been struck. Occa-sionally, she would let out a low moan or protest, muttering, "stop, please," while Cait kept walking, almost uncaring.

After three circuits of this—who knows how many had already been performed—Cait extended the bowl across the circle and poured the contents over Mara's hair. The woman let out a piteous cry, like a rabbit caught in a trap, and all but collapsed. She was crying freely, now.

Instincts warred within Livingston. He wanted to leap forwards and put an end to whatever it was that was causing Mara pain. He wanted to end her suffering, to wrap his arms around her and swear his protection. It was a primal need, raw, one he'd never felt before and he was a heartbeat away from acting on it. He hesitated. Part of him, the detached, academic part of him, recognised that this was magic being performed. It was a ritual of some sort, though he did not know what, and if he interrupted, he would never see its conclusion, never know what it was for. He wished he'd been here earlier so he could have seen the beginning of the ritual. He gave in to academic curiosity and brushed away any shame for it. He was a scholar, it was not his place to interfere but to observe, and that was an end to it.

Mara's cry faded away, and she collapsed on her side, breathing heavily. Cait set the bowl down and carefully smudged the circle with a foot before crossing over and wrapping her arms around her granddaughter. "I know, my sweet little one," she said, brushing back that brownish-gold hair. "I know it hurts."

"How much longer do we have to do this?" Mara whispered, letting her tears fall freely. Cait took a deep breath and shook her head.

"I wish I knew. Each time, though, the protection spell wears off faster and requires more effort to perform. I...I don't think this one will last more than another month. At most. And I don't think I'll be able to perform another." Cait pressed a kiss to Mara's hair and the younger woman whimpered.

"They'll find me," she breathed.

Who would find her? Livingston hated coming into conversations in the middle, but this sounded like one they had been having for a very long time. Was it to do with the protection spell? Why would Mara need protecting; she was a little too vivacious for Livingston's preference, with no seeming desire to curb her mouth, but that could hardly be a cause for a protection spell.

He doubted very much that any mention of this ritual would be allowed in his questions to Cait.

"We'll figure it out," Cait murmured, brushing her hands over Mara's hair while the younger woman cried into her arms.

Then, before Livingston could watch further or slowly back away and leave before anyone was the wiser, his horse stepped on a rock or a twig or something that made enough noise to startle everyone. Cait and Mara's heads both snapped up, and they looked directly at him. There was fire in those gazes and they seared, though they could not have seen more than a flash of his face through the leaves of the trees.

He fell backwards, his heart racing and his vision narrowing sharply. Before he could even think about apologising, or explaining, or anything sensible, he was scrambling back towards his horse. Retreat was as instinctual as that desire to reach for Mara when she was in pain, only this time he gave in. He mounted and dug his heels into his mare's side far more than was strictly necessary. The horse whinnied in fury then leapt into motion, leaving the two women and all of their mysterious magic behind.

Despite the fear that coursed through him, mixing with adrenaline into some heady combination that had his head roaring, Livingston could not help but smile. He had finally found some real magic worth writing about.

CHAPTER 8

Walking up into the hills with Cait felt a little like walking to her doom. Mara knew full well that the protection spell needed to be renewed, knew that she needed to go through with this ritual should she want to survive unnoticed by the ocean and its many spies for a while longer, but there was only so much she could do to stop the trembling in her hands.

The hills loomed around her as the afternoon light changed shadows into terrifying monsters. The wind rushing through the grasses seemed to taunt her, singing a song that Mara could not understand. She pulled the sleeves of her bodice as far down over her hands as they would come, then shivered.

Finally, they reached the copse of trees where they usually performed this ritual. It was out of the wind for the most part, the twisted trunks of the alder trees close enough to block out that dreadful singing. In the middle was a circle that they had carved into the ground over many years' use. Over time, she and Cait had added stones washed up by the sea to reinforce the purpose of the circle. A single point at the northern-most facing point was smudged for entry and exit without breaking the power of the circle.

Cait set down her supplies, a bowl and flask of water, some herbs and a few dried pieces of seaweed. "Alright, my dear, you know what to do."

Mara did know, and she still hated it.

She took a deep breath and closed her eyes, taking that fateful step into the circle. Almost immediately, her inherent sense of the wind's song and the call of every drop of water in her vicinity vanished with a bright and suffocating silence. She was empty, her magical senses dulled and the world around her myste-rious, dangerous, even terrifying. There was a slight tremor through that smudged entrance into the circle, but Cait closed it with a simple motion and the magic that kept Mara there snapped into existence.

The hairs on Mara's arms stood on end and she rubbed her hands over the linen sleeves. "It's sharper than before," she said.

Cait's brows furrowed, but she said nothing. She just poured the water into the bowl, added a few herbs and the dried seaweed, then started chanting her spell. Mara watched as the magic in her grandmother's hands rippled over the water, changing its shape. Were she not in the circle, she knew she would be able to feel the subtle changes in the water, its very essence being filled with magic meant for a singular purpose. To guard. To protect. To keep safe against the forces that hunted.

For a hedgewitch, such a ritual was dangerous to perform. This was not some ritual any magicless buffoon could perform; those were usually destructive spells, since destroying was so easy. If it were not for the pearl at Cait's throat, Mara knew that it would be beyond her grandmother's power. This was deep magic, something that needed more control and more power than most hedgewitches bore. It needed the power of a true witch, but there were fewer of those remaining in the world than ever before. The pearl focused Cait's power, helped her bridge that gap and complete the ritual.

Mara hated that it was necessary.

Finally, the spell cast on the water was done. Cait looked a little wan, and there was a slight rasp in her breath. Mara swallowed nervously. The two women exchanged a glance for a moment, then Cait dipped her fingers into the water and began to walk around the circle. She chanted as she did so in a language that was known only by the lost users of magic in this part of the world. The syllables were harsh and the vowels like wind over rock, but there was power in the words.

Cait spoke, and she stepped, and she flicked water over the barrier of the circle, the magic in the droplets screaming each time she did so. They struck Mara with a force that felt like stones; she was always surprised that she never came away bleeding from these rituals. But the spell stuck, burrowing into her skin and granting her what protection it could. Oh, but it stung.

Onwards, Cait chanted and walked and threw water at Mara. Each subsequent drop was like fire and soon, she was all but doubled over, moaning her pain. She lost count of how many times around Cait walked. Once, only a circuit of three would have been enough to perform the ritual. Over time, as Mara's magic grew, it became necessary for more. And more. And more.

Finally, Cait flung her last droplet of water and let the bowl fall to the ground. Mara let out a cry, her body trembling and unable to do anything about the pain of the spell sticking to her skin. Her bones felt like branding irons and her skin itched madly as it seemed to reform around her. She shivered and yet was warm. Her magic, distant and still subdued due to the circle, whimpered within her. The only thing that felt as it should were the tears falling down her cheeks. Cait smudged the circle and went to her, wrapping her arms around Mara. The touch was startling after the pain, but she leaned into it, unable to stop the tears that leaked from her eyes.

"I know, my sweet little one. I know it hurts."

If only she *did* know, Mara thought. But her grandmother had no true concept of the pain. "How much longer do we have to do this?" Mara asked, her question a plea for all of this to end. Why could she not simply be human? Be normal?

"I wish I knew. Each time, though, the protection spell wears off faster and requires more effort to perform. I...I don't think this one will last more than another month. At most. And I don't think I'll be able to perform another." Cait smoothed back Mara's hair.

While her heart sang at the knowledge that this was the last one, a month was hardly enough time. Her magic was still growing, and if the protection spell didn't last until it was fully manifested, then the spies would find her. Mara had been hunted her whole life, but it would be nothing at all compared to the efforts the sea would go to in order to find her once her magic manifested.

"They'll find me," Mara breathed, a realisation like a stone weighing her heart down.

"We'll figure it out." Cait's words were soft, but they were also resolute. And Mara, foolishly or no, believed her.

At least until a sound broke through the clearing. Mara jerked her head up and turned towards the sound. She spotted eyes—wide, alarmed—staring back at her. She recognised those eyes.

It was the man, Livingston, that sought to ask questions of her grandmother regarding magic. Mara *knew* that he was there to spy, but this was the first time that one of that ilk had actually got so close to their prey, close enough to see the truth. He could not be allowed to return to the sea.

Mara surged to her feet, ignoring the residual pain from the protection spell. She leaped over the stones of the circle, breaking the power that lay within through sheer force. There was a brief resistance, then her magical sense came back to her all at once. She could feel the rain in the few clouds gathering on the horizon. She could hear the song in the wind off the sea as it raced through the hills. She felt the water in the ground, though the connection was weaker there, and therefore felt every tremble from a horse's hooves racing away into the hills. Away from her.

Well, if he sought out the sea, he was going the wrong direction.

Mara ran after man and horse, her steps sure. She had grown up in these hills, even if her affinity was for water. She knew the best places to run. She knew how to traverse the rocks and the crags that opened up suddenly between bracken. She could move faster than a horse who was unfamiliar with these parts. She should have been moving faster even now, but she was still weak and reeling from the ritual.

Still, she made it to a break in the hills that diverted into a gully and stopped, heart pounding and breath wheezing. An instant later, Livingston appeared on his horse. The creature took one look at Mara and stopped, nearly throwing her rider from the saddle. He let out a curse and staggered in his seat. A moment later and he was recovered, but the stormy expression on his face told him he would not soon dismiss this. His eyes gleamed feverishly and he stared at her with something akin to curiosity tinged with desire. Mara wanted to shy away, but she forced herself to stand her ground, her shoulders back and her head high.

No spy would get the better of her. Not here, in her own country.

"Why are you following me?" he demanded.

"Following you!" Mara choked out an indignant laugh. "You are the one following us! I would not try running from me in these hills, Mr. Livingston. You will lame your horse long before you lose me."

"I knew there was magic here," he said, pointing an accusing finger at her. His eyes brightened further with an interest that was almost desperate. That stone in Mara's heart sank further. "Why did you not tell me about this? It would be perfect for my research!"

Mara tossed her head back, her hair catching on the wind. It whispered of the sea to her, still taunting her, chasing her. "You think you have a right to know everything that takes place in our lives, just because you were given permission to ask a few questions?"

"Questions about magic!" Livingston insisted. He was scowling at Mara now. "This is so much more important than you could possibly imagine. Do you know what will happen if magic returns and the world is not prepared for it? People have no *idea* what magic is like anymore. It's all just children's stories and legend. Nothing real, nothing any of these people have experienced. It will cause fear and chaos and I can prevent that with something so simple as a book! Is that not a noble goal?"

"Noble?" Mara nearly choked in indignation. "Oh, yes, I grant you that the world is unprepared for a return of magic, but you think that one book, perhaps only ever to be seen by scholars, is going to change how people react to magic? If it were so simple, then everyone would be educated and enlightened, instead of living in constant conflict with one another. And yet you think that because it is about *magic* that your book will prepare everyone for something they cannot even fathom?"

Livingston drew back, Mara's words striking him with obvious accuracy. He curled his lip at her. "I merely wanted to ask questions of Mistress Del Sol, to understand magic further. And yet when you could have provided me with more direct experience of magic, you denied me. Why? What were you doing that is so secretive?"

Mara lifted her chin. "That is *none* of your business, sir."

"Is it not? This is my entire purpose in life. I have given up my scholarly reputation to chase magic—something that is considered foolish and false by a world so enamoured of science—and you deny me my right!" He was fuming now, the fire in his eyes spreading to his cheeks and highlighting that pale scar. He looked, for a moment, dangerous. But Mara had lived with enough danger in her life, and she had absolutely no intention of backing down.

"Your right?" she asked, her voice quiet. She ached to put magic into her words, to sing him a song that would rend his heart from the pain of loss, or to send him mad with the cawing of ravens in his ears. She wanted to prove to him just how deadly the forces were with which he wanted to play. That, though, would be the height of folly, especially for one that she suspected was a spy, no matter how much he clung to his story about a book.

"Your right?" she repeated. "You think you have a right to follow two women into the hills and spy on them? You think you have a right to peer into the windows of people's homes and record their personal lives for the edification of others? You think you have a right to take what people have protected and kept safe from the judgements of others and throw them into the light?"

"That is hardly what I am doing," he scoffed.

"Isn't it?" Mara waved a hand down the hills, to where her grandmother undoubtedly waited for her to return home safely. "Do you have any idea how people would react if they knew my grandmother was a hedgewitch, had magic? Oh, sure, there are rumours about her—there are about any herbwoman. But rumour and reality are two very different things. Do you truly believe that the people of Tallmadge would react well to reading in your book that they had a hedgewitch amongst them all this time? Would they welcome her with open arms? Would they welcome *me*, who am family to her? Ask yourself precisely how magic disappeared in the first place and give me your answer then."

Livingston was glaring at her, now, his obvious anger making his horse antsy. The creature tossed her great head and seemed to look at Mara with an intelligence that made her wonder if the horse could understand what was being said. It mattered not; the horse could not sway her rider's opinion, only carry him. She turned her focus back to the horse's master, no matter how little she desired to do so.

"You think that my book would cause such harm?" he said, voice low and nearly trembling with anger.

"The whole purpose is to prepare people for magic's return, to help them understand!"

Mara shook her head. "Oh, I'm sure they'll understand just fine when you reveal that they've had hedge-witches and nymphs and all manner of other beings right under their noses. You say you met a Keeper of the Wild? What would happen to them if their magic were flayed open before the world, if there were nowhere else safe for them to hide? It is not your right to push yourself into matters that are private, secret, nor is it your right to put so many people's fates in your hands. My grandmother agreed to answer some of your questions, not to bare her soul to you. You have not earned that, and you likely never will."

Her chest felt tight with fury, her blood burning with more energy than the protection spell had cast into her. She longed to sing Livingston a song he would never forget, had the magic on the tip of her tongue. But that would reveal her own secret. Besides which, Mara had never used her magic to do harm to anyone before, nor had she desired to do so. This man, though, this intrusive, self-righteous man, was sorely tempting her. So she did the only thing she could that would let both of them survive this encounter with their minds intact, if not their dignity.

Without so much as a good day, for fear she would use the words to decapitate the man, Mara pushed her way past the horse and started down the hills. She did not know how much he had guessed about the protection spell, about her purpose for being there, but if he knew, without a doubt, about her magic she would be doomed. For now, her own secret was safe, but if she remained there, arguing with that man, she would be more than likely to do something stupid. Then the spy would tell the ocean where she was and all would be lost. Mara had to leave before she convinced herself that sending him raving into the hills for the rest of his days was a good idea.

So she stalked her way down the hills, trying to burn her anger into her steps and fearing that she failed even as her eyes blurred with tears.

Upon returning to his rented splendour, Livingston wasted no time with such mundane things as conversation or supper, instead going straight to the room he had claimed as his study and writing down every scrap of information he could remember. He wrote about the ritual and about what Mara and Cait had talked about when they didn't think he was listening. He wrote about the circle and how Cait had smudged it, how she had thrown water on Mara while walking clockwise towards the sun. He didn't know how much of this was important for the ritual—a protection spell, he thought they said—but he took down every detail and word they'd spoken. He tried very hard not to think about what Mara had said to him afterwards—how had she managed to catch up with him?—but the betrayal in her eyes and the fury in her words was difficult to forget.

Still, he managed nearly an entire chapter on the ritual, though there were any number of unanswered questions, such as what the stones were for, what the ritual was truly about, the purpose of the water, what the chanting meant, and more. But having more questions was better than having none. At least it meant he had something to investigate, rather than the pointless journey he had half-anticipated.

He wrote furiously until nearly midnight, drawing on his previous research to try to fill in the gaps, coming up with a list of new questions and a further list of things he would like to know but would unlikely be told, then walked out of the room, ankle throbbing slightly, to find that Mrs. Cusper had left a tray of supper by the door. He managed, barely, to keep his feet from the stew.

Such a mundane thing in the midst of his thoughts on magic, it seemed to shatter some spell that he had cast around his thoughts. All the fervour and excitement at the evening's events fell away until he was nothing more than a man who should thank a housekeeper he didn't even like for thinking of him.

He took the tray down to the kitchen—who could have an appetite when the mind was working so furiously—but it appeared everyone had retired for the night. Not that he was surprised; his tendencies to get lost in a line of inquiry were notorious for keeping him up at all hours of the morning. Perhaps he should have warned Mrs. Cusper about his strange hours.

Livingston took a roll and some butter up to his room and settled in to sort through his thoughts, but he could not quite find a way to regain his focus on magic. Instead, his thoughts flew to Mara and the blatant fury in her eyes as she'd confronted him. She had stood before him like a queen facing down an invader, and he was not so pleased to have been cast in that particular role. He was trying to *help*!

Ever since he had stood in the midst of that wild storm caused by Briony, the Keeper, Livingston knew that the world would be unprepared for the return of magic. He himself had been terrified, unable to do anything to defend himself against the onslaught of the wild magic that swirled about him. He never wanted to feel that helpless again in the face of powers beyond his ken and sought to produce this book so that others might be prepared as he hadn't been. He wanted the terrible awesomeness that was magic to be understood. What you understood, you did not need to fear.

Mara hadn't been swayed by his arguments, though, and that puzzled him. Well, more than puzzled him, it frustrated him to no end.

He threw back the bedclothes and paced the room regardless of his sprain, stopping before the window to look out on the quiet street. It was so ordinary, just a street lined with houses. But around this town stood the highlands, the mountains that hemmed them in against the cliffs and the sea. Full of magic, as he had seen today. So why would Mara and Cait try to keep it a secret when it was so obvious?

"None of my business?" Livingston scoffed. He nearly went to the table to write out precisely how it was his business, how he had every right to know about the magic hereabouts, the magic that Mara and her grandmother were keeping from him. Perhaps he could read the speech to her. He tossed that idea aside as soon as it came to him. No, that was not a woman to be swayed by speeches.

"Haven't earned that right?" He rolled his eyes.

Had he not earned that right several times over, first by means of that wild storm, then by the fact that his ancestors were supposedly druids. He had talked to witches and hedgewitches and seen the ruins of times past. He knew the terror of magic, and he yearned for the wonder of magic, and he surely had the right to learn about it.

But there were other things that she had said, and those were the harder words to bear. She had said that his book would do more harm than good, that people would not take it as a means to being prepared for the return of magic. That it would scare people. She did not understand! Livingston was doing his best to make people aware by telling them that magic existed alongside them, and had done all this time. The world at large was unprepared for magic's return, simply because they had forgotten it in favour of the sciences that could be seen, proven, by human hands. And magic, for the most part, had fallen away; that which remained only a shadow of what it once was. But it was growing stronger. People needed to know! Surely the residents of Tallmadge would be glad to know they had a hedgewitch among them, and a trustworthy one at that.

A whisper in his mind, sounding suspiciously like Briony, the Keeper, asked, *Would they truly be glad?*

Livingston dropped into a chair and buried his head

in his hands, threading his fingers through his hands. He stared at the carpet, trying to make out a pattern in the moonlit room and failing.

What a fool he was.

Briony's own father, the Keeper before her, had been strung up by an angry mob when there had been a dearth of crops and hunting that they blamed him for. He had practised magic openly and been killed for it. Briony was more open about her magic than most he had met, but even she hid behind the guise of animal husbandry and ecological welfare when in the midst of polite society. Livingston himself had been terrified when he first encountered the strength of her magic. That had been the moment when he decided to investigate, to learn as much about magic as he could. But how many people would turn to books as their first instinct, rather than fight back and destroy?

"No right at all," Livingston murmured, and this time he agreed. He was no one to these people. An outsider, come in to demand the time and efforts of the Del Sols, and why? Because he was a scholar? That gave him no rights at all, except over his own thoughts and observations.

Mara was right. Every word she spoke had been true, and the barbs that had stung before hurt tenfold now. Livingston knew he was more inclined towards the taciturn than charm, but he had never before been so rude and entitled and wrong before.

There was only one thing to do in a circumstance such as this.

"Tomorrow," he vowed. "Tomorrow I apologise."

Mind made up, he finally crawled back into bed and fell asleep, conscience clear.

———

MORNING CAME TOO SWIFTLY GIVEN how little Livingston had slept the night before. He was groggy and felt more than a little dishevelled. It had been too long since he was taking his degree; staying up the whole night no longer was something easily shaken off, even for someone inclined to late evenings. Instead, he stared down at his coffee and toast for what seemed like an hour before he realised that Mrs. Cusper was talking to him.

"…just such a shame, given how good a girl she is. Solid family, even a dowry worth a fair bit, though of course that means naught to you, I'm sure, sir."

Livingston shook his head. "To what are you referring, Mrs. Cusper?"

Mrs. Cusper's mouth dropped and she flushed bright red. She even put a hand to her chest, though Livingston wasn't sure if that was dramatic effect or actual dismay. "Why, sir, I thought you knew!"

"Knew what?" He desperately hoped that an interest in this conversation wasn't indicative of a requirement to be kept abreast of all future gossip in Tallmadge.

"Miss Sophia Farley is engaged to Mr. Nicholas Guthrie!" Mrs. Cusper made it sound like the worst thing in the world, though, having not met this Guthrie character, Livingston was hardly one to judge.

"Is that all? I shall send her my congratulations," he

said, taking a sip of his coffee. It wanted for more sugar.

Mrs. Cusper gaped at him as though he had suddenly grown a second head. Livingston set his cup down and sighed. He was never going to get through breakfast with his housekeeper hovering like this.

"What is it, Mrs. Cusper?" he asked.

"I…it's just…well…it was thought that *you* were going to propose to Miss Farley!"

Livingston choked back a laugh. "Me?" he asked, dabbing at his mouth with his napkin to hide his smile. It didn't appear to be working. "Preposterous. I have only just met the girl two days ago. How can I possibly know her well enough to propose?"

"It's just…isn't that why you came to Tallmadge? To find a wife?" Mrs. Cusper looked aghast, even horrified, at his cavalier manner. Livingston could see that he was going to have some rumour quelling to do. The townspeople seemed to think he was here to find a wife, and Mara and her grandmother seemed to think he was here to cause them personal harm. All he wanted to do was do research for his book. What was so wrong about that?

"Hardly," Livingston said. He straightened his shoulders and gave Mrs. Cusper a look that was as cold as he could make it. "I did not come here in search of a wife, nor did I come here to spend my holiday wandering about at balls and garden parties. I came to do research for my book. That is the entire story, start to finish. I want only to find out about magic in the area, and that is what I intend to do."

"But…you took this house!"

"Because it was a reasonably well apportioned house." Livingston took a deliberate sip of his coffee. "I do not wish to be cruel, or judgemental about this town, for it does seem to be a good one, but I have been amongst the high society of town. Surely, if I wanted for a wife, I would have found one there. *If* I ever marry—and I stress the if—then I will marry for love, not fortune or family. I would want a companion, not some simpering woman with only a dowry to recommend her. Not," he added, "that her dowry was all that recommended Miss Farley, I'm sure."

"I see." Mrs. Cusper's back was up, and he could see that he had offended her. He sighed and waited for her to clatter the serving dishes a bit, rearranging the spoons and such before stalking from the room. Livingston muttered a few rude things under his breath and picked up a bit of his toast. Barely nine in the morning and already he had the beginnings of a monstrous headache.

He took his time over his coffee and toast, reading the paper with far more attention than he usually paid. He lingered as long as possible before finally giving up and coming to terms with the fact that he was going to have to go to Cait and Mara Del Sol and apologise profusely. It was a decision much harder to swallow in the light of morning than the shadows of night, but he had made it and he was determined to see it through.

No sooner had he risen from the table, however, then the bell rang and someone knocked at the door. Livingston muttered a curse, but migrated to the drawing room, where he would inevitably be plagued with visitors all morning.

Mrs. Cusper stalked into the drawing room, her mouth in a thin line. "A Mr. and Mrs. Bunting to see you, sir," she said with all the formality that true disdain could manage. If he did not wish to be poisoned through his soup, Livingston knew he would have to find some way to make it up to his housekeeper. He seemed to have offended everyone in this town and would apparently be handing out apologies like political leaflets. For now, he just nodded his acceptance of the visitors.

Mrs. Bunting was a short, colourful woman who seemed to make the entire air frenetic just with her presence. Her husband, by contrast, was remarkably bland, his clothes a bit drab though well made, and his expression serenely placid.

Livingston bowed and was immediately pulled into a conversation he would rather have avoided.

"Oh, Mr. Livingston, it is *so* good to meet you at last! We must have missed you at the Rushworths' party; those things are always so crushing you can hardly find the person standing next to you!" Mrs. Bunting said, her voice a little too excited for such a simple first meeting. He detected a gleam of something in her eye and wondered if he could bribe Mrs. Cusper to spread the rumour that he wasn't looking to marry. Given the ire his housekeeper currently felt towards him, Livingston rather doubted it. She would likely find great humour in his predicament.

"It was a close affair," was what he managed instead

of the various and sundry things that would not have gone over quite so well.

"Welcome to Tallmadge," Mr. Bunting said, his smile placid. He took a seat on the sofa without waiting for permission and looked about the room languidly. Livingston gestured to Mrs. Bunting, who sat as well, then he settled into his own chair for what looked to be an unfortunate day.

"We came to greet you, and to also offer you an invitation to my little garden party in three weeks' time. I know it's so early to be thinking of such things, but I do so love putting things on the calendar and I thought you might, too," Mrs. Bunting said. Before Livingston could agree or disagree to the invitation, she swept on, describing some of the guests, the planned activities, and some details of the lives of the families hereabouts.

Livingston tried to listen with polite interest, but he quickly found himself growing bored, his eyes glazing over and his attention wandering. He wondered if the herbwoman and her granddaughter ever attended events such as the ridiculous garden party. He imagined that the vivacious Mara would put the guests of such an event to shame, with her quick wit or a pointed look. Cait would likely just scoff and go about her work.

Jealousy seized him by the throat for a moment at the thought of how happy they must be to be able to eschew social obligations like a garden party, simply because they did not wish to attend. How marvellous to be able to pick one's own direction in life. He wished fervently that he could just settle in to his research with none of the social obligation that he bore. As the day drew on and Mrs. Bunting's ceaseless chatter continued, Livingston resigned himself to delivering his apology another time. Then, he continued to dream of such freedoms as Mara and Cait Del Sol must have. He almost forgot to think of magic at all.

CHAPTER 10

Three days. Mara had been trying to swallow her fear for three days. After she'd yelled—quite thoroughly—at Livingston for his interference in the protection ritual, she was certain that the spies from the ocean would send people to come and get her. She stayed in the cottage, only venturing out when her grandmother was with her. She even avoided the creek for fear that the water nymph would have been drawn into the search, even if reluctantly. She knew that her life was over, all because she felt the need to yell at a man.

Mara had been foolish enough to not tell her grandmother what she had said to Livingston, explaining it away with a simple, "I don't know where he went," after returning from chasing him. She had hoped that Cait would see it as nothing to worry about, and it did seem like she was being surprisingly calm about things. But when Mara went into town with her, carrying supplies for some regular customers who needed salves and tinctures, Cait tucked a sprig of witch hazel into her hair for extra protection.

"Be careful today," she said, tugging at the sprig until it was snug in Mara's braid. "I have to deal with Mr. Francis' rheumatism, so I will be a while. Take the tinctures straight to—"

Mara took her grandmother's hands, wrapping them in her own. They were warm and supple, from years working so delicately and precisely. Only the bones beneath belied their true age. "I know what to do. I promise I'll be careful."

Cait took a deep breath and nodded. "Very well." Then, she took her basket of supplies and started down the street, leaving Mara to make the deliveries on her own.

Despite her brave words, Mara could feel the hair on the back of her neck prickling. It had been three days! Why was it taking so long? She disliked waiting for things—for her father's septennial visits, for the plants in the garden to grow, for summer storms—and waiting for the hands of the ocean to reach out and take her was almost unbearable.

She made her deliveries with as little small talk as possible, trying to hide her fear behind a polite smile. The customers seemed to notice that something was amiss, for none spoke with her beyond a minute or two instead of the customary ten or more minutes. Others just sent her away with a curt thank you. She finished the deliveries with nearly two hours to spare before she was to meet her grandmother back in the square, and she knew she would never survive being this close to the sea and not *knowing* what was coming for her.

So she did something incredibly foolish.

Where the cliffs dropped off to the docks, there was a nice broad estuary where the creek that ran by her cottage flowed out into the sea. The sands were relatively smooth here, and there were plenty of tidepools that captured fascinating life that the waves brought in. It was popular in the summer months with children and governesses. That day, bright and warm, there were no fewer than three young boys running around under the supervision of a rosy cheeked governess. Mara walked along this stretch, close enough to the rocks to be far away from the reach of the water at low tide. She rarely dared to venture this close to the water, knowing full well what would happen if she came into contact with the sea. But right then, with the threat of imminent capture upon her, she just wanted to know the water's mood. She wanted to know what would come for her. And when.

The ocean seemed plucky that day, dancing along the sand with a sort of joviality that had the boys giggling with glee every time their bare feet got caught in the wash of a wave. The sky nearly touched the water and mingled blueness together, making it diffi-cult to tell where ocean ended and sky began. The waters were happy. They were not anticipatory. They were not gleeful in victory. They were not taunting.

It made no sense to Mara.

Unless…

She held a hand over her mouth and nearly stumbled into a tidepool. Careful to keep away from the water, she steadied herself on the rocks and closed her eyes.

"What a fool I've been," she murmured. Then, because it was dangerous to keep her eyes closed around the ocean, she opened them again and tried to decipher the particular song of the waves between the churning of her thoughts.

Livingston must not be a spy for the waters.

Three days had passed and if the sea was not openly taunting her, then it was likely it didn't even know she was there. It didn't know that the thing it and all its peoples sought was standing a shore's length away. It didn't know because Livingston wasn't a spy. He was a researcher, trying to understand magic. His story about the book, about the research, was clung to so firmly that it felt false to Mara, yet must be the truth.

That truth was almost as ridiculous as the one she'd abandoned. This world was not at all prepared for magic, that much Mara agreed with. Even so, she was shocked at Livingston being truly what he said. He was surely almost as rare as magic itself. The realisation did not make her like him much more, true, but it lifted a weight off her shoulders.

She looked around at the water and froze. She should not be there. It had been one thing to stand so close when she was sure that the ocean knew where she was, but another entirely to be so close when she was perfectly safe.

Mara turned her back to the water, though it pained her to do so, and picked her way along the shore, avoiding every drop of water and wet patch of sand, just to be safe. She drew closer to the creek that led up to the hills, the sight of freshwater a relief, if only it meant she was closer to home. Then, she paused.

What was he doing there?

As if her thoughts had summoned the man, Livingston was standing before her. He leaned over a pool at the edge of the estuary, where the creek became wide and met the sea, its fresh water mixing with the salt of the waves. The rocks there were slick and pointed and many a creature who thought to take a drink of the creek had found themselves swept away by the sea. It was notoriously dangerous and everyone in Tallmadge knew to stay away from the spot.

Except, apparently, Livingston.

"What are you doing?" Mara called out, picking her way closer. She was sturdier on these rocks than most due to some inherent ability in her bloodlines, but it was still perilously close to the water. Her heart beat louder in her ears.

Thankfully, this time, her words did not precipitate the foolish man falling into the water. She would not have been able to save him from the savage currents then. Instead, he looked up at her and blinked in astonishment. Mara expected him to scowl at her, but he looked almost pleased to see her. Almost.

"I'm examining the tide pools for any signs of sea life. I've heard that sometimes bits of magical water creatures get washed up as detritus into these pools and they make it more abundant with life," he said. Mara resisted the urge to snort at such ridiculousness.

If any magical creature had washed up on these shores, she would know about it, even if it was only a portion of a fin or scale.

"You shouldn't be there," Mara said, instead of correcting the man. He did frown at her this time.

"I assure you that my ankle is quite well," Livingston said, a bit of bite in his tone. Mara ignored it and watched the draw of the ocean instead. The waves were pulling back a little more than they had been, and the wind was picking up. She knew, instinctively, that Livingston was about to be bowled over by a wave and if he fell into the water, he likely would not be coming out again. The ocean did not easily relinquish that which it took from this spot, except as flotsam up the beach. Several children had been lost to this spot in just that manner.

She moved, faster than she had ever moved before. Her feet were sure on the slippery rocks, her balance perfect. She was made for movement on shores like these. Mara reached out, took hold of Livingston's arm, and all but pulled him backwards, out of reach of the waves and into the waters of the creek. Livingston gasped, likely at the cold or at the strain on his ankle or the impropriety of her hand on his arm or something, but Mara wasn't paying attention. Not anymore.

For in standing in those waters of the creek, she felt where they mixed with the waters of the ocean. It was the first time since she had been pulled from the water by her father that she had come in contact with the ocean. For years, she had begged Cait to just touch the water, once, to know what it was like. Her grandmother had staunchly refused to even teach Mara to swim in the lake, far from the ocean's reach. Now, Mara knew why.

In that one touch of the water, she could hear the entire ocean sing. The song of the sea was like nothing she had ever heard before. No music could ever compare to that depth of emotion, the plunging melodies and the twining harmonies. The currents and winds, the waves and the stretches of smooth water. Fish, darting to and fro. Larger, more graceful whales deliberate in their movements. The swiftness of seals and the staunch solidness of urchins and sponges. It was all there in that song, so vibrant as to be debilitating, so marvellous as to be crushing.

Then, the song changed ever so slightly. It was subtle at first, a wakening of some ancient, monstrous entity older than the ground and broader than the sky. It woke, and it *looked* at her. Then, it looked at the man she had saved and it smiled the smile of one that had swallowed a thousand ships with mad glee.

Mara came back to herself with a start and scrambled from the water, running back along the shore as far as she could before she collapsed in the grasses that grew in the sand, breath wheezing. No song she had ever sung could possibly compete with that, whatever it was. She was nothing but a speck in the face of the vastness of the ocean and yet...and yet she knew that it was where she was meant to be. Even if it was a death sentence.

Livingston caught up with her a moment later, sinking to his knees before her.

"Miss Del Sol? Mara?" he asked, reaching out to touch her arms as though he feared for her sanity. As though he was concerned. She shrugged him off and tried to push him away, thoughts still stuck in that overwhelming ocean song, but there was no moving against the enormity of what she had done.

"Are you well?" Livingston persisted. His dark hair was falling in his eyes and there was a crease between his brows as he studied her. "I admit I am no physician, but you do not seem to be injured. Are you well? You saved me from the wave, and I suppose I should be grateful. But I also much apologise."

Mara blinked. She ran her tongue over her dry lips and frowned. "Apologise?" she asked, slowly, carefully.

Livingston nodded, his shoulders sagging a little with what seemed like relief, though why that would be Mara did not know. "Yes," he said. "I must apologise for the way I behaved up in the hills. You were obviously participating in something private, and I had no right to interfere in such a thing, no matter my desire to learn about magic. You were right on many scores during that particular conversation, but if it is not too much trouble, I would rather not list the entire litany. It does make me look a bit of an arrogant cad."

Mara blinked again. Her mind was too full to cast her thoughts back to the hill, but she nodded anyways. "Thank you," she said, hoping that would suffice for an acceptance of his apology. His shoulders sagged just a little more. Then, his frown deepened.

"Are you sure you are quite well? You look pale. Is it...perhaps a fear of the ocean?" he asked with all the certainty of someone who had read such a thing in a book.

Mara let out a choked laugh. "A fear of the ocean?" She brought up a hand to wipe at her eyes, not entirely sure why she was crying. "I suppose that explains it well enough."

Livingston nodded, his hands once again on her arms, his eyes sympathetic. "I understand. It is difficult to overcome such a fear, but it can be overcome. There are things like learning to swim, or just walking with your feet in the water. A little exposure at a time. It's been studied recently amongst some of my peers at the university, and while it's not my area of study, I am somewhat familiar with the practise. I could write to some colleagues if you wish to know more."

Mara shook her head, pushing Livingston away. "I fear this exposure procedure of yours would do more harm than good. Now, if you'll excuse me, I have to go find my grandmother. Tell her what happened."

Cait would be furious, Mara knew. Not necessarily with her, but certainly with Livingston for putting her in this situation. And, if she were being truly honest, with her for being so close to the ocean. But mostly, Cait would be furious with the hands of fate that kept conspiring to put Mara in danger. It was not a conversation she looked forward to, but she wanted nothing more than to be wrapped in her grandmother's arms right then.

She scrambled to her feet, shedding sand from her skirts and deliberately turning her back on the ocean so she would not even have to see it. Livingston rushed to stand before her. "Mara, wait," he said, looking as solemn as before, though with concern rather than anger. "It is not the end of the world."

"Isn't it?" Mara asked, too far into her own hysteria to realise how much she was giving away. "It knows me, now. And worse for you, it knows that I helped save your life."

Then, without explanation or a goodbye, she fled back to the relative safety of Tallmadge, heart pounding in her ears, not nearly loud enough to drown out the echo of the ocean's song that rang in her memories and her heart.

CHAPTER 11

Livingston made his way back to his rented house in a daze. He was fairly certain that he did not understand a single thing about what had just happened. He couldn't even begin to parse the events, and all thoughts of putting them in his notes were far from his mind. To be pulled from tide-pooling in the face of a wave that might have smashed him against the rocks was one thing. He could even claim to be grateful for that; certainly opening his skull on the dangerous rocks of these northern beaches was not a way he hoped to die. But Mara's reaction to the ocean was like nothing he had ever seen before.

She must have been out of her mind with terror, he decided. It was the only explanation that made sense. And while he didn't share her irrational fear of the ocean or deep water or whatever specific horror gripped her mind, he could see—obliquely—how it might make someone panic. Still, there was something off in the way she had almost scoffed at his question as to whether she feared the ocean.

Something that pulled at his heart as much as his mind.

"What was it she said?" he muttered to himself. "'Something like that'?" He shook his head and nearly tripped on the curb as he crossed the street. He had to remember that this was not the university town, a place where he could walk the streets blindfold and still know exactly where he was. This was Tallmadge, home of hedgewitches who did ritual spells, vivacious women who warned him of nymphs at one turn and saved him from the ocean at another.

"The nymph!" he exclaimed, drawing attention from several people walking by. Livingston pulled out his notebook in the middle of the street and flipped through the pages, only moving when a horse pulling a large cart started bearing down on him. Heart in his throat, he stuffed his notebook back in his pocket. Maybe these examinations would be better left until he was at home.

He practically ran there, and not five minutes later was throwing himself into the chair in his study, thumbing through his scrawl for that piece of informa-tion that he knew held a key to this mystery, if not the entire answer. There it was!

"Nymphs can only be seen by those with a water affinity," he read aloud. If Cait Del Sol was not the one with the water affinity, then it must be Mara. And if she had such an affinity, then why was she so terrified of the ocean? Shouldn't she be happiest there?

It was so frustrating trying to come up with theories without enough information. He knew very little about water magic, or beings who lived in the water. The nymph had been his first encounter and he hadn't even been able to get more than a basic description of the creature from Mara and Cait. If he was going to figure this out, then he needed more information. Which, of course, brought up the question of whether he *should* figure this out.

Mara had been very clear during her berating of him. He was putting his nose where it didn't belong. He had not earned the right to interfere in her business just because he had an overdeveloped sense of curiosity. But at the edge of the ocean, with her feet in the water, she had been so scared. Terrified beyond anything Livingston had felt, even in the midst of that storm of wild magic that had scarred his face. He saw it, clear as day, on her face. He could not in good conscience stand by and let her fear build. Not if he could help. It was, after all, the entire reason for his book.

The only problem was where to find information on water magic.

Livingston shoved his notebook into his pocket and went to the kitchens. He found Mrs. Cusper sitting and eating a pastry with the cook. Both women started and spluttered as he entered the room.

"Mrs. Cusper—"

"Mr. Livingston! Whatever are you doing down here? If you wanted a bit to eat, you should have rung the bell. It's not proper to have you down here in the servant's quarters, not when you have such important business to attend to!" Mrs. Cusper said. Apparently, she hadn't yet got over her offense at Livingston's honest statement as to why he was here.

"I came to ask about the library—"

"Oh, the travelling library!" the cook exclaimed, cheeks brightening as she smiled. "Such a good collection of novels they have there. Nothing terribly fancy, mind you, but a decent enough collection to keep us northerners occupied."

"Have they anything on magic?" Livingston asked. There wouldn't be any reference books, certainly, given it was a travelling library, but they might have some fables or children's stories. He would settle for an illustrated book.

Both women looked at each other, then back at him, obviously flummoxed. The cook shook her head. "No, I don't think so. There was a novel about a bloodsucking demon once, but that got pulled out of circulation fairly quickly for being too incendiary."

Livingston had read the thing at the time of publication, hoping it would be far more accurate than the drivel it turned out to be. That was not what he had in mind.

"And do you know anyone in town who might know of magic? Legends? Stories? Especially about water," Livingston said. This time, Mrs. Cusper actively frowned at him.

"None of us are foolish enough to put stock in such things. Oh, you get the occasional visiting sailor with tales of sea beasties and monsters and the like, and some of the folk up in the hills will spin you in circles with talk of wisps and Faeries and such, but none of us in Tallmadge listen to such nonsense. We have our sense, here."

"I do not doubt it," Livingston murmured, though he was quietly imagining wringing the woman's neck for mistaking his meaning so thoroughly. "Thank you for your time. I do not anticipate going out again this evening, except to post some letters."

With that, he turned on his heel and marched back to his study, quietly fuming. If the whole world was like this, then his book had every chance of being laughed off the shelves once he finally got it published. If they wanted to laugh, then they could laugh. If they wanted to throw his book off the shelf, then they could. If he could help one person understand magic with his research, then it would be worth it. Until then, he would have to persist on determination alone.

Determination enough to bend his pride and ask for help.

He pulled out some paper and began writing a letter to Aidan, and then another to Reggie. Surely Sir Aidan Rouelle could ask his wife, Briony, if she knew anything of water magic. And if she did not know, then the house at Blackwell Downs had an extensive library. The same was true of Reginald Townsend's house in town, one of the only useful things about that ridiculous and enormous pile that his friend had inherited. One of them had to have some information about water magic.

If they did not, he would have to swallow what little

pride he had left and beg Cait Del Sol to tell him what she knew.

He cringed at the thought.

Livingston sealed the letters and threw them on the table with a sense of finality. It wasn't failure, he told himself. Asking for help with his research was not failure. It was just a different means of collecting information.

He cursed and snatched the letters off the table, shoving them in his pocket. He would go post them himself before he lost the nerve. The walk to the postmaster was almost worse than the walk back from the beach. Then, he had been lost in his thoughts, distracted, too caught up in his own world to see the eyes that followed him as he walked. Now, mind too full for thinking, he couldn't help but notice the attention. It was the way the milliner eyed him as he passed, the couple walking with linked arms studied him with an intense scrutiny. It was the whispers that started in doorways just before he was out of earshot, the giggles of the young girls standing outside a tea shop.

Something had changed in the last day or so to make Livingston more than just a topic of idle gossip. He had a sinking feeling that Mrs. Cusper might have something to do with this new development. Either that, or the gossip mills worked in far more mysterious ways than he knew. No wonder she'd been so snippy with him in the kitchens. He wished he were confident enough to just lift his head and stare down the gossipmongers. Instead, he kept his gaze straight and did his best to ignore them as if he didn't even see them.

Finally, Livingston stopped in the postmaster and general store. He fumbled the letters and put the appropriate amount of money on the counter. Then, ignoring the side eye, he fled.

"It's like everyone's gone mad," he muttered.

A giggle sounded behind him.

Livingston whirled, only to come face to face with a young girl clutching a raggedy doll, her hair shining but scraggly, her dress neat but a little short in the hem. There was a scrap of linen tied around her leg from a healing injury. A working family's child, most likely.

"Are you lost, little one?" Livingston asked, crouching down. The girl shook her head and clutched her doll.

"They're staring at you because Miss Sophia is going to marry someone else," she said, far more eloquently than he would have expected of a child her age. Her words were not encouraging, either. Then again, at least they weren't discussing him because of his interest in magic. Although, he almost preferred that than his marital intentions.

"Why would you say that?" he asked, wishing he had a sweet or an apple or something to give the girl. Maybe he could bribe her to spread other gossip. She also might enjoy a treat.

"Because that means you're a challenge," the girl replied, hugging her doll close. "That's what my ma says, that you're a challenge. She says that all the young ladies will be trying to catch you now that Miss Sophia is engaged."

Wonderful. Depressing news delivered from the mouth of a child.

"I'm only here to do research on magic," Livingston said. This seemed to catch the girl's attention.

"I like magic. The herb lady does magic, sometimes, when I get hurt. My ma says she's better than the doctor. And I like it when Miss Mara comes, too. She sings to me. She's pretty." The girl smiled, showing a gap in her teeth.

Livingston smiled back. "She is, indeed," he said. It was the truth, if only a very small part of it. "What do you know of magic?"

"Are you going to marry Miss Mara?"

He drew back a touch, nearly falling on the ground with his legs bent as they were. He steading himself against the wall of a building. "Why would you ask that?"

"My ma says that just because you're doing a search on magic that doesn't mean you're not looking for a wife," the girl said. Livingston wondered who this girl's mother was, and how in the world he could set her straight. "She says you're just looking for someone special, but you just don't want to say so in case you're swamped with ladies. I think that's a funny thing to say."

"So do I," Livingston said, perhaps more darkly than he should have, considering his audience. "But I am not looking for a wife at all. I really am only here to study magic."

"What kind of magic?" the girl asked, looking at him with big, expressive eyes.

"All kinds," Livingston answered. He probably should be trying to return the child to her mother, but it was refreshing to have an audience that believed him, that let him discuss his ideas and who actually seemed interested in magic. Even if that audience was a child. "I'm especially curious about water magic right now."

"Water magic? Like selkies and sirens and stuff?" The girl's eyes got impossibly bigger and her mouth rounded in astonishment. It was as if he'd pulled the stars from the sky and handed them to her. In fact, he had a feeling she'd done it for him.

"Selkies? Sirens?" Livingston knew—vaguely—of sirens supposedly able to sing sailors into rocky waters, but he had never heard of a selkie.

"Selkies. Seals that can take off their skin and be human," the girl said. "My ma says they're just stories, but sometimes she tells me bedtime tales about them. Fishermen would capture the women and bring them ashore and hide their skins and force them to be their wives. But when the selkies got their skins back, they would swim away, leaving their children behind. Isn't that sad?"

"It is," Livingston murmured. "Incredibly sad."

"Hettie!" A woman with an apron splattered in water and the harried look of someone who has lost something precious came running up. "Where have you been? I'm so sorry, sir, she doesn't normally run off like that!"

"It's perfectly fine," Livingston said, straightening. He made sure to smile at the mother. "Your young

Hettie has been regaling me with stories of selkies and sirens."

"Hettie!" her mother scolded. "What have I told you about such things?"

"But he asked about magic!" the girl insisted, hugging her arms tightly around her doll. She looked at Livingston in desperation.

"I did," Livingston said. He didn't want the child to get into trouble on his account. "And I appreciate her help."

Now, he had a place to start. Something to ask about. Selkies and sirens. Perhaps there were truly monsters living in the ocean after all. Perhaps Mara had good reason to be afraid. He tipped his hat at the girl and her mother, tucked a coin into the girl's hand, then walked away, wondering who he could ask for stories about sea monsters.

CHAPTER 12

Mara dreamt of the sea.

She stood on the cliff's edge and stared out at the horizon, the waves below her crashing into the rocks with rhythmic force. Each time a wave came in, the song that played in her mind grew louder, stronger, deeper. She heard the beauty in the water, in every touch of its drops to the rock, carving away minuscule pieces and carrying them away. Everything returned to the sea; it was only a matter of time.

In her dream, she was not afraid of the water. Not afraid of its call, the song that reached out to her. She knew its touch, the salt that clung to her skin when she swam, making her buoyant. She knew the creatures that swam in its depths, each one coming up to greet her as if meeting a long lost relation. She was a part of the ocean in a way that she had never been part of any human society. She could understand its moods, the reasons for its actions. She could understand the true depth of the waters, in all senses. The storms that raced across its surface could not touch the stillness below, moved only by gentle currents that were, even so, inexorable.

The ocean was her home and her family and it missed her. Did she not miss it as well?

Mara took a step closer to the edge of the cliff, her bare toes slipping just past the edge of the rock, tiny bits of stone plummeting to the waves below as a precursor to the jump that would take her to the water's soft embrace. There were ripples out there, just beyond the spot where water met rock. Then, two beings appeared, looking up at Mara. She knew them immediately.

One was her father in his seal form. His body was sleek and made to slice through the waves with impossible speed. His whiskers twitched at the sight of her and he let out a joyous bark, the sound both a greeting and request that she join them.

The other being was someone she had never met and yet could not help but know. Her mother. A siren, her voice pure and strong and magnificent. Mara's voice paled in comparison to that magic. She was a beautiful creature, her golden skin sun-kissed with freckles, her hair dark and lustrous, despite the water clinging to her tresses. Her shoulders and arms had the faint outline of scales that Mara knew continued down her body until they culminated in a tail. Not a true mermaid, for she was more spirit than fish, the siren still had enough of those features to be confused with those dwellers of the sea.

Mara beamed, waving. Her father leaped out of the

waves in a feat of acrobatics while her mother giggled. The ocean churned around them, amused and eager.

Mara inched closer, knowing that if she fell off the cliffs, she would not die, not be crushed by the force of the water and the rocks that lay beneath the surface, but be carried by the ocean and her parents to safety. To the home that she had always longed for but never known. To a place where she belonged.

Her feet were halfway off the cliff when she was suddenly jerked back. Her vision shattered, the ocean and her parents vanishing in a swirl of darkness. Mara collapsed onto the ground, hissing as she hit her elbow on a jutting stone.

Awareness rushed over her all at once, nearly drowning her in alarm. She wasn't at the cliffs. She was inches away from the creek outside her cottage, the nymph blowing angry bubbles at her, her grandmother standing above her with wide eyes, her nightdress smudged with dirt and grass, her feet bare.

"What were you *doing*?" Cait demanded, her voice a harsh screech against the quiet of the night sky. Mara flinched back and stared at the creek. What *had* she been doing? Before yesterday morning, it might have been alright for her to play with a few droplets of water, to touch the creek for a minute even, but now? With the entire ocean calling for her so loudly that she heard it in her dreams?

"I was...I was asleep," Mara said. She scrambled to her feet and huddled in the safe shelter of her grandmother's arms. That shelter might not remain after what Mara had to tell her, but she clung to it all the same. "It's all my fault," she said, tears slipping from her eyes.

"What is?" Cait asked, her voice still harsh with fear.

"I…The ocean," Mara whispered. "It's singing to me in my sleep. It knows where I am, now. That I still exist. And it's all my fault!"

Cait stiffened, her arms around Mara pulling back as she stared. She must have seen something truly terrible in Mara's eyes, because she tossed her braid of grey hair over her shoulder and stalked back to the cottage as though propelled by the wind, Mara trailing dutifully in her wake. With a few swift movements and a muttered spell, Cait soon had the fire in the kitchen going, the kettle hanging over its roaring flames. She went through all the motions of making tea, measuring out the leaves precisely, putting them in the pot, preparing the mugs and saucers and even going so far as to take out some scones that she had purchased from town at the same time that Mara had been ruining her life. It was a ritual, this tea making, as much a part of Cait's magic as the spells she used in her preparations.

Once the kettle had boiled and the tea was poured, Cait sat in her seat with a huff and crossed her arms. "Speak. Now."

"I…I thought that Livingston man was a spy, especially after he watched the ritual and…well, I figured that if he was a spy, and he had seen you doing the protection ritual, that he already knew who I was and it was only a matter of time before the ocean's people came for me. So I—" Mara sucked in a deep breath, her fingers automatically reaching for the scone and tearing it to tiny pieces, just for something to do. She forced her hands still. "I went to the shore—not in the water, just the shore—to see if I could hear what mood the ocean was in, so I could know how much time I had left."

Cait said nothing, only took a sip of tea, but there was judgement in her eyes. Mara lowered her gaze.

"The ocean didn't even know I was there. It didn't seem frantic or frenzied or excited or anything. It was just a normal day. Which means that Livingston wasn't a spy, which means that I was wrong. I was just about to leave the shore when I saw him…" She closed her eyes and relayed the rest of her tale without once opening them. Seeing Livingston, saving him, accidentally touching the water, the realisation of the ocean as its song filled her blood. All of it.

Finally, when she was wrung out, her dream a nightmare that still loomed over her shoulder with the false promise of joy and hope, she fell silent. Not daring to look up at her grandmother, she took a sip of her tea, the cup shaking in her hands.

"I've ruined everything," Mara breathed, nearly dropping the cup to the table as she covered her eyes with her hands.

A moment later, warm arms encircled her, Cait's sturdy frame strong and safe in the midst of the tempest. "It's not your fault, my child. You were doing a good deed, and if there's ever a reason for the ocean to find you, I would rather have it be over a good deed than some stupidity on your part or mine."

Mara swallowed a laugh she didn't feel. "It's singing

to me even now. I can hear it in the creek, though it's only an echo."

"And it will get louder. You know full well that your magic is growing. It will manifest soon, and if you had not accidentally stepped into the water, I think the ocean would have found you, regardless. Your magic is too strong. Even I can sense it growing, and you know I have no affinity for water magic as you do."

Mara did laugh at that, the sound dry and bitter. "My magic? A few tricks with the water, and a voice that can mesmerise. How is that ocean-stopping? Why am I the one who has to live out of the water for fear of what my *magic* might do?"

Her grandmother smoothed back a strand of hair from Mara's head. The motion was meant to be comforting, but all Mara felt was an empty fear.

"Your father would not have brought you to me if your gifts were nothing more than a minor talent for water and a passable voice. Those are just what leaks over from your spool of magic, my dear. You won't know the full shape of your gifts until they manifest. Mine manifested when I was fourteen, but they are only a *fraction* of what you can do, even now."

"Your spells can heal," Mara sniffed.

"And your songs don't?" Cait huffed and sat back down, handing over another scone. "This one's for eating, so don't tear it apart. If you think that this is all your gifts will ever be, then you're wrong. No two ways about it. I will tell you this; if the ocean is calling to you in your sleep, then it is still not strong enough to send its people for you. Or, more likely, the selkies and sirens are still warring and can't spare the effort for you. But that will change. They will grow desperate."

"What do we do?" Mara asked, staring at the scone, too afraid to look up and see the defiance in her grandmother's eyes. Cait was far braver than she. All Mara wanted to do was curl up in bed and pull the blanket over her head. But that would do nothing. Solve nothing. "Should I flee inland?"

Cait shook her head. "You cannot. Your father told me years ago that you must stay at least *near* the water or your spirit will falter. No, if you wish to live, then you must stay here. All the same, you cannot continue as you have been."

Mara hunched her shoulders. "What can I do against the *sea*?"

Cait sighed. She tossed her braid over her shoulder. "Up until now, we've been very cautious to keep you quiet. I think the time for that is gone. We must hone what magic you have, so that you at least have *some* control when your powers fully manifest. You must practise your water talent. And you must sing with the full effect of your voice."

Mara choked on her tea. "I *can't*! People will get hurt if I do!"

"Not if you have precise control," Cait said. Her gaze was steely, resolved. Mara had never seen her grandmother like this, and it frightened her almost more than the sea. "You will practise on the hills and its creatures until you can put them to sleep without fail. Then, you can practise on the people of Tallmadge. We must still be careful. We wouldn't want the people here to go on the offensive just as you're readying to fight the water. So good songs only for them. Love songs, reels, happy things. Nothing dangerous. Do you understand?"

Mara nodded. Her heart sank as she agreed. She had spent her entire life avoiding her magic, and now she was meant to hone it? It was enough to send her reeling.

Cait huffed again and downed the rest of her tea. She pushed herself standing, leaning against the table, and stared at Mara for a moment. "Good. Now, be a dear and do the dishes. I'm too old to be getting up at odd hours of the morning for war councils."

It was nice to have family that cared. She knew that her father cared, else he wouldn't visit as often as he could. But seven years between visits was too long for Mara, and she knew she would have been lost years ago if it hadn't been for Cait.

Her grandmother paused in the doorway. "Did... you happen to tell anything to this Livingston character?"

Mara blanched. "Of course not! I had enough sense for that. Though, I may have been a little indiscrete in my description of the ocean."

"Indiscrete how?"

Mara pulled her hair over her shoulder and started re-braiding it, anything to distract her from the intensity of her grandmother's stare. "I may have assigned a sort of sentience to the ocean. He thought I was afraid of the water, of swimming, and I just sort of laughed."

Her grandmother nodded, sagging against the

doorframe. "Well, at the very worst, he knows you have a water affinity. There are far more dangerous things than that. I fear, though, that if he remains in Tallmadge for any length of time that your secret may come out. I hate to ask this, but do you think we can trust him to keep…keep quiet? To the villagers, I mean."

Mara pressed her lips together to keep from blurting out all her fears. She tried to take his apology seriously, tried to believe that he meant what he said. But a niggling feeling in the back of her mind suggested otherwise.

"I don't know, Grandmother," Mara whispered. She shivered. A few minutes ago, the ocean had been the worst of her problems. "I do not know."

"Well, then we had better find out. The next time you see him, in town or wherever, invite him up for tea. Promise him that I'll show some spells or other such nonsense. Anything to get him up here. We'll find out more, and if need be, I'll bind him."

Cait fingered the pearl at her neck and Mara's heart sank. Even with the added power of the pearl, she was barely strong enough to perform the protection ritual, and that was a ritual spell. Powerful, but not impossible for those who were not witches. A binding was something else entirely. Yes, there were some bindings that could be done by ritual, even by people without magic, but they were cruel and dangerous. A proper binding was a delicate thing.

"We'll talk to him," Mara said, voice low. "I have to believe that he means well. After all, he keeps saying that the entire purpose of his book is to help prepare the world for magic."

"And if he does not mean well?" Cait asked, brows raised.

Mara shook her head. "I do not know." She wanted to believe in his good intentions, but those could go awry with ease.

"Clean the dishes, then get some sleep. We have many things to do tomorrow."

With that, her grandmother left Mara alone in the kitchen, the fire warming her and the scones filling her belly. For all these comforts of home, Mara could not help but shiver.

CHAPTER 13

When attempting to learn about the sea, it is generally best to speak with those who spend time there. Livingston was, therefore, in a pub with low ceilings and a pervasive fish smell, situated as close to the docks as it was possible to get. Most of the clients there were sailors or dock workers or fishermen, men who spent their entire lives on the ocean. They were a little hesitant to open up to Livingston at first, but after he stood a few rounds of ale, and lost badly at cards, they were more willing to talk with him.

"Selkies, you say?" a gruff, weather-worn older man said. He had a neatly trimmed beard and only one ear, but was certainly the most knowledgeable of the lot. He had ported in many parts of the world, from the northern climes to the tropics, and had seen just about everything there was to see on the waters. "Oh, yes, I've heard of 'em."

"Who hasn't?" This was from a boy, perhaps creeping towards seventeen, who had a few scraggly hairs to serve as a beard. He had been on ships since he was a lad, running lines. He downed his ale like a practised man and hardly looked flushed for it. Livingston envied his youth for a moment. "There are stories about them everywhere in these waters."

"Never seen such nonsense," a third man, with dark skin and a patch over his left eye, grumbled. He curled his arms around his pint as though someone might take it, and he had a mean eye for cards. "Seals is seals, nothing else to it."

The first man, Gates, scoffed. "Don't you remember that time over by Langstroth Point? We nearly had to abandon the dinghy what with those seals being so aggressive. They nearly capsized us!"

Livingston's fingers itched to pull out his notebook and take down every word, but he had learned that people didn't much like it when you took notes at a card game. Or in friendly conversation. Or on the street. Instead, he looked at his hand and tried not to wince.

"Pshaw. That was naught but bad weather and mating season, you know that, Gates!" the man with the patch said. He watched Livingston for a moment and played a card. It would appear that he was about to lose another round to this group of sailors.

"Langstroth Point?" the youth, Sam, asked. "My captain always says to avoid that place by at least a boat's length, or you're liable to get caught in some bad currents."

"Aye, not a good place for a landing," Gates said, nodding slowly. He finished off the last of his ale and Livingston took the unspoken cue to gesture the barkeep for another. These people sure could drink; he wondered if they were used to this sort of fare, or if they, too, would wake up to headaches in the morning.

Gates continued about Langstroth Point, shaking his head in disgust. "I've only met a few people willing to risk it, and was unfortunate enough to be on the dinghy every time. There're rocks under the water, see, that make it a dangerous place at a good time. But something strange happens there with the currents. If a boat gets caught in it, then you'll spin and spin until the tide drops and you get smashed into the rocks. The seals do right well there, no doubt about it."

"But are they selkies?" Livingston asked. He tried to keep the desperation out of his voice, but he didn't *care* about rocks and currents. He cared about magic.

Gates rubbed his beard and pulled a face. "Hard to say. Stories will tell you that selkies are only known in seal form for being highly intelligent—smart as people, they say, and twice as cunning. And they're meant to be mighty protective of their females and young."

"That's because fishermen used to steal the females for wives. Supposed to bear strong sons and be beautiful as a sunrise." The man with the eye patch chuckled. "I've seen a few women like that, but not bearing sealskins."

"I had a captain once, when I was just a boy, that said they were nothing but trouble, disrupting good fishing just to keep the spoils for themselves," Sam said.

No one pointed out the irony of his reminiscing about his youth.

"Nonsense, Sam," Gates said, roaring with laughter. "Selkies don't care a jot for our fishing lanes. They protect their families, same as people, and like to play in the water. They're just seals that can turn into people by shedding their skin. Nasty fighters when provoked, though."

"And," the man with the patch said, lifting a finger, "they're irresistible to humans. Male or female, doesn't matter. If you see a selkie without their sealskin, it's impossible not to fall in love with them. That's why they were so popular for wives, or lovers. Human and seal offspring are said to have webbed fingers, like this." The man drew lines between his fingers and waggled them. "Makes it easier to visit their underwater families."

"Syndactyly?" Livingston asked. "It's a relatively infrequent birth defect, but it's not uncommon. I know several doctors who have dealt with the matter."

"Don't matter what it's called, only what it means. That there's a selkie somewhere in the family tree," Gates said with a firm nod. "I've never seen a selkie myself, in human or seal form, but I've been in Tallmadge ports long enough to know when they're about."

They came to Tallmadge? This was enough to have Livingston sitting up straight and listening for every word, not that he hadn't been before. He completely forgot about his pretence of playing cards.

"Oh, yes, they're about. Can only come ashore every seven years, or so the legends go, but when they're about, you know it. There's a definite smell in the air, like the sea turned into fog and filled the streets. Not fishy, but not just salt water. It's more than that."

"A tang of brine," Sam said. "I smelled it when I was ten. It was my first time in this port. It was a full moon, I think."

"Nonsense, doesn't matter what moon it is," Gates said. "Isn't that right, Uriah?"

"Hmmm, I suppose. The more interesting question is why they come ashore at all. Most stories I've heard have them sitting on the beach, or on rocks near the shore. But in the last couple of decades, it seems like every story I hear has them coming into the villages near the coasts, stealing washing off the line and poking about. They don't need clothing or human things, and they don't eat more than deep-water fish, so stealing washing seems out of character."

"Pah! That's faeries!" Gates protested. He threw his cards down onto the table, to the collective groans of everyone there. Livingston was losing a tidy sum to these people—mostly because he wasn't paying any attention to the game—but it was worth every bit to get such information. "Everyone knows it's faeries that steal washing."

Uriah shook his head. "Not in these stories. The laundry is always returned, smelling of brine and salt. What faerie does that?"

The others considered for a moment then gave up. Sam took the cards to shuffle and deal out again, his chest puffing up slightly as he did so.

Gates eyed Livingston as he looked at his cards. "Why are you so interested in selkies, anyways?"

Livingston had a better chance with this hand, especially if the grimace from Sam was any indication. "It's not just selkies. I'm interested in all magic. I'm doing research for a book and am in Tallmadge based on rumours of a lake monster—yes, I know they're just rumours. Cait Del Sol, the herbwoman, has put me straight on that front."

The men laughed, as seemed to be the normal reaction when Livingston brought up the lake monster. Sam even had the gall to wipe at his eyes in the hilarity. It was very difficult not to resent the boy for his confidence bordering on arrogance, as well as the energy he possessed, but Livingston liked the lad. He would go far.

"You'd be surprised how many people come to Tallmadge looking for the lake monster," Uriah said, the only one who managed to recover his senses long enough to talk reasonably. "Not all of them have the herbwoman to put them straight. There's almost a tourist industry from it!"

"That Cait is a good woman." Gates nodded his head firmly and took a deep drink of his ale.

"I sense a story there," Livingston said, only half bluffing.

"No story. She just treats those of us who get injured for half of what it would cost if we called on the doctor. Himself gets airs, see, and charges more than any sane family could spend for treating little things, like fish hooks to the hand."

Livingston winced. "Does that…happen often? No, perhaps you shouldn't tell me."

Gates guffawed. "Don't tell me you're squeamish! You won't get very far interviewing people about sea magic if you can't stand the sight of a little blood. What if you ever have to go to the fish docks? Ha!"

Livingston muttered something and tried not to let his embarrassment show. Unfortunately, his cheeks were warm and he had a feeling that his fair skin was showing every flush. At least the lighting in this place was dim enough that the others might not see. All he'd wanted was a discussion about selkies, not an interrogation about his aversion to blood. There was a reason he'd never taken up boxing or hunting, much to his father's disappointment.

"I think you'd better stick to talking with Cait Del Sol, and her pretty granddaughter," Uriah said with a wink. "They're not likely to bleed you."

There was almost a collective sigh. The three sailors exchanged a glance, their expressions warm. Livingston felt like he was missing something.

"What?" he asked.

"Tis nothing. Just that half of us wish Miss Mara would accompany her grandmother to the docks more." Gates grinned, showing the decaying teeth that still remained in his mouth. "Now there's a woman full of life. And knowhow, too. She's almost as good at healing as her grandmother."

"More than half of us with those wishes, I'd say," Uriah murmured into his drink. Even Sam blushed, the tips of his ears turning red.

Livingston did not know what to say to that. Mara Del Sol had not struck him as the sort to have a string of suitors following her about. She was pretty, certainly, even beautiful when she got that fierce look in her eye. But every interaction he'd had with her had either resulted in her shouting at him, or an unreasonable protective instinct on his part, neither of which recommended her as someone he should fall in love with. Then, perhaps these sailors were merely swayed by a pretty face.

"Oh, no need to look indignant, lad." Gates waved him off. "She's nothing but honourable, that girl. But there's no denying that she's captured the hearts of many a man on the docks."

"It's her eyes," Uriah said. "They're like the sea. Changeable and endless."

"And when she sings." Sam all but sighed. "Bliss."

"I didn't know she sang," Livingston said, and was surprised to find that he was disappointed by that. Granted his few interactions with her had been contentious, to say the least. There was still a part of him that wished to hear her sing.

"She sings at lots of the parties that the toffs give," Uriah said. "They wouldn't invite her otherwise, though she's good enough to be walking among them no question. They just think that she's not worth as much because she was a foundling. Adopted by Cait Del Sol. Rumours say that her mother was a fallen woman, but there's no chance of such a thing. Orphaned with no family to take her in, more like."

There was too much in that statement for Livingston to unpack, and he wasn't sure he wanted to, or had the right to do so. Nor did he want to discuss Mara with these people; was it unreasonable to want his relationship with her, whatever it might be, to remain his alone? Instead, he turned his attention back to the cards and to magic. "So, are selkies the only creatures of magic in the sea? Or are there monsters there, like there are in the lake."

This launched a discussion of creatures known as kraken, gigantic squid-like beings with tentacles large enough to take down a galleon without much thought. The descriptions were made especially graphic for Livingston's benefit; the sailors each laughed when he started to look a little green. By the end of the evening, when he was walking home and bidding his new friends a goodnight, all discussion of Mara Del Sol had been forgotten.

Well, not forgotten exactly.

Livingston recalled the fear he had seen on her face as she stood in the place where the creek met the ocean. He was mostly sure that she had a water affinity, but based on his discussion this evening, that didn't necessarily explain anything. In fact, he was more confused than ever. Why had she been so afraid?

And, more worrying to his mind, why did he care so much?

Livingston put the latch key into the lock and pushed the door open, leaning against the wood as he closed it.

"You look exhausted."

He jumped, cursed, and put a hand to his heart. "Mrs. Cusper! I thought you would have gone to bed hours ago."

The housekeeper, wearing a dressing gown and slippers, her hair braided over one shoulder, held a candle in its holder and looked him over. "Been drinking, have you?"

He straightened his waistcoat, trying not to feel affronted by the interrogation. "If you must know, I was interviewing some sea faring gentlemen about magical creatures from the deeps. They were more than happy to tell me what stories they know."

Mrs. Cusper sniffed. "You university types sure do go to strange places. You could have just asked my nephew about that and got all the information you needed without spending time in such company and coming home smelling like a distillery."

He was growing tired of this woman's interference. She came with the house, though, and he could not dismiss her. He could, however, give her a stern talking to. He straightened and looked at her with a stern expression he had borrowed from a professor who delighted in strict obedience. "There is nothing wrong with spending time with sailors or dock workers or anyone who works with their hands. My research will take me to many places, and I have no qualms about such things. The fact that you do, Mrs. Cusper, tells me a great deal. Now, if you don't mind, I am quite tired and am going to bed. I shouldn't expect to be down to breakfast before nine. Good evening."

With that, he stalked up the stairs and tried not to think of his fury at his housekeeper, whether she deserved it or not. Instead, his thoughts turned to Mara Del Sol and what her singing voice might sound like. Frankly, that train of thought was not much better.

CHAPTER 14

Despite it being far closer to the reach of the ocean, Mara made it a point to run all her grandmother's errands in Tallmadge—staying away from the water's edge, of course—just so she might accidentally run into Livingston. She told herself that it was easier than actually knocking on his door, but accidental meetings were not something easily arranged, and she spent two days tending to patients and fetching supplies and avoiding the docks and the beach and the cliffs before she managed to find him. Why she was so desperate to find him, she wasn't entirely sure, but he occupied more of her thoughts than she expected, it gave her an excuse to delve into her own magic, and any distraction from the threat of the ocean was welcome. Even if it came in the form of a man with dark hair, fine features, and bright grey eyes that were a little too observant.

She was sitting in a small garden near the edge of town, surrounded by folk who could not afford the services of Doctor Thompson for such simple complaints as Mara could treat. She had just finished checking on Hettie's bandages—now ready to be removed—and was examining a cut on the hand of a blacksmith.

"I tried to keep it clean, really, but there's so much soot and metal around my forge," he protested. Mara smiled and nodded, wiping the wound with a cloth and some water.

"You don't need to explain to me, Mr. Hendricks. I only wish you would wear gloves or something. This cut is fairly deep." She cleaned it out as best she could, then pulled out a small flask and poured some whiskey on it. Her grandmother rarely approved of such methods, but Mara found it effective for cleaning such things. She then dabbed some honey mixed with yarrow onto the wound and wrapped linen around it. "Change those wrappings once a day at least and try to keep it clean. If you still have problems, come back and see me. And for goodness sakes, invest in some sturdy gloves."

"I will!" Mr. Hendricks cradled the hand to his chest. "My hands are too important to lose. Thank you, Miss Mara. Tell your grandmother I'll be by in a few days to see about that window latch."

He went off smiling, which was the best she could hope for.

Most of her patients were those with minor scrapes and cuts, the occasional fever, and stomach complaints. She also had teas especially for women, some remedies for rheumatism and all manner of preparations for skin issues.

Of course, though, her straightforward day would go wrong when she was dealing with her most difficult patient. The girl was maybe sixteen, a milkmaid who spent her time with cows and other livestock. She was dealing with an outbreak of cowpox, and for all that Mara could provide a soothing balm for her sores, there was little she could do for the underlying issue.

"I'm sorry, Lyra," Mara murmured, spreading ointment on the girl's arm. "There's not much more I can do. My herbs and balms will only help so much. I can lower the fever with willow bark, which will help a little with the pain, but you can't take too much."

"Anything will help, Miss," Lyra murmured, her throat raspy from fever. "I appreciate you taking the time."

"Drink plenty of water, broth if you can keep it down, and try to rest. I know your family needs your wages, but they will be worse off if you die." She hated to scare the girl, but cowpox could be very dangerous if ignored.

"That is the advice you give such an ill patient?!"

"Oh, no," Lyra murmured, eyes wide. Mara was inclined to agree with the girl.

Doctor Thompson was, in general, a capable physician. Sometimes. He was overly fond of remedies that were foul tasting and tended to cause more nausea than otherwise, but he knew how to treat serious fevers and broken bones. He also charged a small fortune for his remedies, claiming that no one else could replicate them and that his patients would die if they did not hire him to treat them. His efforts were shown in the number of expensive waistcoats that he owned, as well as the fine watch and cane that he bore. He outright loathed Mara's grandmother, and only regarded Mara the courtesy that her beauty required, which to him meant he was both condescending and dismissive.

"As far as I am aware, there are no known treatments for cowpox besides treating the sores to prevent infection, rest and plenty of fluids," Mara said drily. Lyra, a smart girl, wisely curtseyed to Mara and fled home. She took the bundle of willow bark tea with her.

Doctor Thompson sniffed and leered at Mara's basket of herbs and tinctures and balms. "Certainly none of that frippery will do any good."

"Is there something that I can do for you, Doctor? Surely a man of your stature must be quite busy," Mara asked, trying to maintain at least a semblance of polite refinement. Doctor Thompson waved his hand about at the few people still lingering in the garden. They were diminishing in number by the moment.

"I heard a rumour that you were here, doing 'good works' for those who cannot afford my treatments." He glared at the few stragglers, who quickly followed Lyra's example and fled. Mara was glad for it; the doctor's tongue could do as much damage as those things he claimed to cure.

"I was only offering such herbal remedies as I could to alleviate the suffering of those with minor complaints," Mara said. She wondered what Doctor

Thompson would do if he knew how many of these remedies had her grandmother's spellwork woven into them. Probably something terrible. He hated standard herblore; knowledge of a hedgewitch being involve would probably send him into apoplexy.

"You were wasting people's valuable time with foolish nonsense! Old wives' tales at best, false hope at worst. What is this?" Doctor Thompson plucked out a sachet of lavender and chamomile petals.

"It's to help reduce headaches," Mara said. "You boil it in water as you would tea and the aromatic steam calms and soothes."

Doctor Thompson tossed the sachet to the ground and twisted his heel into the bundle. "Absolute nonsense. Do people *pay* you for this ridiculousness?"

Mara said nothing. Some people paid with coin, certainly, but most offered trades in exchange. Like Mr. Hendricks, who would fix the window latch on the cottage, or Lyra, who often paid in fresh milk. Some gave cloth, others time, even others chickens or eggs or meat. It was all these people could offer, and Mara would not turn them away for not having enough. Not when the herbs were freely provided by the hills in exchange for just a little care.

"I should have you drawn up on charges for fraud," the doctor said, voice trembling with rage. "You are doing irreparable harm to these people!"

Mara rose, tucking the basket onto her arm. She was facing imminent danger from the ocean, a being who was far older and more dangerous than any human doctor. Within the ocean were the armies of the selkies and sirens who laid claim to her, as well as any other creatures who might want such a morsel as Mara represented for their own gains. She had been hiding all her life, and now she was actively being hunted. There was nothing this man could do that she feared. She was tired of pretending to be demure and obliging for these humans.

"Am I?" she asked, putting just a touch of her own magic into her voice. It was enough to give the slightest impression that Doctor Thompson should be wary. "Or am I just a threat to your *reputation*, Doctor? To your pocketbook? Proving that people can get good, effective treatment without paying enough to feed a family for a month? Did you know that Lady Grey praised my grandmother's teas last she was in Tallmadge for the summer? They helped her headaches immensely, enough that she could go riding. Your… potions…only made her dizzy."

"Lady Grey said no such thing!" Thompson snarled. The woman in question only visited Tallmadge during the end of the summer, to get away from the oppressive heat in town, but she was always well regarded and kind, even when suffering from her persistent headaches.

"Did she order more tonics from you after the initial dose?" Mara demanded. She was well beyond the limits of propriety and class, but she could not find it in her to care that Doctor Thompson was considered a gentleman and she was an orphan with no apparent background, adopted by the local herbwoman. She just burned with indignation. "No? You should know better than anyone the benefits of herblore, yet you continue to try and attack me and my grandmother for performing an ancient tradition that has helped countless people."

"Because modern science has put that nonsensical idea where it belongs! In the gutter, with you and your patients." The doctor raised his cane, shaking it with fury. He advanced on Mara, reaching for her basket, fire in his eyes. Perhaps she should fear humans as much as the ocean. They could do harm, too, even with her own temper to match the doctor's.

"I would think that a man of science, as you claim to be, would be well aware that many modern medicines come from the natural world." The voice that interrupted was smooth, deep, just a little dark. Still, the sound of it made Mara nearly sag with relief. Doctor Thompson drew up short, spluttering, his face going bright red.

Livingston was there, dressed in fashionable clothes of shadowy fabrics that seemed incongruous for the bright warmth of the garden. His dark hair was combed back and the scar on his left cheek was in sharp relief to the slight tan on his face. His eyes, though, bore barely concealed fury. And they were directed at Thompson.

"There are superior synthetic materials—"

"That are derived from natural compounds, most of which must be cultivated and grown rather than created in a laboratory setting," Livingston said. He walked forward as casually as if he were out here to have a conversation about the weather. He even stooped to examine a yellow clover flower growing between the rocks near the garden's boundary. "There were several articles about it in last year's scientific journals. Surely you read them."

"I, ah, well—" Doctor Thompson spluttered.

"I, myself, have been treated with Mistress Del Sol's remedies—being foolish enough to sprain my ankle during a walk in the hills—and am fully healed, none the worse for wear. In fact, it feels quite remarkable." He extended his foot. "Would you care to examine it yourself?"

This was the last straw for Thompson. Recognising that he was outnumbered, or perhaps outmatched, he huffed, gave a swift bow to Livingston, a glare to Mara, and then marched off with his chin lifted high.

Mara sagged, letting out a breath, and sat back down. "I genuinely dislike that man."

"I cannot imagine why," Livingston replied drily, sitting beside her without so much as a by your leave. She was a little surprised to find that she didn't mind. "I can see why I was warned off of him by my housekeeper."

"Thank you for your assistance." Mara picked up the ruined sachet and tucked it amongst the herbs in her basket. She would have to see if it could be salvaged. Perhaps she should bill the doctor for the lost materials. He would likely march up to her cottage and shout some more. It wasn't worth a few pieces of lavender and some chamomile, though she would take great satisfaction from such a sight.

"I only wish what I did could be equal to the service that you gave to me."

She looked up in alarm, but he was looking at her not with fear or triumph at discovering her magic, but with gratitude.

"Saving my life?" he asked. "Or is that such a common occurrence that you so easily forget?"

"That wave," Mara said, trying to chuckle. She feared she failed dismally. "Yes, of course. I recall."

"I…gather that you were not entirely pleased with that situation," Livingston said. His tone was gentle and Mara was not sure she liked that. She didn't want gentleness from this man; she wanted answers.

"What is it, exactly, that you want from me and my grandmother?" she asked, perhaps more bluntly than she should have. She was definitely still riled from battling with Thompson. Livingston, though, merely smiled, continuing in surprising her.

"I would love it if the secrets of magic were revealed to me, but, alas, I know better than to ask for such things. From anybody. I have been informed, in very precise terms, how invasive my previous methods were." He shrugged one shoulder and had the gall to look contrite.

Mara huffed. This man needed to stop apologising to her or she might find herself liking him.

"I am attempting to mend my ways," he said, flicking his eyes to hers. They were stormy and uncertain, but there was something else in those depths. Mara looked away before her curiosity could overcome her sense. "In doing so, I would like no more from you and your grandmother than you are willing to offer."

Mara eyed him. "That sounds…"

"A little too good to be true?" Livingston gave a wry laugh. "I fear I set myself up for your doubt. I do apologise, truly."

Mara wished she had answers for this, had a solution that would make dealing with Livingston easier, make it so that she could understand this man without the turmoil that she currently suffered. Somehow, she doubted that would happen.

"I…appreciate your apology," she said at last. Then, huffing out a breath, she looked at him and tried not to show her guilt at still not trusting him. "My grandmother wanted me to invite you up to the cottage tomorrow for tea. She said that she would show you a spell, if you're really so keen."

Livingston perked up, the shadow that seemed to perpetually hang over him fading slightly. He was a subdued man, quiet and introspective, easily overlooked by society even for all his charm and good looks, but when he felt a true interest in things, he was very nearly bright. It was impossible to ignore him when he was like that, shining with interest and curiosity. What it must be like to only spare energy on those things that you truly enjoyed?

"I would greatly appreciate that," Livingston said, very nearly smiling. Then, his expression faltered slightly. "I, ah, don't mean to pry, but…why were you so frightened of the ocean the other day?"

Mara rose to her feet, shoulders back, chin high.

She may have decided he was not a spy, but she did not appreciate being interrogated. There were some secrets she was still too afraid to share. If she spoke them to this man, it would make everything so much more real. She feared she would shatter if that happened. "If you have no wish to pry, then I suggest you do not ask such questions. I will see you tomorrow for tea. Do try not to sprain your ankle again."

Then, basket tucked in close to her side, she left that warm, pleasant garden to go and brood over her fate and an unfortunately likeable man who had too much curiosity for his own good.

CHAPTER 15

*L*ivingston realised, as he adjusted his cravat for the third time on the walk up to the cottage, that he was nervous. It was nothing more than tea—and perhaps a demonstration of magic, which he was trying not to get overly excited about—but he was undoubtedly nervous. He cleared his throat and wondered how best to apologise to Cait for his previous crimes. Mara was one thing; he felt like he could talk with her openly, even if it meant being snapped at. In fact, he rather liked her honest opinions. Cait was an entirely different matter. She scared him a touch. Perhaps more than a touch.

He knocked on the front door of the cottage and straightened his shoulders to try and control his nerves. It was a trick learned long ago, when forced into situations he would rather avoid, and while it didn't always get rid of his discomfort in certain social circumstances, it at least gave the illusion of surety. In society, even the illusion was enough to make do.

Mara opened the door, actually smiling. Livingston blinked a moment, a little shocked. Her eyes—a striking blue green on a regular day—were bright and cheerful. She had a sprig of lavender tucked into her hair. There were, perhaps, shadows under her eyes but she looked almost joyful. He had been expecting just about anything but that, and his heart skipped a beat at the sight of her.

"I, ah, brought some chocolates," Livingston said, holding out the box. He had thought about bringing flowers as a gift for his hostesses, but given the multitude of blooms that surrounded this cottage, he figured it would be commonplace. So he had sought out the only purveyor of chocolates in Tallmadge and purchased a box. Mara stared at it with a little line of suspicion between her brows.

"Chocolates?" she asked.

"Yes," Livingston said. "It seemed better than flowers."

Mara huffed a breathy laugh, looking at the garden behind him. "Perhaps you are right. My grandmother abhors hothouse flowers, says there's nothing like what nature provides right where we are to be beautiful. Come in, please. You can explain to my grandmother why you brought chocolates while I hang your hat."

Livingston entered into the tiny cottage and found it a much more pleasant experience than the first time he had been there. He wasn't in a sour mood from tripping into the creek—he'd asked permission from the nymph this time, even bowing to the air where he hoped she would see. There had been no problems crossing. He could look at the house with interest instead of disdain and desperation. It was…comfortable, and that was enough to melt away some of his nerves. The windows let in abundant light, the air smelled of herbs and there were signs of cheer everywhere, from the knitted blanket draped over a chair to the fat cat that lounged in a patch of sunlight.

He found Cait in the kitchen, prodding at the kettle over the fire with a poker as if that might make it boil the faster. "Good day, Mistress Del Sol," Livingston said. "I brought chocolates for our tea."

"Chocolates?" Cait turned and looked at him with an appraising raise of her brows. "Mara has told me about them. She had some once, when she sang at a ball. She said they were quite good. Never had much reason to buy some myself. They seemed an awful waste of money."

"Then let me be the first to present some to you," Livingston said with a bow. Inwardly, he winced. They were simple folk living simple lives, these two women. Whatever money they made off of Cait's spells and their combined herblore likely went towards food and clothing, whereas he could simply go and purchase a box of luxury chocolates without so much as batting an eye. He had even silently lamented at the lack of variety in Tallmadge. He knew there was nothing wrong with having money, so long as he used it for productive good, but he did need to be more aware of how everyone else managed. His father, at least, had instilled in him some sense of philanthropy while quietly emanating his disappointment about Livingston's scholarly bents.

Cait took the box tentatively and opened it, setting the silk ribbon aside. She plucked out a piece and bit into it. Her eyes widened. "It has raspberries in it!" she exclaimed around the mouthful of chocolate.

Livingston nodded and pointed to some of the candies. "Yes, those are filled with raspberries, and I think those are creme. The rest are plain. I wasn't sure which you would like, so I got a variety."

Cait gaped at him, only stopping when she realised that the treat was melting in her fingers. She ate every last morsel, even going so far as to lick her fingers no matter that Livingston was standing right there. "Mara!"

"Yes?" Mara entered the kitchen, eyes dancing.

"If this is how he apologises, then I think you should invite him around more often," Cait said, gesturing to the chocolates. "You did not say they were this good!"

The last remnants of Livingston's nerves dissipated at that and he felt himself relaxing for the first time since starting out that morning. Cait studied him, the corners of her mouth lifting in a smile, and he realised that she had done that on purpose, to make him more comfortable. It was a kindness, one he had not expected given his previous interactions with them. He managed a slight smile to show his thanks.

The women led him into the drawing room for tea, each working around the other as they plated biscuits and chocolates and poured the water into the pot. It was like a dance, practised and easy, the movements memorised and the knowledge that the partner would be there sure and certain.

Abruptly, Livingston wondered if Mara liked dancing.

He coughed at the thought, his smile a little strained when he accepted his cup of tea. Mara frowned, her eyes darkening slightly.

"I hear that you intervened when that buffoon Doctor Thompson tried to prevent my Mara from helping people," Cait said once everything had been served. She settled into her chair and appraised Livingston with shrewd eyes. Apparently, the gift of the chocolates had not won her over quite as much as he thought.

"Grandmother!" Mara said. A touch of colour tinged her cheeks and she stared into her tea.

"I am certain that Miss Mara had no need of my services. She seemed quite capable of arguing the medical treatments with the doctor. I merely thought the man quite rude, and must admit I have a hard time standing by when confronted by such poor manners," he said smoothly. Mara's cheeks were still bright, but she lifted her head a bit, the sunlight streaming through the windows catching on her hair.

"You have a silver tongue," Cait said. Her eyes narrowed. "Or did you think that I had forgotten *your* poor manners when it came to spying on our ritual?"

Livingston winced. The cup he was holding rattled in his saucer and he took a moment to steady his hands and his head. "That was a grievous error on my part.

I…was eager to learn about the magic in the area and overstepped. You have my sincerest apologies."

"Hmph." Cait watched him over her tea. Then, finally, she softened slightly. "I still say you have a silver tongue, but at least your heart seems to be in the right place."

It was as though a collective sigh of relief left every person in the room. Mara relaxed a touch and Livingston felt he could actually enjoy the tea, which had hints of lemon and chamomile.

"Are you the only one with magic hereabouts?" he asked. He was trying not to pry, but he really did want that information for his book. He needed to have considerable more about the area before he could conclude his chapter.

"So far as I know," Cait said. She sighed.

"Magic is rare," Mara agreed. "I remember when I was a girl, there were a few others with the gift. I learned of the nymph from a washer woman who claimed to have a gift for rain."

"Old Widow Leighton, you mean?" Cait asked. She nodded. "Yes, I remember her. She died in a flood during a particular bad storm, oh, it must be a decade ago."

"Twelve years," Mara corrected. She wrapped her hands around the cup of tea and inhaled. Livingston pretended that the steam rising from her cup masked the sadness in her eyes. He was thankful to be far enough away not to instinctively reach out and squeeze her hand. He wondered when the last time was he had so casually thought about touching a person, even to provide comfort. His fingers tingled and he realised he didn't know. He remembered his mother squeezing his hand when he was sad, but she had been dead for some twenty years.

"And there was an old man—Withering was his name, and yes, it was his real name. He claimed to have the gift of sight and prophecy." Cait snorted a laugh. "I remember he used to climb to the top of the hills during the full moon and beseech the stars to give him answers to questions people had paid him to unravel. Said it was some old druid technique, though the man was no druid. I'm amazed he actually had any magic at all, the foolishness he got up to."

Mara smiled, then, the sadness almost gone. Livingston clenched his hand against his knee and released the tension there. Any thought to comfort was foolish and should be put out his mind.

"Withering was a kind man," Mara said. "He gave me apples from his tree."

Both smiled fondly at the memories of a time long past, and Livingston felt like an intruder. He wanted to ask more questions about the man, his gift of sight, or the woman with a gift for rain, but somehow the words got stuck on his tongue. He couldn't interrupt these memories, not when he was the outsider here and everything he had done so far felt intrusive.

And yet, the book he was writing *would* change things for a lot of people when magic emerged from hiding once again. That much he believed.

"It's been a long time since Withering died, and now I am the last, at least in these hills," Cait murmured. She set her tea cup down and smoothed out the linen apron over her skirt, the fabric hiding some of the trembling in her hands. Mara pressed her mouth into a tight line and flashed a look at Livingston. When their eyes met, it was like a jolt. A flash of communication, something more than the worry that she felt for her grandmother.

"Do you…you are certain that magic is returning to this world?" Mara murmured. She looked nervous, as though she desperately wanted Livingston to answer yes, and was afraid also that he would.

"Everything I have seen would seem to indicate that," he said. "It's counterintuitive, with so many people like your friend Withering, or the Widow Leighton dying. Even my friend, Aidan, his wife is the last Keeper of the Wild—at least in this part of the world. The druids are gone, the Fae have vanished, and yet I do not doubt that magic is wakening once more."

Mara shivered.

This time, he moved without thinking. There was a scant few feet between their chairs, but Livingston crossed it in the blink of an eye. He knelt before Mara and took her hand in his. Her skin was warm, yet there were goose pimples on her arm. She shivered again and once more he looked into the wild waters that lived in her eyes.

"What are you so afraid of? Let me help you. Please," he whispered. Mara sucked in a breath. She tried to hide her reaction with a gentle smile, but he saw the truth. He squeezed her hand, and to his surprise, she squeezed back. Then she delicately slipped her fingers from his and lay her hand in the folds of her skirts.

"Many things, scholar," she said. Her smile turned sad. "None of which, I fear, you can help with."

"There are some things which should not be put into your book," Cait agreed, a touch of bite in her tone.

He pulled back, standing, shoulders stiff. "I had no intention of putting your troubles into my book," he returned, his voice cold. "You truly have a low opinion of me if you believe that I would use someone's fear in that way. As such, I think it probably better if I go. I do not wish to cause any further discomfort to you."

He bowed and turned away, legs eating up the short distance to the door. He had made it outside, the stems of the flowers brushing against his legs. He pushed a particularly clingy thistle away and was just about to step onto the green of the hills when Mara came running after him.

"Wait!" she called, her steps far more sure than his. In her hands, she held his hat.

"I thank you for bringing my hat," Livingston said stiffly, taking the piece from her. He turned away again, only to halt entirely when Mara touched his hand. He stood perfectly still, hardly able to breathe, at the shock that travelled up his skin. He did not turn to look at her, nor did he walk away. He just stood there, her hand on his.

"Wait," she breathed.

He turned. She looked up at him, then looked away.

"I apologise for my grandmother," she murmured. "She only fears for our safety."

"I am not trying to jeopardise your safety,"

Livingston growled. He raked a hand through his hair. "I do not even need to use your name, your specifics, in my book. I only want to know about magic! I just want to *help* people!"

"I know that," Mara said. She took his hand again and this time he did not freeze. He stepped closer, just a hair, but enough that he could pick up the crisp, clean scent of ocean water, as though she had just been swimming.

"Then why will you not talk with me?" he breathed, reaching up to tuck a strand of hair behind her ear. The movement was forward, so improper for someone with whom he had only had a few conversations. It set his skin aflame. He took a step back. "I apologise. You must be busy, and I, ah, have some work to do. Good day."

"Wait," Mara called again. She closed her eyes and took a deep breath. "Why is it, really, that you are researching magic? And please, don't tell me that it's because you want people to be aware of what is coming when magic reawakens. I have held my tongue about enough secrets involving magic to know when people are hiding something."

Livingston sucked in a deep breath, head spinning. He looked towards Tallmadge, so far away, and the hills, impossibly daunting. Neither had him as unsure as the woman standing before him.

"Why?" he scoffed, a front of confidence he did not feel. "Because it terrifies me."

"Terrifies you?" Mara asked. She knew enough about terror to last a lifetime. It seemed odd that this man, so assured and ready with a quick word for any situation including arguing with her, should be terrified of magic.

Livingston's jaw tightened. Whatever it was, it truly bothered him. Mara knew she would get nothing out of him here, standing before her grandmother's cottage, not when the words they had passed there were so close behind them. It struck her, then, that she wanted to understand this man and his fear. Perhaps that was all he wanted to do with her. She studied him for a moment longer and her resolve softened.

"Follow me," she said, then started off towards the meadow of wildflowers. She nodded to the nymph in the stream and watched carefully to see that Livingston made it over without harm. He did, though there was something in his expression that spoke of a deep mistrust of the nymph. He even went so far as to give her a bow, though he could not see her, which had the nymph in giggles.

Mara led him into the hills, the gap between them hiding the cottage from view as it opened into the field of wildflowers. It was warm, and the bees were happily buzzing about. There were a few butterflies, but on the whole the only noise came from the wind and the bees. A world unto itself, far away from any fear.

"What is this place?" Livingston asked as Mara sat on the ground with her skirts spilling around her, some daisies tickling her face. "A sacred site for magic?"

"It's just a field," she said. "Sometimes I gather herbs from here, the sort that grow better wild than cultivated. But it's mostly just quiet, away from the world. A field. There does not need to be magic here to enjoy its peace."

"A field," he repeated warily. Mara patted the ground beside her and he hesitated. Then, letting out a deep breath, he sat, his long legs stretching out before him, the dark fabric of his trousers in stark contrast to the greenery. He would have looked out of place there, Mara thought, if he weren't so solid and grounded. If there was a scrap of magic in this man, he surely had an earth affinity, she was certain of it.

"It's a bright, sunny day," Mara said. She added a touch of calming tones to her voice, the magic as subtle as she could make it. He hardly twitched, just settling in to the song of the flowers and the sun. "There are no people about, just you and me and the flowers and the bees collecting for their honey. Nothing to terrify."

Livingston snorted. "Nothing to terrify, indeed. If you were not so insistent, then perhaps."

Mara felt her cheeks warm. She forced herself to keep her posture relaxed, her expression neutral, rather than react to his forward words. He seemed to realise what he had said just as the words slipped out, and he winced.

"I apologise. I should not have—"

"I prefer honesty to a great many things. And it would appear that we both have a bad habit of insistence in the place of patience," Mara interrupted. She smiled. "Now, are you going to tell me why you were so…well, rude isn't quite the correct word. So overly cold with my grandmother? She was a bit harsh, yes, but your reaction was, ah, unexpected."

"I thought we were being honest." He tilted his head back and closed his eyes. "You want to know why I said that magic terrifies me, not why your grandmother's barbs struck me."

Mara held her tongue. He was right, after all. Livingston chuckled, but he kept his eyes closed, head tilted towards the sun.

"It seems ironic that you would pry into my secrets when I have been scolded for prying into yours," he murmured. Then, he lay back, resting his head on a cushion of grass. He was close enough that Mara could run her fingers through his hair if she wanted, but she refrained.

"If I apologise, will that make you feel better?" she asked. "I know that my grandmother and I keep secrets. It is what we have done since I was a girl, and it was—is—the only recourse available to us. Our secrets are dangerous. While I would love nothing more than to shout it from the hills and let the world know, the repercussions would be…"

"Frightening?" Livingston asked.

"Violent," Mara breathed. He cracked open an eye, then, and stared straight at her. Something in her expression must have told him that her confession was the truth. He looked fully at her, his eyes curious and yet restrained. Then, some barrier between them broken, he spoke.

"Last year, I went to stay with my friend, Sir Aidan Rouelle, at his estate Blackwell Downs. South of town, right in the middle of a forested area. He was taking stock of the place in a determination of whether to sell. A woman, Briony, stopped him. She was a Keeper of the Wild."

He had mentioned this Keeper before. Mara had never met one, only heard the stories, but knew that they were possessed of some of the oldest magic, a sort that was barely tame.

"I like Briony. She is smart, fair, generally even tempered. But there were some…issues she had with Aidan that had been cultivated by his mother. In the process of learning more about Keepers and helping Briony integrate with society in town, the three of us came across a witch who could help." His expression became closed at this, something more than a guarded nature keeping him quiet. "She was a true witch, not a hedgewitch, and she knew a great deal about Briony and Keepers…enough that when we returned to our dwelling that evening, Briony accidentally set off a wild storm."

Mara hissed in sympathy. Wild storms went hand in hand with the stories of the Keepers. They were dangerous, a natural defence mechanism that could fell trees and make any animal ravening. There was a theory that the control over the wild storms was why so many Keepers had been picked off, in the time when magic first began to die. There were similar theories about many lines of magic, and no one knew how many were true or just fear and paranoia that kept those who remained silent.

Livingston fingered the scar and his face, his eyes shuttered.

"That's how you got that, isn't it?" Mara asked, lifting her hand to touch the deep line on his cheek. She paused a few inches away and lowered her hand again. It was too much, that desire to brush her fingers against his skin. If she did, something would change. She knew it, and hesitated for it.

"Aidan, and my other friend Reggie—Reginald Townsend—told me that it made me dashing, even more so than my brooding usually managed. All I could think about was that moment of terror, when I thought that I was going to die." He laughed drily. "I *have* to learn about magic, don't you see? It's the only way I can truly understand what happened to me, how I can make sense of the world. Because if there are these great and terrible forces out there that I can't understand..."

"It feels overwhelming, like a weight is crushing you and you can't move." Mara nodded.

"Yes." Livingston looked surprised. "You're the first person I've talked with that understands that."

"You would be surprised what people understand if you bothered to explain things to them." Mara sighed, knowing she was likely guilty of similar lapses. "It's okay to be afraid, you know. And there is a great deal of magic out there, most of which is not understood. I fear that you will be searching for a long time."

To her utter shock, Livingston flopped onto his back, making a disgruntled sound in the back of his throat. "Talking with you and your grandmother is thoroughly depressing. Don't you ever talk about happy things?"

Mara laughed. "Generally, that's *all* we do! You're the one who keeps bringing up difficult topics. If you want to discuss happy things, then you shall have to ask different questions."

He blew out a breath as if considering, then turned his head to her with pleading eyes. Mara laughed again, harder.

"Fine! I'll come up with the topic," she said. "Have you been invited to Mrs. Bunting's garden party yet?"

Livingston groaned and covered his eyes with his hands. "I asked for happier topics, not an incessant parade of gossip."

"You need to relax. The parties and dinners aren't all that bad. Yes, people are inclined to talk, but only if you give them reason to do so." Mara nudged him and he cracked an eyelid to glare at her. "Have you given them reason to do so?"

"Not intentionally. I apparently leased the wrong house, in that it was the most expensive house I could take. By the standards of town, it was hardly a fortune, but here in Tallmadge? It means I must be extremely wealthy and obviously looking to find a bride. Why else would I come?"

"Knowing Alder house, yes, it does give that impression," Mara agreed with mock severity. The man laying in a field of wildflowers at her side growled, the sound hardly ferocious. "I assume you set them right?"

"Only after having to entertain a good number of families with eligible young daughters at the Rushworth ball. Yet they still come after me, the mamas with eager expressions and the daughters with simpers that hide empty minds. No one seems to believe that I am here only for research!"

Mara hummed her amusement so he wouldn't have to deal with the shame of being laughed at again. "Yes, I do see how that would set you up for gossip and attention at the garden party. I was going to suggest that you be as boring as possible, but somehow I think that wouldn't matter much, given the house you took. All your struggles in Tallmadge are going to stem from that one error. Ah, the life of a travelling scholar!"

Livingston growled again, this time half-heartedly. "You may laugh, but *you* aren't forced to attend for the sake of politeness."

Mara smiled. "No, I am attending to be paid for lending my voice to their entertainment. A far better proposition, for at least I have worthwhile recompense for my presence than social niceties and gossip."

"You sing? That's right. Someone mentioned it, but I had forgotten." Livingston propped himself up on his elbows and looked at her, as though assessing her for more hidden talents. He wouldn't find any, not unless he had the magic to see her for what she was. Mara was grateful that she was just a normal person to him, not a magical oddity. He wouldn't be so free with his conversation then. Or would he? He had heard enough of her slips to perhaps guess that she was hiding magic, and he still spoke with her as an equal. She felt her face grow warm at that.

"If you're asking me to sing for you now, I won't," Mara teased. "I have a specific routine for my voice and cannot merely sing when I am demanded to do so."

"Oh? And what is this routine?" He quirked a brow, obviously disbelieving her.

"I must *want* to sing," Mara said, sniffing. This time, it was Livingston who laughed, the sound considerably lighter than she had heard from him. It suited him well.

"You would do well with my friends," he said, leaning back into the grasses again. "None of them put up with nonsense just because society tells them to, either."

"What is town like?" Mara asked. She brushed aside a bee that was crawling up her skirt and watched it fly back towards its sisters. "Is it really as colourful and loud as everyone says?"

"Have you never been?" he asked, sounding surprised. Mara shook her head.

"You will find that a great many people in Tall-madge have not been into town, outside of those who grace the garden parties. Even they only go occasionally. It is very far away, after all."

Livingston nodded, his attention on the sky. He seemed to still, to become part of the grass and flowers around him, a more solid part of the world than anything else around him. Yet his eyes were distant, as though they could see the stars. "It is very far away, isn't it?" he murmured. "Sometimes I forget that it's all just a place, somewhere people gather en masse, instead of this tangible thing that dictates the social graces, the behaviours of its residents."

Mara hesitated. "Do people really expect so much of you?" she asked, her voice quiet.

"I am fortunate in that my parents never argued too forcefully against my academic pursuits. My father made certain I could manage the family money, and my mother made certain that I could navigate any social situation with finesse, if not ease. But they largely left me to my own devices on how I chose to live my life." Livingston turned his eyes away from the sky to a butterfly flitting from flower to flower. "I know not all have my luck in that regard. It's perhaps why I dislike the expectations of society so much; it comes from a place of insecurity in the future, which shouldn't be what determines how people live or who they love."

"I imagine there is more than insecurity in the future which determines people's lives," Mara said. Such as the terror of two magical races coming to hunt her down, to capture her power or to kill her for it. If that were insecurity, then she was nothing more than a regular human girl.

"I suppose." Livingston looked at her again with those eyes, part sky and part distance that could never be crossed. "What determines your future, if not insecurity?"

Mara sighed. He was prying again. She couldn't blame him. She hated the burden that this secret made her wear on her shoulders. It was impossibly difficult, being able to only talk about this with her grandmother. How nice it would be to tell all to this willing ear. Instead, as always, she deflected.

"I am adopted, you know."

"I have been so informed, though I do not know how accurate the stories coming from my housekeeper are." His expression was serious, solemn even. "Do you…wish to know your parents? Is that was drives you?"

Mara shook her head. "No. I was given up for a good reason, I'm sure." She was sure, too, for she knew the reason. "I sometimes wonder what might have been, though, if my life were different. If my grandmother hadn't adopted me, raised me." If the ocean had kept her in its clutches, or she'd been left with an ordinary human who didn't know a drop of magic. "But I am happy here, with her. No matter what the rest of Tallmadge thinks of me, that they would rather shun me than include me, except for my singing. I am happy here."

Livingston frowned, the movement creating a furrow between his brows, adding just a hint of care to his features. "Are you worried that it will be taken away from you, this happy life?"

Mara shrugged. "Aren't we all? No, we're getting into dark and depressing questions again. We should go back. You should really see the spell that my grandmother had prepared. She was going to—"

His hand covered hers, the touch firm and safe and warm. "Mara," he breathed.

She closed her eyes. Just as when he'd touched her hand in the cottage, when she'd reached for him as he walked away, there was a spark that was nothing to do with magic. Or perhaps it was everything to do with magic, just of a sort that was older and deeper than anything she'd never known. She revelled in the touch for a moment. Then, carefully, slowly, she pulled her hand away. "Come, let us go."

Livingston nodded, and suddenly that guardedness that stood between the two seemed insurmountable, a wall made of secrets that would tear the world apart if they had a chance.

Mara wished she could go back a few seconds, leave her hand in his, and relish that brief moment of safety. It was too late, the moment gone.

CHAPTER 17

*L*ivingston wanted to say that witnessing the simple longevity spell that Cait performed was all he could think about, but he would be lying.

He had gone with Mara back to the cottage and ducked his head in silent apology for his outburst. Cait responded with a similar motion and then they went about with tea as though the interruption had never happened. Mara watched all of this with a sort of twinkle in her eye, though there was something guarded there, too. Livingston knew, because he kept studying her, his eyes inevitably drawn to hers. There had been a moment in that field where the guards had fallen between them, and he didn't know how to get that moment back. So he just drank his tea and listened while Cait talked. And every few seconds, he searched Mara's bewitching gaze.

"Now, most true witches might use a longevity spell to help with ageing, but I haven't nearly that sort of power. Hedgewitches tend to use it for preserving breads, meats, and the like. I'll be using it on a tincture for arthritis so that it stays better longer." Cait eyed him, her hands wrapping tighter around her cup. "You're not going to take notes?"

Livingston nearly choked on his tea. He set the cup down and gave a weak smile. "I, ah, could if you would prefer. But I find it better to observe and then take notes so that I can take in the full effect."

Cait sniffed. Then, "Very well. At least you have some sense. Come into the stillroom. It's easier to demonstrate in there."

She rose swiftly and bustled off before Livingston could even ask a question. He shot a bewildered glance at Mara, who laughed, then rose as well.

"Come on. She doesn't bite."

Livingston followed, admittedly a little nervous. He was finally going to witness some magic. It was diffi-cult to quell the rapid beating of his heart. He stayed as close to Mara as was polite, wanting nothing more than to reach out and take her hand to wrap around his arm, as though he had any right in the world to escort her anywhere. He was close enough to smell the ocean in her wake, and that was simple detail distracted him from the sight of the stillroom. At least until he was hit with the overwhelming scent of herbs and dried flowers.

Immediately, he put a hand to his nose, eyes water-ing. "What *is* that?" he gasped.

Cait cackled at his response. "That will be the seaweed you're smelling. It can be a bit pungent when freshly gathered."

"Seaweed?" Livingston asked, breathing through his mouth.

"It's good for restoring the skin to health," Mara said. He nodded and tried to pay attention through the overpowering smell, which he suspected was a great deal more than seaweed. His eyes watered and he went so far as to pull out a handkerchief to wipe them dry. Breathing through the fabric helped some, but not enough.

Cait pulled out a bottle containing a yellow-gold liquid, the tincture for arthritis. She eyed Livingston to make sure that he was paying attention, and he nodded, blinking away more tears. Then, Cait put her hand on the bottle, closed her eyes, and muttered a few words in a language he did not understand. It was like the language she had spoken during the ritual but softer, somehow, like she was asking of it a different result.

There was a slight crackle in the air, as though lightning was imminent, and a brief surge of heat. Then, everything went back to the way it was. Had Livingston not been paying attention, he would easily have dismissed the atmospheric change as a result of the growing clouds on the horizon. But he had been paying attention. And there was no doubt it had been magic.

Still, he was vaguely disappointed.

"Expecting something flashier?" Cait asked. He winced. His disappointment must have shown on his face; he was usually much better at controlling the outward display of emotions. The last hour—no, the last few days—had done enough to strip his defences away.

"No, I...that is..."

"It's alright, lad. Magic is often thought to be this grand, spectacular thing, meant to awe and inspire or terrify. The reality is a little more mundane, I'm afraid." Cait replaced the tincture on a shelf. He could have sworn there was something sad in her eyes.

Mara turned and bustled him out of the stillroom. He took a deep breath, glad of the freshness of the air. It occurred to him that there must be a spell on the room to keep the odours from permeating the entire house. Useful trick, that. He wondered if he could have Cait perform the same thing on his kitchen so he wouldn't have to hear his housekeeper's conversation when Mrs. Cusper wanted him to be paying attention. The thought made him smile.

"Did you see anything?" Mara asked, refilling his tea. A strand of hair fell in front of her face so he couldn't see her expression clearly, but he thought she looked eager. Why would she care if he had seen anything?

"No," he admitted. "Though I felt the air crackle, as though with lightning. And there was a moment of heat."

Mara blinked, cradling the teapot. "Oh? You felt it, but didn't see it?"

"Is that not normal?"

She shrugged, flushing when the teapot sloshed in her arms. She set it down and sank into her chair, close enough that he could reach out and touch her if he wanted. He refrained. "There's nothing *normal* with magic, though you can sometimes see definite patterns. But I've never met a person who can feel a spell and not see it. People who don't have an affinity at all can't even feel magic."

"I'd say there's a hint of magic in you," Cait interrupted, plopping into her own seat. She took a deep drink of tea, as though the spellwork had exhausted her. Livingston wondered if she were putting it on a bit for him, given the twinkle in her eye, but he decided not to ask. "Probably so diluted in blood that it barely registers, even as a true affinity. But it's there, somewhere in your ancestry."

Livingston tightened his grip on his teacup, almost enough to break the delicate china. He did have magic in his ancestry, according to the witch he had spoken with last year. He had left that piece out of the story relayed to Mara, not because he didn't want her to know, but because that tiny scrap of magic that marked him as druidic scared him even more than the wild storm Briony had conjured. He had scoured the country for word of the druids, trying to understand what they stood for, what their magic did, who they were, but all he could find were ruins and stone cairns and a few carved whorls in rock that had been all but etched away with time. Even those with magic who were willing to speak with him hadn't had any further information than that.

His own life was a mystery to him, and it did not appear that he would solve it. And that terrified him.

"Really?" he said, forcing his voice into blandness.

He made his fingers relax their grip on the cup and took a measured sip of the now room-temperature liquid. "How interesting. Disappointing, I suppose, that I can't do magic or even see it, but at least I can feel it. It would be so much more useful to describe what magic looks like. For my book, that is."

Mara frowned, brows furrowing together. She looked as though she wanted to say something, then shook her head. She clasped her hands together in her lap. He wanted to reach out and hold them again, and wondered if she felt the same.

Foolish, he thought.

He had intruded on her life and now he wondered if she might wish to get closer to him?

"It wouldn't matter much to your research, anyways," Mara said after a moment. "Everyone sees magic differently, even those with a similar affinity. The manifestations, the final products, are all that matter in the end."

If only it were that easy. If only he could say such a thing in his book. It was meant to be an academic piece—though easily read by the masses—and saying that magic never appeared the same to any two people was unhelpful. He needed at least a few examples of how magic *might* appear, so that those with an affinity could recognise it. Mara had described her vision of magic, perhaps he could get others to describe their own. Of course, finding people like Mara and Cait was difficult enough, let alone finding enough for a wide array of examples. His research, and his investigation into his own ancestry and ties with magic, were decidedly more difficult than he had anticipated.

"I wish I could be of more help," Cait said, interrupting his thoughts. She actually looked regretful, as though she would offer more if she could. "It feels differently for each person with magic, too. Some say it is a rush of energy, others like they're pulling thread from a spool. Most, though, just do it naturally and couldn't describe the process if they tried."

"Is that how it is for you?" Livingston asked, desperate for more information. This trip to the north could not be for nothing, even though he had spoken to several hedgewitches already. If this was all the information they had, then he was wasting his time. He glanced at Mara. Well, perhaps not *wasting* his time.

"I may not have the power to do great and impressive feats, but what little I do have is as innate to me as breathing." Cait held out her hands. "I'm sorry if that is not as useful to your research. The truth is, though, that there will always be those who have magic, and those who do not. It will mark some people as different, as other. There will be lines drawn between worlds. I very much doubt that your book, no matter how grand its intentions or how eloquent its words, will change that fact in people's minds. It is not like money that you can earn or lose, no matter how alike we are."

Livingston nodded. He was beginning to think she was right. Nothing he seemed to learn was key to changing people's opinions of what would come. Yes, he could educate the masses, but no matter how much he described or researched, there would always be that fear or jealousy of things that someone had and you did not. Rarely did anything good come from such a situation. He flicked his eyes to Mara and found her studying her own tea with a seriousness that was just a touch darker than the conversation warranted. What sort of life had she lived, where this dividing line between magic and no magic was all she had known? He, at least, had made a choice, even if it was motivated by terror.

"I thank you for your time, and your words," he said after a moment. "It would appear that I have a great deal to think about."

"You won't give up on your research, will you?" Mara asked. Cait threw her an alarmed glance, but the vivacious young woman didn't seem to notice, merely waited for his response.

"It has consumed the last year of my life," he admitted. "I have never felt such a pull to any other topic before, and yet…it feels futile."

He should not be saying such things out loud. Perhaps in the freedom of that meadow, he could voice these words. But here? So close to the real world? No, he needed to consider, to weigh the consequences, to plan and debate, not produce such unfounded claims. Not to mention these people, despite his badgering over the last while, were practically strangers to him. No matter how he was beginning to feel about Mara.

Livingston stood and bowed, trying his best to be more respectful in the movement than he had been earlier. "Again, Mistress Del Sol, thank you. You have been everything gracious."

"You are welcome," Cait replied, looking bemused. She exchanged a glance with Mara.

"Good day, Miss Del Sol," Livingston said, bowing again. She smiled and nodded, but the movement was hesitant, confused.

"And to you, Mr. Livingston," she murmured.

Then, he left. This time, no one followed him.

Outside, the storm that had been building on the horizon had crept closer, nearly blanketing the bright summer sky. The wind was picking up, too. Perfect weather for brooding, he thought, then was disgusted for feeling sorry for himself. He had chosen the academic life. He knew that not all research worked out. How many times had his old professor switched topics before finding something that worked and was worth pursuing? How many experiments or theories were proven false?

Livingston growled and ran his hands through his hair. He *hated* feeling like this. Inadequate, like all his work over the last year had been wasted. He knew that magic was real. He knew that without a shred of doubt in his soul. Yet the world had forgotten that, had let magic become nothing more than children's stories. It should have been a fairly straightforward thing to collect the information that the world at large had forgotten and present it.

Livingston knew a great many people who had built their lives on should have beens. He never thought he would be one of them.

By the time he reached Tallmadge itself, he was fully aware that he was wallowing in his own misery. A couple of people waved or tipped their hats at him and he tried to do the same, at least pretending that he was aware of the world around him.

Then, he met Mr. Farley in the street. The man seemed a great deal less absentminded amongst the group of gentleman around him than he had been with his family.

"Ah, Mr. Livingston!" he called. "I see you're out and about. Your ankle must be better."

"It is, thank you," Livingston replied. Now he had no choice but to talk with these people, if only for a minute or two. The gentlemen in their silk waistcoats and brushed hats parted to let him in. Despite the fact that he was considered to be quite wealthy, he felt a bit shabby beside these dandies. His black attire was suitable for any occasion, and that was all he cared for when it came to fashion.

Rather than the business he expected them to be discussing, though, the gentlemen were all talking about the weather. And they were doing it with more trepidation than he had ever seen for such a topic.

"You had better get in before the storm comes," an older man with an impressive white moustache said, his eyes on the sky. "This one looks like it will be bad."

"Indeed," Farley said, and the others echoed him. They all looked a little nervous, eyeing the sky warily.

"It is just a summer storm, surely," Livingston said, grateful for the distraction from his own thoughts. "I have experienced plenty of those in my life."

"If you've never experienced a summer storm on a northern coast, then you've never experienced a storm," the older gentleman said. He gripped the head of his cane tightly. "I had better get home, make sure the wife has boards for the windows."

Boards for the windows? It was just a storm!

"You had better do the same, though Mrs. Cusper is a capable woman, and been through many a storm in her life I imagine," Mr. Farley said with a firm nod. "You'll see tomorrow just how bad the damage is. Stop by for lunch, maybe, and tell me what you thought of your first storm."

Almost before he had properly joined the conversation, or even got introductions, the group scattered, leaving Livingston once more alone with his thoughts, and doubly unsettled. Thunder, still quiet and a bit distant, rumbled through the sky. The wind picked up, blowing debris along the streets with gleeful abandon.

Had he been possessed of an air affinity, Livingston would have sworn that the storm was laughing at him. He shook his head and put all thoughts of magic from his mind. It was time to move on. The storm would cleanse this nonsense from his thoughts and he would return to town in a few days, ready for a new topic of research. Ready to leave behind women with bewitching ocean eyes.

CHAPTER 18

The storm blew in more rapidly than Mara had ever seen before. She had seen many storms in her life, and knew the song of each one. Some were fuelled by the ocean's wrath, others by a cheerful boredom. Some, even, were fuelled by nothing more than the wind and the currents of the water. This storm, blown in with a swiftness that was terrifying and an intensity that stole the breath, was something else entirely.

"We need to get to town," Mara told her grandmother. Their conversation had been subdued after Livingston left, as if he had taken all their thoughts with him. The two had gone through their usual evening routine, tending to the garden and preparing supper. Then, Mara's instincts had started to prickle, her stomach churning. Her unease grew worse as the storm blew in. It was barely past supper, the skies considerably darker than they should have been that summer evening. The rain was already beginning to pummel the hills, and lightning flashed vehemently.

"The safest place for you right now is *here*," Cait insisted, flinching at a flash of lightning. "I don't want you anywhere near the water when the storm is this bad."

"No, you don't understand," Mara pleaded. Thunder roared loud enough to shake the cottage. She wrapped her arms around herself. "We *need* to get to town."

"Why?" Cait reached out a hand and wrapped it around Mara's. She shivered. The song of this storm was wrathful and had one purpose, which was sung in every drop of vengeful rain and every crack of thunder.

"They're bringing down a ship," Mara whispered. "I can hear the waters calling for the souls of the sailors. The song..."

She closed her eyes and tried not to listen, tried not to panic. Carefully, she drew in deep, even breaths. When she opened her eyes again, her grandmother was staring at her with all the concern of family. But there was something deeper in her gaze, a wariness that hurt Mara more than she could say. But she understood. Never before had she been able to put words to the song of a storm over the ocean, only general feelings. Her magic was coming in, manifesting. And this new understanding of the storm was only the beginning.

"I still think it safer for you here," her grandmother whispered. Mara shook her head.

"If we do not go, more will be hurt than saved. You don't understand, grandmother, the waters—the sirens and the selkies and all the creatures that swim beneath

—they're out for blood tonight." Mara was already crossing the room, reaching for her cloak, though it wouldn't do much good against the lashing rain.

Cait said nothing more in argument, just pressed her mouth together and nodded. "Let me grab my supplies," she said at last. "The weather is too bad to take the cart. We'll have to walk."

"Then we best move swiftly," Mara whispered.

Move swiftly they did, slipping and sliding down the hills until they reached Tallmadge. There were no people out on the streets, and most of the houses had their windows shuttered or boarded over. There were branches and leaves all over the cobbled streets, making an already slippery journey nearly perilous. Mara kept moving, though, her feet sure on the rain-slicked stones. She had her arm wrapped in Cait's, keeping her grandmother steady as much as protecting her from the wind and the rain. Her own dress was plastered to her body, her hair sticking to her face, droplets falling into her eyes. She should have been shivering and terrified, but she was not. She moved on, the song of the storm practically screaming in her ears.

"The beach," Cait gasped, shuddering at the pull of a particularly strong gust of wind. "I hear them on the beach."

Mara hadn't heard the human voices that were yelling to be hard over the storm; she had been too caught up in the ocean's song. She shook her head to try to clear her mind. Now she heard them, men's voices yelling as loudly as they could. Her grandmother tightened her grip and the two of them made their way to the beach.

"Stay away from the waves," Cait ordered once their shoes hit sand. Mara needed no such direction, taking the supplies of the herbwoman and preparing them as best she could in the midst of the storm. She found a rock that sheltered her from the wind a little, enough so that she could actually get out the supplies they would need for injured sailors. Only once that had been done did Mara turn her attention to the water.

The waves were furious and maniacal, refusing to give up the bounty they had dragged from the wreck just beyond the shore. In calmer waters, the sailors could have swum easily to shore. In the roiling waves, they were barely keeping their head above water as they paddled desperately inland. Some clung to boards —all that remained of their once great ship. Cargo boxes and bits of detritus muddied the waters, making a clear path to shore almost impossible.

Someone from Tallmadge had built a bonfire on the beach to serve as a beacon, the flames reaching high even in the rain. Others were running back and forth along the beach, rushing into the water to pull drenched sailors out of the sea. There were not many brave enough to venture out in this storm, even to save the souls of those shipwrecked sailors.

Even with all the activity, all the people being saved, Mara could see that the men being carried out of the water were only a small fraction of those who had been on the ship. In the water, decimated as it was, the remains of the ship hardly looked like much, but she had not grown up in a fishing and port town for nothing. That was a ship large enough to carry nearly two hundred men as well as all the cargo. She saw barely twenty on the beach and in the water.

"Miss Mara?"

A voice cut through the rain, pulling her from her dismal thoughts. She saw Livingston there, hair void-black with water, shirt sleeves rolled up to reveal his forearms, his boots speckled with sand. He was staring at her with astonishment, which she could not help but mirror.

"What are you doing here?" she asked. Her voice did not have to carry as far; the storm was lessening, its initial wrath dry and now only waiting for the moisture it carried to be spent.

"I could ask you the same! A crier came through town, asking for any able-bodied person to help pull survivors from the wreckage." Livingston gestured to the men huddled before the bonfire. He looked sure in his movements, despite the lashing rain and the chaos that surrounded them. Mara knew precisely what she was doing, preparing herbs and dressings, but she still felt relief to know that he was there to help. She reached out and touched his arm, feeling the strength there.

"My grandmother and I are here to treat the injured," Mara said. Indeed, Cait was already hurrying her direction, a large man with a gash across his forehead leaning heavily on her shoulders. Livingston saw the struggle and went to help, taking the man's weight with a surprising ease, given the sand and the debris in the way.

With Livingston's help, Mara set to her work immediately and the next few hours became a blur. She did not know from one moment to the next whether she was treating a gash or a bruised temple, a broken bone or mangled limb or the inhalation of the sea. She only looked at the immediate problem, applied what herbs she could, waited for her grandmother to mutter a spell, before she wrapped the injury in linen strips. It would have to do until they could be seen by a proper doctor—and *not* Doctor Thompson—but none of those souls who were pulled from the water died on their watch.

Finally, the rain ceased entirely, the clouds departed to leave stars in their wake, and the last living soul was pulled from the water, a boy of about thirteen who was shaking with cold.

Mara kept well back from the waves, ignoring their tempting call, and minded her work. To keep her from listening to that song, she focused instead on the conversation of those around the bonfire. The sailors were mingling with the townsfolk, eagerly drinking hot toddys, ale, tea, whatever could be had, and scarfing down bread and pies.

"A dismal night, this," one townsperson said, nodding his head to where the prow of the ship still jutted from the water.

"We were blown off course," a lieutenant said, likely now in charge since the death of his captain. He was large, with night black skin and eyes that bore the weight of the world. His hands wrapped delicately around a mug of warm tea. "Meant to make port several leagues south of here when the storm blew in. Something unnatural about this, I'd stake what's left of my sailing career on it."

Livingston, handing out drinks and bread, cast a glance towards Mara. She did not look away.

"Unnatural?" he asked, as she knew he would. Still, something in her sank at his question. She knew this storm was unnatural, given how the ocean had been acting, how the water in the winds sang. But Livingston was not one to give up that easily, no matter how subdued he had been that afternoon. Mara's throat tightened.

"Stronger, faster, than other storms. I don't know," the man said, shuddering. He drew closer to the fire, the light making shadows dance on the beach and raising the hairs on Mara's neck. "I could not tell you why, only that it was. The sirens will be pleased."

Mara closed her eyes and turned away, bile rising in her throat.

"Sirens?" Livingston asked, an edge of uncertainty in his voice.

"Aye, sirens. They can sing a sailor to his doom, dashing a ship against the rocks or causing him to jump overboard and drown. They say that the creatures use the souls of the drowned to fill their ranks, that their armies are made up of those who used to sail the ocean and now live beneath its waves. Others say that they eat the souls to fuel their magic like you throw wood on a fire."

Every person within hearing distance made a move against the description the lieutenant gave, some crossing themselves, others muttering prayers or kissing pendants they wore. Cait placed her hand on Mara's arm and squeezed. Mara tried to smile back, but could make no move at all.

"I have heard a great number of tales of terrible magical things," Livingston said, his voice a growl against the crackle of flames, "but this may be the worst. Abominations."

"They are at that," the man agreed. "They are indeed at that."

Something in her broke apart.

Mara stuffed a bloodied rag into the basket she had brought with her from the cottage. It would be burned along with the rest of the soiled material. She hoisted the basket and turned from the beach, not even waiting for her grandmother to follow.

She made it only as far as the point where sand met stone when a hand on her shoulder stopped her. Mara jumped and whirled, dropping her basket and spilling bloody cloth over the cobbles. Her breath hitched and she took a step backwards.

"I'm sorry for startling you," Livingston said, his voice low, soothing, even after everything he had said. He stooped and gathered the rags, handing the basket back to Mara. She took it and wished her hands would not tremble so. "I came to see if you were alright. After everything that happened this evening, that is. I...so many dead. Even those we managed to pull from the waves do not feel enough to mitigate such loss."

"No," Mara agreed, keeping her eyes down. "I have seen many wrecks in my life, though none this bad, and it is always...I'm sure the survivors were grateful for your help."

Livingston sighed and ran a hand through his hair, flicking out some of the water. "Have I made a misstep? I feel as though things have been strained between us since this afternoon?"

Mara managed—barely—a sharp bite of laughter. "I had not realised things were ever *not* strained between us, Mr. Livingston. Though, I do truly wish you well in your magical research endeavours."

"They may not be my endeavours for much longer." The confession was said in a casual voice, as though it mattered little whether such things occurred or not. Mara froze. His eyes were downcast and there were fine lines around his eyes and mouth which had not been there earlier, each one screaming of disappointment. He was hurting.

"You would give up on your dreams so easily?" Mara asked. She did not mean for the words to be a barb, but the way that Livingston flinched meant they had struck deeply. "I'm sorry, it's none of my concern."

"I had thought to give up, yes," Livingston said, still not looking at her. He had a hand on the basket handle, his fingers close to hers. She did not move them and neither did he, as if the basket was the only connection holding them together in the midst of the storm that had just passed. "Until...did you hear the lieutenant's words? About the storm being unnatural? About the—"

"Sirens?" Mara interrupted. It took all of her control to keep her voice steady. "I heard."

"How can I give up on my dream with things like this can happen? When storms can appear out of nowhere and the souls of innocent people can be taken to fuel an army or feed a desperate and depraved hunger."

Mara tugged at the basket and Livingston released it, as if he hadn't realised he was still holding it. He blinked and finally looked at her, taking a step back into a distance that was far more proper.

"I do not know," Mara said, and she was not certain what unspoken question she had been answering. "I am tired and must find my grandmother."

Immediately, he straightened and bowed. "Of course. I bid you good evening."

Mara inclined her head and turned away from the man. She did not know why she cared, but the knowledge that he would disavow her should he know of her true parentage, the siren's song in her blood, hurt more than she could say. Enough so that she wished it were still raining on her walk back to the cottage, so the water could hide her tears.

CHAPTER 19

The fervour of Livingston's curiosity had been ignited by the aftermath of that storm, and he spent the next two weeks interviewing those sailors which remained in town, healing from their injuries and fishermen at the docks of Tallmadge. Some refused to believe that the storm which downed their ship had been magic. Others were vehement in their belief that it *was* magic. Livingston gathered stories about such creatures as sirens, selkies, monsters that lived beneath the waves and were as old as the oceans, creatures with the tail of a fish and the body of a human, and more. Often, one story contradicted the next almost immediately upon the telling. One thing remained constant amongst those who chose to speak: the ocean was at war with itself, and that war was spilling out of the deep waters.

Surely, Livingston had argued, that if the ocean were at war with itself, someone else would have noticed before now. The response to that was almost unequivocally a wry look and a subtle shake of the head. No one believed in magic anymore, except as children's tales and superstition. And this particular war was beneath the waves of the ocean, with the creatures that swam its waters fighting for dominance. The winner would gain control of the seas, and the ships that sailed upon them.

That was enough to dash any further questions Livingston might have.

What time he did not spend out interviewing the injured sailors or those fishermen and seafaring folk that lived in Tallmadge, he spent writing up pages and pages of notes. He outlined the storm and the story of the sirens, including various descriptions that sailors had given of the creatures. Some described them as beautiful, almost impossibly so. Others thought they were vicious and sharp, like some sharks that swam these waters. Still others said they were little more than water spirits who took what shape pleased them. Livingston made certain his notes were thorough, that they could stand up to the academic scrutiny his manuscript was sure to experience, but easy enough to understand that any person, lay or otherwise, could read and know the truth.

Only, he still wasn't sure what the truth was. Were these creatures dangerous? Did they care about the humans who walked the earth, or were they only concerned with the lives of those beneath the waves? He didn't question that they existed, though it would be nice to witness a siren with his own eyes, no matter how dangerous their song. He had been sure to reference certain classical myths about the power of a siren's voice and—

"Your bath is ready."

Mrs. Cusper's voice cut through Livingston's thoughts like a butcher's knife. He flinched, his pen splattering ink across his latest page. He blinked a few times and turned to look at the housekeeper. She was standing in the door to the study, looking unimpressed with him.

"And I've asked Mr. Keeting from downstairs to see about a razor and strop. He's a fair hand and won't cut your skin."

"What?" Livingston asked. His voice croaked a little and he cleared his throat. When had he last taken anything to eat or drink? He didn't remember, though there was a vague idea of a scone and some tea, though that could have been from the day before.

"Mrs. Bunting's garden party is this afternoon. You accepted the invitation weeks ago." Mrs. Cusper smoothed out her apron, looking at Livingston quite sharply.

He rubbed his jaw and was surprised to find stubble there. If he hadn't shaved in that long, he likely needed the bath and shave that Mrs. Cusper was all but throwing at him. It was always a shock to return to reality after being drawn into the joys of research. He could barely remember what day it was, let alone drum up interest in society. If he were going to visit Mara, then that would be different, he thought. She might actually be interested in his work. Though, the last time they'd spoken, she had dismissed anything between them.

He rubbed at a spot on his chest. The sting of her dismissal was, he admitted, to account for some of his dive into the realm of research and study. Though after that storm, he did not blame her for being upset. He just wished she would *talk* with him, instead of hiding behind those walls she continuously put up.

Mrs. Cusper cleared her throat and Livingston jumped. He had nearly been drawn back into his own thoughts. A pity, for that would surely be better than this garden party. He wished for little more than to beg off from this social engagement, but he had been too well conditioned to the requirements of society, even if he did not care for them.

"Very well," he said, rising. "Thank you."

Mrs. Cusper just sniffed and strode off.

THE GARDEN PARTY felt stifling almost as soon as Livingston arrived. The weather had been obstinately bright and cheerful since the storm, as if summer were enforcing its dominance. The result was a day that was just a little too warm to be pleasant, with air that was still enough to make one long for a breeze. Add that to the large number of people there wearing their summer finery, gathered about sipping lemonade or edging towards the shade of the finely pruned trees, and it was exactly what Livingston had wanted to avoid.

"Mr. Livingston!" Mrs. Bunting rushed forwards, her bright purple gown almost enough to hurt the eyes in the sunlight. She was smiling and the redness of her cheeks told Livingston that she had been outside a while already. "Oh, it is so good of you to come! I hear you've been asking anybody and everybody about magical sea creatures for your book. Isn't that just wonderful!"

All he could do was bow and mutter a greeting. The woman—and likely most of Tallmadge—obviously thought him an eccentric academic, but that was a sin easily forgivable for anyone with enough money. It was a sin he'd never be able to overcome, here. It was almost enough to make one long for town.

"You've come just in time for drinks and cakes. I have tea, but it seems that the lemonade is far more popular. And I have ices! Elderberry and mint, if you have a preference. They're quire refreshing on a day like today."

"Thank you, Mrs. Bunting, I think I'll just—"

"And you *must* come talk with some dear friends of mine. This is Mrs. Garing and her daughter, Miss Regina Garing. And Mr. and Mrs. Timkin, with their young lady, Miss Elody Timkin and..." the list that Mrs. Bunting rattled off seemed endless, though there were perhaps only ten people in the little cluster, with four daughters of marriageable age. Livingston was going to extract himself to partake of an ice, and try to find somewhere else to linger until he could reasonably leave, but got roped into bringing refreshments for as many as he could carry. The young ladies simpered and blushed as he promised to return with drinks.

It was going to be a dreadfully long afternoon.

He tried to enjoy the summer sun and the cool refreshments, the beautifully cultivated gardens and the birds which flitted about, but all of it seemed drowned out with the annoying buzz of conversation around him. He could barely even think on his manuscript or further questions about magic for all the simpering questions and demands on his attention. He was moments away from simply leaving, claiming a prior engagement or something equally important, when Mrs. Bunting called out above the noise of conversation, her hands clapping together frenetically.

"Everyone! Please gather your attention to the pavilion. I have arranged for some entertainment on this fine summer's day!"

Marvellous, Livingston thought. Some ridiculous dance performance or a troupe of acrobats or some such nonsense. It was too hot for such nonsense. He nearly slipped away then, when everyone's attention was diverted. Something stopped him and he, too, turned towards the pavilion wrapped in climbing flowers. There, looking quite at home amongst the greenery, was Mara Del Sol. She wore a dress in a filmy blue, the colour so unlike her usual tones of grey and green and brown that he almost didn't recognise her. Standing there, her back straight, her chin lifted, her gaze just a touch haughty, she looked as though she belonged amongst these society darlings. And yet, there was something there, a wildness, untamed, that made her stand apart. He had missed talking with her and seeing her there was a blow, indeed.

This was the entertainment? Livingston felt his mouth go dry, and wondered at it.

Then, she began to sing and he did not wonder at all.

At first, all he could hear was the words sung in a delicate soprano, a poem about a young girl in the hills seeking a rare rose, watched unbeknownst by a hunter and a wolf. It was a popular ballad, especially in this part of the country, but Livingston had heard it enough times from the lips of untrained girls showing off for potential suitors to be familiar with the tune. Then, the hairs on the back of his hands rose on end and he stopped simply hearing the words. Instead, he felt them.

He felt the desire of the young girl for the rose, a symbol to her of her future love and of innocent beauty. He felt her steps over the grasses of the hills, the wind on her face. He felt, too, the eyes of the hunter as he sought out a dangerous wolf, jaded and wary, until he came upon the young girl bathing her feet in a stream to soothe them while she sought the rose. He felt the longing of this hunter, the simple joys of the girl, even the furious fire of the wolf as it sought its prey and revenge on the hunter.

He no longer knew who he was, the wind or the sun in this drama, only that the world around him was anything but real and the world taking place inside his head was all that mattered. His heart beat faster for the first meeting of the lovers, for the stalking of the wolf.

His breath hitched as the hunter and the girl climbed to a mountain lake and took in the impossible beauty. He wanted to dance when they finally found this flower. And when the wolf struck at the young girl, all he could see was a blind rage as her blood sprinkled the petals of the very same flower she sought.

In the end, they all died on that hillside, the hunter and the wolf fighting until their very last breath. It was not a happy love song, though the tune was haunting and the sentiment perhaps even a bit ridiculous. It was only after the last note hung in the air that Livingston could acknowledge this. He had been so caught up in the music that nothing else had mattered. He even felt dampness on his cheeks, which was something he had never experienced for any music. He looked around and saw that everyone else at the garden party, from the stern-faced men to the eager mamas and the taciturn footmen, was similarly affected.

Livingston shivered, rubbing his hands over his legs to try and shake off the residual emotions from Mara's music. Simultaneously, he wished she would sing again, just so he could be caught up in her music, the swell of her voice. He looked at her and found her smiling, bowing her head to the applause which her audience was finally giving. But the smile did not reach her eyes. And when she flicked her gaze to him, Livingston saw only wariness there. Fear even.

The fear stung. He had no wish to cause her harm, no wish to do anything but talk with her, make her smile. And she looked at him with fear? Why?

Mara opened her mouth to sing a second song and

the hairs on the back of his hand rose again, this time accompanied by just the slightest shock. His astonishment was the only thing he could hold on to as his emotions took another adventure through music, this time a hero's quest against a ferocious dragon.

Mara Del Sol had magic.

His eyes watered as he tried to hold on to that thought while her magic swept over him, coaxing him into giving in, to listening to her music, to taking the journey that she offered. Beauty and triumph, adventure and pain, all of it beckoned at the edge of her music, not quite strong enough to completely overwhelm him, but enough to beckon and tempt.

Mara Del Sol had magic, he thought, then closed his eyes and allowed himself to be swept up in it. If she had magic, then it was a wonder indeed to be able to sing it into being. He let himself sink deeper into the music, letting go of his astonishment and his shock.

Three more songs, two in languages he did not know but whose emotions were just as strong, and Mara finally closed out her concert. The guests of Mrs. Bunting slowly returned to their conversations, though most of them were discussing the music and the songs. A few eyes, mostly male, followed Mara as she strode through the crowd, looking even more as though she were something ethereal merely trying to wear the finery of these foolish peacocks.

She walked right past him, her attention fixed on the refreshment table. Livingston reached out and touched her arm. "Wait," he murmured.

Mara tensed. Then, putting on a smile that was

entirely false, she turned to him and curtseyed. "Mr. Livingston, what a pleasure to see you again."

"Mara," he breathed. Took a step closer to her. Her eyes widened and she looked about, as if she could possibly care what these people thought. "Please."

"Please what?" she asked. There was that fear again, and it stung even more for knowing the cause.

"You have magic," he breathed, reaching up and brushing a strand of hair back from her face. "Is that why you and your grandmother were doing that protection ritual? I know why you did not tell me; I have hardly been an upstanding citizen when it comes to my interest magic. I have been insensitive and invasive. But…surely, Mara, you know that I have tried to change. That I would never hurt you."

Mara let out a breath that rattled, then took a single, deliberate step back. When she lifted her eyes to his once more, Livingston saw no trace of the fear that had been there. Now, there was only resolve. That look stung more than her words on the beach, than the last two weeks of silence that he'd buried himself in his books to ignore.

"I know no such thing," she said, her voice even and perfectly polite. She bowed her head and walked away, leaving him to watch after her and wonder how he was to prove her wrong.

$\mathcal{M}$ ara couldn't help but feel she'd made a mistake, singing at that garden party. It was something she'd done many times before; all of Tallmadge knew of her singing and were eager to hire her for their own parties. But with Livingston there, eager to seek out any magic, it was a far more dangerous proposition. Especially given his recent fixation on sirens and other monsters of the deep. Rumours of his current interests had circulated around town so many times that it was impossible for Mara to not hear of such things. Not to mention the sinking feeling in her stomach when she'd been almost, inexplicably, happy at the sight of him.

What was worse, though, was that it was the eve of her birthday.

She dug into the dirt with a trowel, using perhaps more force than was necessary to pull out the weed that had begun sprouting. With a vicious yank, Mara took it from the dirt, shook off the excess from the roots, then tossed the offending weed onto a pile. The garden around the cottage was often friendlier to those plants that many respectable gardeners would consider foul invaders, but there were some that still required culling.

"Be sure you get the mint before it overtakes—oh, you've already done it." Cait stood in the door, wiping her hands on her apron. She surveyed the garden and frowned. "How long have you been out here?"

Mara stretched her back. "I don't know. A while."

"All I asked you to do was general pruning. I didn't mean for you to weed the whole garden! Come inside and wash up. It's almost time for tea."

Mara winced. "I'm almost done. There's just the strawberries to gather and the cold frames to—"

"Inside. Now." Cait fixed her granddaughter with a stern look, one that could wither the strongest of flowers. Mara, already hot from being out in the sun so long, exhausted from the thoughts that kept swirling inside her head, and feeling more than a little defeated, could not have withstood that gaze for anything. She sighed and rose, her limbs protesting the sudden change in position. Mara stretched, replaced the trowel in its spot, and shuffled inside, sure to remove her dirt-stained shoes and apron.

When she finished washing up, even going so far as to rebraid her hair, Mara went to find tea and instead found a celebratory affair. Her heart sank.

Her grandmother stood before the table, wearing a

bright pink dress that she only pulled out on holidays, the lace at her neck starting to yellow with age. She had made cakes—for there were at least two, as well as several smaller pastries—with bright blue frosting and decorated with flowers. Even the tea was being served in her best service, the delicate pattern worn with time. It was a celebration, a party, meant to commemorate her twenty-eighth birthday, and all Mara wanted to do was run for the hills.

"Many happy returns, my dearest child," Cait said, stepping forwards and kissing Mara on the cheek. Mara tried to return her hug and feared she failed miserably.

"Thank you, Grandmother. You did not have to do any of this. I have no need of parties or cakes." Mara sat at the table and tried to ignore her grandmother's stung expression. It only made her feel worse. Then, Cait clicked her tongue and started pouring out the tea.

"Nonsense! Everyone needs parties and cakes," she said, practically tossing a tea cup in Mara's direction. "Now are you going to tell me why you're so worried that you cannot even enjoy your favourite cake, or shall I simply take it away?"

Mara sighed and studied the table. "Very well. Thank you."

Cait harumphed, but cut Mara a large slice anyways. Silence settled over the table while the two of them ate. Mara tried to enjoy the treat, the care that her grandmother had taken in her meal, but anxiety kept churning in her belly, tightening her throat.

Finally, "I think my magic…I think it's manifesting."

Cait set her fork down with a tiny clink. "I see. How do you know?"

Mara shuddered, wrapping her arms around herself. "Yesterday, at the garden party. I sang, like I usually do, only this time it seemed like my magic had a mind of its own. It tried to wrap everyone into the song, and I think I nearly cast an illusion over them."

"Siren magic is very powerful," Cait said slowly. Mara shuddered again, recalling each terrible word that Livingston had said about the sirens. About her own mother, not that he knew such a thing. And how concerned he had been afterwards!

"I think it's more than that," Mara admitted. She lowered her gaze, focusing on the cake. "The water has been louder, too. I can hear the ocean even from here. I haven't…I haven't manipulated any water in more than a month, but I know it would be a simple thing to do so. And those are just the things I can feel, that I know exist in my magic."

Cait took Mara's hand and squeezed. To Mara's surprise, there was a smile in her gaze. "We knew this day was coming, my dear. Your father always told us that your magic would manifest later in life, but that it would be strong. That is, after all, why he hid you away here."

As if Mara needed further reminder of her peculiar bloodline. "I should leave," she said. "I should get as far from the ocean as I can, so that it can't find me and I can't hurt anyone and—"

"You cannot. I tried, once, years ago and you grew

dangerously ill." Cait pulled back, grabbing a small box that lay wrapped on the counter. She handed it to Mara as if it might break. In turn, Mara unwrapped it with equal care. Inside, nestled on a bed of silk, lay a pearl. No, not *a* pearl. The pearl that normally hung at her grandmother's neck. The pearl whose own inherent magic was enough to make Mara's magic sing.

"I cannot!" Mara protested, pushing the box away.

"You must," Cait said, pulling out the pearl on its necklace and handing it to Mara. "You must always have a piece of the ocean with you, now that your magic is manifesting. You have lived here with me, safe and sound and the most miraculous thing in my life, but there is no changing the fact that you are a creature of the sea. It *calls* to you! You may not live in the waters, but if you do not live near them, you will die. The pearl is a piece of the ocean—a powerful one, yes —and it will provide you with enough protection here on land to keep you safe, so long as you do not go into the water."

"But this is yours! It was your price for taking me in, a pearl of great power to amplify your own," Mara said, though her fingers closed around the pearl.

"What use could I have for such a thing, beyond using it for protection spells for you? I'm nothing more than a hedgewitch. My powers cannot be truly helped by that pearl. I have no need for great power." Cait closed her hand around Mara's and smiled gently. "It belongs with you."

Before Mara could stop herself, tears filled her eyes. She wrapped her arms around herself and tried to hold back the water, but she could no more do that than she could stop her magic from manifesting. "I'm terrified," she said through the tears. "The ocean…it knows where I am, surely it knows, too, that my magic is…and then there is the fact that he despises sirens. I know it shouldn't matter, shouldn't change anything—I do not even know why I care, but I do! And it's infuriating and terrifying and…"

"Mara, child, what *are* you talking about? Who hates sirens?" Cait frowned, her gaze sharp.

Mara felt more than foolish, the heat from her blush warming her tears. She should be worried about what the ocean would do once its creatures found her, but instead, she was more concerned with the opinion of a man who annoyed her as much as he challenged her. She shook her head. "It's so stupid, Grandmother. We were at the beach during the storm and he heard the stories that the sailors were telling about sirens devouring the souls of the drowned and said how terrible creatures like that were why he was writing his book, so he could warn people. I feel like an idiot, like one of those girls with the simpering mamas, so unaccustomed to society, batting her eyes at the first person to pay her attention, only to find out he's…he's…"

"Oh," Cait said with surprising calmness. "I see. It's that Livingston fellow. I thought you two were uncommonly easy in your conversation."

Mara wiped the tears with one hand, the other still clutching her pearl. "I felt like there was someone who finally understood me, and instead it's just like everything else in my life: dangerous. He even approached me at the garden party, wanting to know why I hadn't told him of my magic. Siren magic! As if I ever could reveal such a thing."

"Mara! Stop feeling sorry for yourself," Cait scolded, voice as sharp as it ever was. "You have had a life more difficult than most, surrounded by secrets as you are. But that is no excuse for not finding happiness. Yes, you have to find someone who either embraces you and your magic and is happy to let you be yourself regardless of who and what you are, and I know that can be difficult. But never *ever* think that you are less than you are because a man—a human man with human faults—knows less than he should about magic. If you wish him to act appropriately, then educate him!"

Mara choked out a laugh. That one brought about more until her tears were from laughing, not sorrow. "You're not even shocked at my interest?"

"Well, he's certainly better than that Rawlins fellow you were so keen on," Cait said with a dainty sniff. Mara wanted to cover her face with her hands, but she did not.

"I was sixteen and he was very handsome. It is not his fault that I did not find his poetry to my tastes."

"He compared you to a boulder!" Cait snorted. "Surely a boy with as many tutors as he had could come up with a better comparison than a boulder."

Mara laughed again. "Yes, very well, Kyle Livingston is far better than Theodore Rawlins."

The two women laughed a little longer, until the awkwardness and fear had completely dissipated. Mara was in the midst of helping herself to a second piece of cake when Cait spoke again, once more changing the mood. "I am glad that you care for this gentleman, *if* he proves worthy of your respect, that is. But at the very least, wait to educate him on your particular brand of magic until after this evening."

"This evening?" Mara hadn't planned on venturing into Tallmadge this evening. She wanted to finish the garden before she could even contemplate being amongst other people again. A sense of accomplishment would at least lend her that confidence.

"Your birthday," Cait said. Her voice went quiet. "Your twenty-eighth birthday."

Mara tightened her fist around the pearl, then quickly put the necklace on and tucked the beautiful piece into her bodice, so no one with prying eyes might see it. Even here in the hills, she felt nervous, doubly so since Cait's reminder.

"I forgot," she whispered. "It feels so long ago that he visited, but I thought it was still another year or two off before he came again."

"Seven years since the last time," Cait murmured. She smiled, but the gesture was weak. "He will be so glad to see how you have grown, how tall and strong you stand."

Mara wasn't so sure about that. The last time her father had visited was on her twenty-first birthday. She had been feeling the depths of her separation from the society of humans then, when most of her peers were marrying or finding their own way in the world and she was being left behind. Her loneliness had since transformed into a comfort with her own companionship, but she had been miserable company for her father. He hadn't understood her longing to fit in with the humans, instead regaling her with stories of what selkies her age might be doing, not realising that only made things worse.

"Do you think…" Mara took a deep breath, trying to release all the nervousness in her body at once. She let the breath out in a rush, then shook her head. "Never mind."

"He may have the answers about your magic that you seek," Cait said, answering the question Mara was too afraid to ask. "But he may not. I'm not aware of any previous pairing between a selkie and a siren. Your birth would not have been forbidden if it weren't a powerful thing, and yet there are no stories that I know. And I've searched."

Mara shrugged one shoulder. "I suppose I'll discover it for myself soon enough."

As if that were any consolation.

"My dear, forget all of this. Just for one night, be pleased that it is your birthday. Enjoy your father's company. Pretend that none of these problems with the ocean or your magic or this Mr. Livingston exist. None of them will, for one night, if you do that."

Mara nodded, tried to smile. She failed. "Well, if I'm going to meet my father after seven years, I might as well change. I wouldn't want him to think that I spend all my time in the garden getting dirt everywhere, even if I do."

"Child, you could desire nothing more than to live

in a cave in the hills and your father would still love you," Cait said, reaching forward and smoothing a thumb over Mara's cheek. "For that matter, so would I."

Mara tried to smile again, and this time, she succeeded.

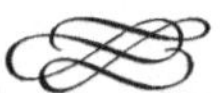

CHAPTER 21

*L*ivingston was happy to admit that he was not terribly social on the best of days, preferring to be closeted with a book instead of out at a dinner or ball or walking around with the intent of conversing. So when even he felt as though he was deliberately hiding away from the world, it was saying something.

After returning home from the garden party, he avoided his housekeeper and her interrogations, any servants who might be wandering the halls, and even his own reflection in the mirror. His thoughts were just too tumultuous for other people, even himself.

Mara had magic.

And she hadn't told him about it.

Had he not tried to mend the barriers between them—mostly caused by him, he admitted that much—she would likely never have told him. Livingston had been certain that some sort of understanding lay between them. He was interested in magic, not to harm, not to hurt, but to help people on both sides of the divide. Mara had listened to his fears and not laughed at them. She had been kind and understanding and yet when he tried to do the same, tried to be there for her because of her magic, all he received was distance.

She had *magic*.

It made so much sense, in retrospect. The protection ritual, the discussions with her grandmother, the way she knew so much about magic when Cait was the hedgewitch of the two. Tiny clues that Livingston should have seen, should have been able to name. The party had been the first blatant use of magic in front of him and, truth be told, he was entranced. Her voice inspired wonders, sang up emotions that he had never thought to experience in such intensities. She had mesmerised an entire party. None of them recognised it for what it was, instead just thinking her exceptionally talented. But Livingston had felt the magic. He knew what it was. And yet, when he tried to talk with her about it, tried to ask her to trust him, she pulled away.

That, more than any curiosity he might have over the form and range of her ability, stung.

So he hid.

The next day, he crept down the stairs to try to avoid Mrs. Cusper and her questions about the party, hoping to grab some bread and cheese and slip away from the house before she even knew he had awakened. He would spend his day walking the cliffs, if nothing else, so that he could avoid more questions and stares. Somewhere people did not often go. Instead,

Livingston came face to face with one of the footmen holding a platter of letters, topped with two thick parcels.

The two of them blinked at each other for a moment.

"Good morning, sir," the footman said, bowing slightly and showing no hint of surprise. "The post has come. Would you care for it in your room, or the dining room? We haven't yet received the newspapers from town."

Livingston winced inwardly. "The dining room will be fine, thank you."

There was no hiding now he'd been seen, so why bother?

He followed the footman into the dining room and heaped his breakfast plate full of food. He wasn't the least bit hungry, but at least no one would bother him while he was eating. He took a cup of strong tea and set to opening the parcels.

They were both books, one from Aidan and the other from Reggie. The first was a volume on Tales from the North, a story collection featuring magic and monsters. The second was a more detailed discussion on sea creatures and their sightings in the logs of naval captains.

Two of the letters were from his friends, as well. Reggie's was short and to the point, stating that he had found the book on sea creatures in the library of his family home and that his housekeeper hadn't even noticed it was gone, so to keep it as long as he liked. Oh, and please say there were entertaining happenings in the North, because town was so dull and full of simpering ladies and their mamas all eager for the Townsend fortune.

The second letter was longer, more thought out, and included a note at the end from Briony, Aidan's wife. Aidan was reporting on life at Blackwell Downs, how Nesren, the wolf that he had adopted was carrying a litter, having been accidentally bred with a local shepherd dog. He talked of the weather, the land, and Livingston genuinely believed him to be happy in his new life, this man who had once disdained the country. Aidan also touched on magic, though he said little more than the fact that he had found the book of stories, and for Livingston to be careful. Briony's note was more informative, if it did put a sour taste in Livingston's mouth.

BE CAREFUL, Kyle, when dealing with magic of the water. Keepers such as myself, and my father before me, rarely had to deal with such things as we were more concerned with the wilds in the forests and marshes and grassy places. But when we had a chance to interact with those who had an affinity for water, or who were water spirits, or others entirely, they were always changeable as the sea. Deep and steady, and yet dangerous when riled. Constant, yet untameable. If you win their loyalty, know how to navigate them, as it were, then you will have a full relationship, but a misstep could have you drowned. I asked some of my wild friends what they knew about creatures of the sea, and even the wind was reluctant to answer. They said only that the sea was preparing for war. I do not know what any of it means, but I hope you take care. Aidan and I would miss you sorely should anything happen.

LIVINGSTON CRUMPLED the letter and shoved it into his pocket. He would save it for his book, but just then he couldn't bear to look at Briony's words. It was hardly anything he had not already learned from the sailors and Cait Del Sol, but the words stung all the same.

Of course he would take care. He felt he had been doing nothing but taking care since Mara had scolded him on the tops of the hills. Yet he still managed to earn her mistrust somehow. Briony's words were certainly accurate in that regard. Mara was strong and sure, but heaven forbid you cross her, rile her temper. She could be as calm as a summer's day on the ocean, as bracing as a storm on the sea.

Livingston stilled.

He had only just discovered that Mara had magic. He did not know anything about her having a water affinity, and yet Briony's words were so accurate, so perfect in their depiction of Mara, that he did not think it could be anything else. He did not even know a person could have both an affinity and magic, though it made sense. They were related, magic and affinities, though he hadn't quite worked out the details on how. Cait had been remarkably unhelpful in that regard.

Sometimes a person had one, or the other, or both, or none at all.

He had none at all.

Mara had both. She must have both.

"Water affinity," he murmured, thinking of the way her voice swelled over the crowds, transfixing them. He recalled the illusions she spun. The way her song created something out of nothing and was nearly impossible to ignore.

Combine that with her apparent water affinity and…

"I've been so *stupid!*" he growled, slamming his fist onto the table. She must have siren blood in her. That was the only logical explanation. And he had, several times and in her presence, decried the viciousness, the terrible nature of the sirens. No wonder he had earned her mistrust! She must have felt like he would attack her if he knew, when the opposite was true. He did not care one jot that she had siren blood.

He started to rise from the table, gathering the attention of the servants waiting to clear up. Then, he hesitated. His first instinct was to go to Mara directly, to ask her as many questions as he could in order to understand. That would earn him no favours with her, given her reticence on magic thus far. It was his own fault, but the situation still rankled.

He would have to find another way to talk with her, to gain her trust and to assure her that he would not do anything to harm her, even if it meant leaving some information about sirens out of his manuscript. He would do anything to make things right between them.

"Where is the florist in town?" Livingston asked, startling the footman.

"Ah, it's over near the market, next to the haberdashers and green grocers." The man gave a hesitant bow, as if not certain what he would next be asked to do.

"No, wait," Livingston said, silently cursing. "I can't give her flowers, not when she has a whole garden."

"A gift for a lady?" the footman asked. "My mam always suggests that useful things make the best gifts. Of course, she never says no to a pretty bauble or two, when my dad has been especially bothersome."

Livingston smiled. "Baubles nearly always do the trick, but I do not think it will mean much this time. The lady in question is far too practical for such things."

"Do you mean Miss Mara?" the footman asked. He must have spied Livingston's astonished expression, because the man gave a wide grin in response. "You've been up at the cottage several times, and surely your book can't be taking that much time from the herbwoman. You were also seen at the garden party with Miss Mara, touching her hair."

"Does the whole town know?" Livingston asked in dismay. He knew how insidious gossip was in town, and Tallmadge seemed to have speeds just as swift, if not more so. Of all the times for gossip to be about him, it had to be now, when it actually mattered that he keep silent. He doubted very much that Mara would like her name bandied about.

"Very likely. It will put a great number of hopeful

mothers out, but I think Miss Mara is the best sort of person. She deserves to be happy, what with how kind she is to them as need her help. Those toffs don't treat her half as well as she deserves, calling her names based on her birth, which no person can help." The footman's passion was growing, and he must have realised his misstep, because he cleared his throat, cheeks bright. Apparently more than the few people in the tavern were half in love with Mara Del Sol.

Livingston couldn't blame them.

"Well, what would you recommend as an apology gift for our lovely Miss Del Sol?" Livingston asked. He couldn't quite help the teasing tone in his voice.

The footman, though, seemed to take his question seriously. "She doesn't much care for jewels or ribbons. And her garden does have plentiful blooms. Maybe… maybe a dog to keep her company on the hills? Or a nice roast from the butcher?"

Livingston winced. A dog, while a wonderful companion, involved a great deal of care from its keeper and he didn't want to do that to Mara unless he knew she would not mind. And he was certainly not going to buy her a cut of meat! That hardly conveyed the message he was trying to send. No, he needed something more. Something deeper, which gave his apology and told her of everything else he could hardly put into words.

He stilled, an idea springing into his mind. "Do you know, by chance, where I could purchase some books?"

THAT EVENING, after having hunted down a shop that sold books of poetry and prose, none of which were remotely scientific or related to magic, Livingston marched up the hill towards the cottage. He was getting more used to climbing this way, no longer feeling like he needed his horse at every rise in the terrain. Perhaps it was the fresh air that made him feel energetic enough to take on the world. Somehow, he doubted it was due to the northern cooking.

The sun was setting, casting its light over the hills and onto the ocean in an array of reds and golds. The air was still warm from the day, but cool enough for walking. Perhaps he could convince Mara to take him back to that field of flowers. They could talk, just the two of them, safe from prying eyes and ears.

He paused a scant few hundred feet from the cottage, the stream bubbling before him.

He was being foolish. He had never behaved this way towards any woman, and certainly not one he had first considered a subject of research. Could it truly be that he was, dare he say it, falling in love?

Livingston gulped in a deep breath of air as his dreams of being a retiring, solitary academic shattered before him. Yet, when he considered their loss, he did not mourn. Instead, he straightened his shoulders, adjusted the book of poetry in his hands, and lifted his gaze towards the cottage.

He froze.

A figure approached the cottage, slightly shadowed in the dying light. It was a man, broad in the shoulder and powerful in the leg, though Livingston could not make out any of his features. He could see that the man was hardly clothed, his chest bare and his nethers wrapped with some sort of bulky cloth. Whoever he was, he was heading straight for the door, opening it and slipping inside as though he had a right to be there, though he seemed a little uncertain in his steps.

Livingston was not a man drawn towards the physical sports of boxing or fencing, always having preferred a pleasant walk to anything more vigorous. He did not hesitate though, leaping over the creek with a single bound, running for the door to the cottage, mind completely empty of anything except the need to get to Mara and Cait. He would protect them, even if it meant having to fight like he'd never been able to before.

He threw the door open and burst into the drawing room. Mara and Cait were there, but so was the man. He was inches away from Mara, his arms wide. Livingston could see now that the cloth around the man's waist was fur, and that his skin was decorated with pale scars. His hair was short and unruly and he had a wild look in his eyes.

"Get away from her," Livingston snarled. He lunged.

"No, wait!" Mara stepped between him and his target, pressing her hands to his chest. Behind her, the man flashed his teeth and let out a low sound that was more animal than human. "Wait!"

"Mara?" the stranger growled.

"Father, this is Kyle Livingston. Livingston, this is… my father." Mara looked up at him with those oceanic eyes, telling him silently that she was revealing all her secrets to him, that she was trusting him with this most closed off part of her heart. Livingston fell back and stared again at the stranger.

"Your...father?" he asked. This wild, strange man who walked around with no clothing and had so many scars as to be almost unsightly, surely he could not be father to the beautiful, effervescent Mara. He narrowed his eyes, mind wracked with confusion. "He is not a siren."

Mara shook her head, her eyes wide and watering. She looked away from him and his heart ached for it. Then, she let out a low whisper, "No, he is a selkie. My mother was the siren. And now you know. Judge me how you wish."

CHAPTER 22

Mara had already been struggling with the manifestation of her magic and the feelings for Livingston she'd never wanted, but now, standing between her father and the man she had grown perhaps stupidly fond of, she was in desperate need of something far stronger than tea. There were things to be dealt with, first.

"Judge you? I would never…A selkie," Livingston said, rocking back on his heels. His gaze flickered between her and her father, studying them both in turn as if searching for a resemblance that was magical as well as physical. "And your mother—"

"A siren, yes," Mara said.

"Mara," her father said with a growl, the sound animalistic. "You should not be telling a human such things."

"I'm afraid it's rather more complicated than that," Mara said with a weary laugh. "Now, can we sit and talk like civilised people or are you going to fight?"

Livingston took a step backwards, though he was still glaring at Mara's father. In turn, the selkie too retreated, sitting in a chair close to the fire. Cait handed her father a blanket, which he wrapped around himself, and some of the tension in the room dissipated. Mara sank into the couch and twined her hand with her grandmother's. She needed the extra strength. Livingston was forced to sit on the lone stool, the house not really being made for that many people.

"Perhaps…" Livingston began, then hesitated. He looked at Mara, then her father, and his shoulders straightened. "Perhaps introductions are in order. My name is Kyle Livingston, and I am a researcher of magic. I also happen to be quite fond of Mara, regardless of her heritage, and would care to know why you are here."

Mara's cheeks burst into flames, the heat so startling that she was sure she flinched. Cait squeezed her fingers and gave a wry smile to Mara. "Breathe," she mouthed. Mara nodded.

"I am Othed, commander of the armies of the great selkie nation. Mara's father." The man narrowed his eyes. "And I would like you to elaborate on your 'fondness' for her."

"Enough," Cait snapped. "We do not need you posturing like two drunken men at the tavern. It is Mara's birthday, and that is all that matters. Unless, Othed, you have *other* news you wish to share?"

Mara instinctively reached for the pearl at her throat, which now throbbed with insistent energy. It had been startling to put it on and realise how in tune it was with her own magic, but now, it seemed to read her fear and was moments away from acting on its own. Her father followed her movements with his eyes, which widened with surprise.

"You have given her the—"

"Yes," Cait said simply. "It was time."

"Then it is true, what the currents whisper," Othed said, leaning forwards to stare at Mara. "Your magic is manifesting."

"The *currents* whisper?" Livingston asked, his tone caught somewhere between curiosity and indignation. Othed sneered at him; Mara's heart sank at the display.

"Do you not know, human, what is going on beneath your very nose?" he demanded. He waved a hand at Mara, fingernails pointed like claws. "Do you not know what the offspring of my people and the people of song are capable of? The very *ocean* seeks her to control her power, to tame the weapon before anyone else can do so. Why do you think she lives here and not in the sea with me? With her mother?"

Mara shrank back. She eyed Livingston from beneath lowered lashes, afraid to look at him directly and see what he thought of her now that he knew the full truth. He just sat there on the stool, as composed as he had been at the garden party, a perfectly civilised man in the midst of such disorder.

"A weapon," Livingston said, his voice low. Mara recognised fury when she heard it, but it took her an extra moment to realise his fury was on *her* behalf. "Do you honestly think of your daughter as a weapon? I knew the ocean to be careless of the lives that it encounters, but I never thought it cruel."

Othed reared back and rose from the seat by the fire, the flames casting dangerous shadows on his skin. "You *dare* judge me, human? Do you know what I have given up? Do you know what I have done to protect her?"

"Enough," Mara said. Her voice was not loud, but she infused it with enough of her magic to prove how serious she was. She glared at her father until he sat back down and once more pulled the blanket around his bare shoulders.

"You would use your power on me?" he asked, as if he had a right to be hurt.

"This is my *home*," Mara snapped. "You have no right to threaten anyone beneath its roof. I know why you gave me up, Father: to protect me. But in doing so, you relinquished all right to judge me for my decisions. I choose to invite Kyle into this house. Just as you are invited."

"He knows nothing of the true dangers you face!" Othed protested, throwing an arm out to point at the man.

"Because I have not told him," Mara said, holding her chin high. "And I would have done so had you not shouted my entire magical history for him to hear. Is that what you do when you are with the other selkies? Do you talk about me as a point of pride, or as a casual conversation piece, regardless of my actual life?"

This time, the selkie remained silent, his expression

sullen. He hunched his shoulders. "I apologise, daughter."

Mara gave a quick jerk of her chin, then turned to Livingston. He was studying her with a calm expression, but for one single line that formed between his brows. She did not know what the expression meant, if he were studying her as something to write up for his book, or if it were more. She swallowed back her hope.

"If you have questions," she murmured. "Best ask them now."

To her surprise, Livingston did not immediately start voicing his questions. He studied her for a moment, reaching up to adjust his jacket as if it were uncomfortable. He pulled out a small book from the inside pocket and studied it for a moment. Then, he set it on the side table closest to her. He looked at her father, at Cait, then sighed and shook his head. "I have no questions, only that you tell me what you wish to tell me. It is your life, Mara, and you are allowed to choose whom you involve in it, and to what extent."

Mara blinked, and she was fairly certain she was gaping at Livingston. This, coming from the man who had been pestering her with questions from the moment they met—invasive, intrusive questions—like he had every right to know them. Had the revelation of her parentage, her own magic, changed that much between them, whatever it was that actually lay between them? Or was it something else? She hoped it was something else.

Mara knew, then and there, that she wanted to tell him everything. "I was born to a siren by a selkie father. Such unions are forbidden by oceanic law, for fear that the children will acquire such power that would imbalance the order of the waters. So my father brought me here, twenty-eight years ago, and left me in the care of Cait Del Sol. I always had an affinity for water, pulling bubbles into the air, making ripples in still waters, stilling the waters that were frantic, even speaking to the nymph that lives in the creek outside. And I could always sing, not merely with skill, but with enough power to draw certain emotions out of people. I could make a love ballad tragic, bring smiles to the faces of people through a dirge, it did not matter. But these are...trifles to the powers of the ocean. Hardly enough to qualify me as a hedgewitch, even. I was told that this was because my power had not yet manifested."

Mara lowered her gaze to her hands, resting so calmly in her lap. Her fingers felt like they belonged to someone else, tingling as they were with power. Even now, she could hear the call of the ocean as its waves beat upon the shore. "Once my powers manifested, that was when I would be able to tip the balance. But if the creatures of the sea caught me before then, they could kill me, train me, make me their own. I have been hunted my whole life, terrified to dip so much as a toe into the ocean for fear it would find me. I have been so careful that even the spies the ocean finds and sends to the coastal towns haven't so much as looked twice at me. Until you came, that is."

"Mara, I..." Livingston trailed off and she gave him

the best smile she could manage. It felt watery, weak, and she let it slip away.

"You were not to know. But saving you from the ocean, that day on the beach, it alerted everyone to my whereabouts. That storm was the ocean's way of telling me it knew where I was, and it was going to come for me." Mara shuddered and wrapped her arms around herself. "And now, I can hear it calling to me. Like a bell, signalling that it's time to go back."

"You cannot go back," Othed said, his voice harsh against the cosiness of the room. "I heard it when you stepped into the water, but so did everyone else. They know where you are, Mara, and they will come for you."

"Is she to be in danger her whole life?" Livingston asked, and it warmed Mara a little to know that he cared.

"No," Othed murmured. "The summer equinox is in two days' time. There is also to be an eclipse, a passing of the moon between the sun and the earth. The waters will be at their strongest during this time, unlike what has been seen or will be seen in a thousand years. If we can keep Mara away from the ocean until then, she will be safe once more here in this human town."

In this human town. Mara's breath caught in her throat. Before she could ask for clarification, Livingston spoke again. Apparently his decision not to ask questions of her out of respect for her life and her choices did not extend to his suspicions of her father.

"So I will take her to town. It is far from the coats, she will be safe there," Livingston said, and he looked quite ready to spring from the stool and whisk Mara away in that very moment. She felt her cheeks warming again.

"You cannot," Cait said, a quiet murmur. "I tried it once, when she was but a girl, knowing that she would only be truly safe far from the gaze of the ocean. I could take her a day's journey inland, but no farther, before she fell ill. She is a creature of the sea, my boy, and though she may walk amongst us here in Tallmadge, she must always remain close to the waters."

"So, what, once this equinox has passed, she'll just go back home with you, selkie?" Livingston demanded. Othed bristled, but shook his head.

"No. I would give many things to see my daughter more than once every seven years, but even after the equinox, her power will be great. She will always present a threat to the ocean, just as much as she will always be a part of it. She must remain on land."

Mara had known this almost her whole life. She had known that her father would never come for her to bring her home, to let her live amongst his people, or her mother's. She had known, when he never even considered staying more than one night per visit, when he never suggested giving up his seal skin to be with her, that she was always meant to be apart from that life. But no one, not even the honest-tongued Cait, had said that fact in such clear words before. Her father had truly abandoned her when he gave her into Cait's care. His visits may have been borne of love, but they were continued out of obligation.

Mara rose, her movements jerky as she tried to get

her thoughts under control. She opened her mouth to speak, acutely aware of everyone's eyes on her. Nothing came from her throat, not speech, not magical song. Just silence. She shook her head violently, then fled from the cottage into the star-flecked night.

She half-imagined that she heard her father calling after her, demanding that she stay, that he wanted to see her and spend time with her still, but there was only silence. Silence and the quiet snick of the latch on the cottage door. A few moments later and strong arms wrapped around her, sure where once they would have hesitated. Mara turned into them and wept, burying her nose in Livingston's chest. He said nothing, just held her and let her cry.

And that, she realised, was the moment she knew she loved him. When he asked no questions, told her no stories, only stood with her when the world felt particularly cruel.

CHAPTER 23

Livingston remembered distinctly how it felt as if the earth had fallen away from his feet when he first learned that he had druid blood in his ancestry. The world had gone a little blurry and his heart pounded in his ears, a reminder of what ran through his veins that was impossible to ignore. He remembered the feeling of being alone and afraid when he had been in the midst of the wild storm. Of being so cut off from the world that nothing existed outside the terror of that moment, the leaves and branches swirling around him, the animals prowling towards him with deadly intent in their eyes, growls in their throats. He remembered these things and thought he understood a tiny piece of what Mara felt in that moment.

So he held her and watched the stars and asked nothing of her.

After a while, her shaking and tears subsided and she pulled away from him far enough so that he could look into her eyes. In the darkness, they were as vast as the deepest parts of the ocean, and held just as much mystery. How he could ever have mistaken her for an ordinary person, he would never know. She was everything extraordinary. He never wanted to let her go.

"Thank you," she murmured, lowering those tantalising eyes.

"I will always be here," Livingston said in response, brushing back a strand of her hair as he had done at the garden party. It held a great deal more meaning, now, though he was not sure he had the words to describe why. "I don't care whether you're siren born or a creature who just appeared on the hills to tempt wayward scholars."

Mara snorted. "I've never heard of creatures designed to tempt wayward scholars, unless you refer to books."

"Yes, well, it is a particular failing of ours," Livingston said with a dramatic sigh. Mara smiled, and he thought that it was genuine. "Do you want to stay out here a little longer, or do you want to go inside? I cannot speak for your father, but I imagine that Cait will be worried."

Mara sighed and wrapped her arms around herself, a gesture Livingston recognised as one she used to soothe and comfort herself when she believed that no one else would do so. He knew that he was breaking all bounds of propriety—and had been since almost the moment he met Mara—but he wrapped his arms around her waist and held tightly, just where her arms were. If she needed comfort, he would be all too glad to provide.

"It's been seven years since my father visited. He can only come onto land once in a seven-year period and he always visits on my birthday, for one night. I used to think that it was a special thing, that I was like a princess in a story who had been cursed to only see her family once a decade. And for a while, it worked, and I could be happy, joyful even, when he visited. But now…I've seen the man four times in my existence, spoken with him for perhaps a grand total of five hours, and I'm realising that I know nothing of him, or of what he wants from me. My magic hadn't manifested before, so it never came up. And perhaps I was too young to understand. Or to know what to ask. Now, though…" Mara trailed off with a sigh and leaned her head back to rest against Livingston's shoulder.

"As someone who had parents, I can tell you that their expectations are no easier to meet when you know what they are than when you do not."

Mara tilted her head to look at him. She still had shadows in her expression and he wanted nothing more than to cast them aside. It was easier said than done, however. "I thought your parents understood your scholarly ways."

"They did, to a point," Livingston said with a nervous laugh. "It took many years before my father gave up on his dreams of me being a great man, and my mother hers of seeing me charm society into eating out of my hand. I still do more with society than I would prefer because of the many lessons that my mother drilled into me. It is a difficult habit to break, that deference, especially when it is not necessary. Your father's expectations for you, whatever they are, matter very little in comparison to what *you* want. It is your life, Mara Del Sol, and you have a right to live it."

Mara lifted her head higher and Livingston realised she was looking at the stars. He knew, generally, the constellations that lingered above their heads, but much preferred studying Mara's features in the starlight.

"I've never actually considered it," she whispered. "What I want from my life. I've only ever been concerned with hiding from the ocean, with the consequences of my magic, with keeping my head down. I…I have wanted to fit in with the humans of Tallmadge, but even if I were fully without magic and human, then that would still be unlikely given that I live here with Cait, and the stringent rules society seems to follow."

"You do not have to bend to their whims. You can be extraordinary without them. Nor do you have to decide now," Livingston said. He shifted his weight a little and turned Mara so that he could set her down onto a rock in the field just beyond the garden. He sat beside her. "That's one of the benefits of youth. Taking our time."

Mara chuckled, then did it again until the solemnness she wore like a shroud seemed to fall away, leaving her vivacious self there. "Don't tell Cait that! She'll set you to grinding herbs for a month!"

Livingston smiled broadly. "I would like that."

Mara blinked, looking up at him. She seemed

confused, or perhaps uncertain. But she twined her fingers with his and replied, "Yes, I believe you would."

They sat together a few minutes longer, saying nothing and listening only to the wind over the hills. If Mara had asked it of him, he would have stayed there all night long, waiting for sunrise with her. She was far more sensible than he, apparently, because she rose to her feet and pulled him with her.

"Come, let's go back inside. I *know* you have questions for my father, and this will be your only chance to ask them for seven more years."

"It does not sound like we have that much time," Livingston said, trailing behind her. She hesitated, going still enough that time itself seemed to stop.

"No, I don't think we do."

He wished he had said nothing.

Inside the cottage it was warm, almost stuffy, and everyone was exactly where they had been. Othed sat beside the fire, his hands cupped around a cup of steaming herbal tea. Cait was knitting, which Livingston had never seen her do before. Neither seemed to be talking to the other; the air crackled with tension.

As Mara and Livingston reentered, Othed's shoulders slumped and he seemed relieved. Cait, on the other hand, just shoved her knitting aside. "There, I told you so. You didn't need to send scouts off to the ocean to find them. They were just in the back garden."

"You cannot be too careful right now," Othed countered, sneering at Cait. "Mara is a valuable—"

"Mara is right here," she snapped. "And I am my

own person, not some tool to be traded about like gold. I *know* that the ocean and all its players are seeking me. I have been hunted my entire life! There is nothing more I can do than I have already done except wait. Or have you some way of fighting back that you haven't revealed all these years? No?"

Othed's mouth opened and closed, but he seemed at a loss for words. Livingston rather thought he looked like a fish, wide eyed and gaping; he decided it would be better not to voice that particular statement out loud. Instead, he sat once more on the stool, moving it a few inches closer to Mara's spot beside Cait. This did not go unnoticed by the selkie, and he narrowed his eyes.

"I do not know what interests the sea holds for *you*, son of the earth," Othed sniffed. "Your presence here is highly suspect."

"I am here because I care about Mara," Livingston said, lifting his chin.

"Son of the earth?" Cait asked, quirking a brow. She peered at Livingston as though he were some stranger. "That is a name I have not heard in many decades."

"What is it?" Mara asked. Her voice was perhaps too eager, ready to latch onto any conversational topic that was not centred around her. Had she been anyone else, Livingston would have changed the subject, but he knew her secrets and it was right that she knew his last. Not to mention, he was glad to save her the scrutiny.

He opened his mouth to reply, but Othed got there

first, and he was derisive at best. "Druid born," the selkie spat. "He reeks of it."

"I have been told that I have druid ancestors," Livingston told Mara, determined to keep his voice calm despite the selkie. She widened her eyes a bit. "It is part of why I am so interested in studying magic, because there are no druids remaining left to talk with. Only their ruins."

"Father? Do you know of the druids?" Mara asked. Othed made a huffing sound and wrinkled his nose.

"Druids are not the providence of the sea-born, but I know enough. More than this human, it would seem, though his ancestors are the ones of whom we speak."

The selkie obviously did not like Livingston, and he didn't know whether it was because he was human—druid born, at that—or if it was because he cared for Mara.

He put a hand to his chest and bowed his head. "I would be most grateful if you would tell me what you know, sir," he said in his most charming and humble tone. The selkie blinked as if taken aback.

"Ah, er…The sages of the seas would know best, but I can tell you what I learned when I was but a pup." Othed scratched the back of his neck. "The sons and daughters of the earth were humans who, ah, how was it described…who existed between. They spoke for the earth to the humans and for the humans to the earth. They listened for the words between the land and the stars, the sun and the moon, the day and the night. They lived in the places between light and shadow, and they could interpret between the living and the dead. It's a powerful thing, being between, and dangerous."

A shiver travelled up Livingston's spine, like he was hearing truth for the first time since his quest to discover magic began. He wet his dry lips and tried to formulate the thousand questions that were spinning around his mind. "Do you know why they disappeared?"

Othed snorted. "Why does anything magic disappear? They were forgotten. The humans decided one day that the world no longer needed them, and the druids went to the far-off places between old and new. And there they waited to be called back and resume their place as the ones between. Instead, they were forgotten. At least the Fae chose to leave. And we creatures of the ocean had less need of the humans than the ones who walked among them. We will still exist, even if the humans forget all about us."

"Fool," Cait said sharply. "For generations, your people—*all* your people—have been growing weaker. That is why you so seek after dear Mara, because she stands for a new age that you want to usher in and control."

"I gave her to you!" Othed snarled. "Yet you accuse me of wanting to use her?"

Cait did not rise to the bait, instead sinking deeper into the couch cushions and folding her fingers together. "Perhaps you gave her to me because you *knew* you wanted to use her. It may have been the one decent thing you did, Othed of the selkies."

Othed growled, the sound reverberating deep in his

chest. His features seemed to change slightly, shimmering as if touched by firelight. The pelt wrapped around his waist looked as though it would melt into his skin. But he held onto whatever scrap of humanity allowed him to take this form, instead reaching out with hands to strike at the hedgewitch.

"Enough!" Livingston was on his feet, between the two warring factions before he even knew he had moved. "Your motivations are irrelevant right now. All that matters is keeping Mara safe until after this eclipse on the equinox. If neither of you is interested in putting aside your arguments about Mara's fate, then I suggest you both leave."

"Stand aside, druid," Othed growled.

"I will not," Livingston snapped. He straightened his shoulders and lifted his chin. "You said my people stand between, well that is what I will do. I will stand between the earth and the sea, and I will do my best to protect Mara. That is *all* that matters!"

"Kyle," Mara whispered, reaching out to twine her fingers with his. "You do not need to do this. I can't…I don't know what dangers may wait for you if you do."

He knelt before her, trusting that Cait and Othed would refrain from killing each other for a moment at least. Mara's eyes were once more filled with unshed tears and he could tell she was so close to falling apart completely. He squeezed her fingers.

"I will do this," he murmured. "Because in this life, we get to choose how to live, and I choose to live mine with you."

Mara smiled. She pressed her forehead to his. There

was a moment where he thought she would say something, but instead, a harsh crack filled the air, reverberating from a great distance off. Everyone jumped, but only Cait gasped, her face pale.

"What was that?" Livingston asked, looking around for broken crockery, though he knew it had been no such thing.

"It's been years since I've heard a sound like that, but I'd say that a piece of the cliffs near Tallmadge just fell into the sea."

Othed nodded grimly. "The ocean grows impatient. It will not wait much longer before it demands you return to it, as it demanded the stone break beneath its power."

Mara shuddered, her eyes fluttering closed. Livingston kept a firm grip on her hand; he would not leave her now, no matter what the ocean demanded. What one man, druid born or not, could do against the entire ocean, he did not know, but he was going to do it.

CHAPTER 24

Mara was not certain she had the energy to remain awake for her birthday night, as she had done in the past when her father visited. She was so tired of arguing, of discussing what was to come. She wanted to sleep until all of this was over, and then wake and go about her life. She wanted Livingston by her side, and all of this business with the ocean to just disappear. She wanted to *live*, not just wait interminably.

"Do you plan on staying until the eclipse?" Mara asked her father, perhaps bluntly. She was trying to keep her eyes from closing, some few hours after her father arrived. The hour was well on its way to midnight, yet still they talked. And talked. And talked. Mara remained silent most of the time.

"I imagine I will be called back to the waters to lead the army against the sirens when the time comes," Othed said, leaning back in his chair with a sigh. Livingston shifted on the stool, and it gave Mara a sad sort of gladness to know that he was willing to risk the discomfort of sitting on the uncomfortable old thing for her.

"Then what?" Mara asked.

"What do you mean?" Othed tilted his head.

"My magic is sought after. That's what my entire life has been about. When the time comes, when this eclipse happens, what then? Will you defend me against the selkies and the sirens?" Mara couldn't quite help the bite that clung to her words, though she did regret the flinch from Othed. She was tired and had no patience for dancing around any longer.

He looked between her, Cait, and Livingston, eventually lowering his head. "I do not know. The only defiance I have been able to manage against the others was to bring you here. The others are suspicious of me, have been since they learned of your existence. I thought I was saving you."

"You did," Mara said, though she knew he had not quite understood what it meant to save her life by depositing her amongst the humans. She could tell that decision alone pained her father. A human life, one of loneliness and solitude and learning of human ways and human magic and losing her heart to a human. She may have been born to the sea, but she was more human than siren or selkie. "You did save me. But there comes a point where I will have to save myself from whatever fate awaits me."

Silence rang loudly throughout the room. Mara could tell that everyone there wanted to protest. Cait knew better than to argue. Livingston seemed to be holding his tongue only out of deference to her, though he would likely speak his mind as soon as they were alone. Othed simply seemed to be at a loss for words.

"Father," Mara said, standing and walking over to him. She put a hand on his shoulder. His skin was warmer than any man's and he had a wildness about him that would never be tamed. "You gave me to Cait so that I might live. You do not need to put yourself in any more danger for my sake. I will be alright."

Othed nodded and swallowed. "You will be. You've always been alright, every time I've seen you. Just fine, so happy here, making a life for yourself in ways that I never could have imagined. It gives me great joy to see you grown and strong. As strong—stronger, even— than any selkie."

Mara smiled and kissed her father's forehead. "Thank you. For saving me, and for letting me stand on my own, now."

Othed said nothing more, just smiled and squeezed her hand. Then, with a rush of movement, he stood and threw the blanket back. He nodded his head to Cait, to Livingston, then strode out into the night without a backwards glance. Mara was left wordless in his wake.

"He never was one for long goodbyes," Cait sniffed. "Not something magical creatures really need to worry about, I suppose."

Livingston's fingers twitched, and Mara wondered if he was going to include that tidbit in his book. She sighed and shook her head. This was all too much.

"I'm exhausted. I am going to bed and intend on sleeping until at least noon," Mara announced. When this was met by protests from Cait and Livingston both, for reasons entirely unknown, she just ignored them both and swept from the room to do exactly as she had said.

Only then did she notice that the book Livingston had left on the side table at the beginning of the evening was not one of magic or monsters, but poems. Love poems. She smiled and took it with her, feeling just a touch lighter than before.

***

GIVEN that she had spent her whole life hiding from the ocean, waiting for the inevitable to happen, Mara was exceptional at going about her life. The two day deadline seemed to bring things into sharp focus, and while she knew that the threat lingered constantly in the back of her mind, she was also perfectly content to continue on as before. She felt almost serene in her life, even knowing what was to come. There was a peace in facing a definite deadline, in knowing that all of this would soon be over, one way or another. She felt no need to worry.

The others were worrying enough as it was.

She prepared sachets and tinctures, linen strips for bandages and other such things as were necessary in the business of herbwomen. She gathered herbs for the stillroom and performed her chores around the cottage.

And she ignored her grandmother's pointed looks every time she walked into a room.

On the second day, the day that the eclipse was to happen, Cait kept such a close eye on her that Mara was inches away from throwing a pot of tea at her. Cait was staring at her over a plate of scones, her gaze vivid and direct. Mara did her best to ignore the look, simply reading the morning's post and buttering her own scone. Cait opened her mouth like she was going to say something when someone knocked on the door.

Mara leapt up. "I'll get it!"

She practically flew to the door, ready for any distraction, and nearly slumped in annoyance when she saw Livingston standing there, holding a sad bunch of wildflowers he must have picked on the way up from town. Half of them were weeds.

"Not you, too," Mara sighed.

"Pardon?" Livingston asked, furrowing his brows. He looked to have dressed with special care that day, wearing his usual dark colours, but in clothes that were meant more for sporting than social visits.

"Grandmother has been staring at me all morning, and now *you've* shown up to check on me, too," Mara said. She stepped back from the door and swept her arm widely. "You might as well come in, then. Grandmother has prepared scones."

"I do like a good scone," Livingston said, giving her a sly grin. As he passed her, he paused and kissed her cheek gently. His mouth brushed by her ear and Mara's breath hitched. "I only came to check on you because I care, not because I don't think you can handle whatever this day may hold."

Mara nudged him aside. "Cheeky," she said, and

walked back to her grandmother with her chin held high.

"Ah, Kyle Livingston!" Cait was overly cheerful, her enthusiasm marred by the droplets of tea she spilled trying to fill a fresh cup. "How good of you to come. And you brought flowers!"

"I'm afraid the game is up, Mistress Del Sol," Livingston said with a dramatic sigh. He sank into a chair and handed over the flowers. "Your dear Mara knows that I am here to keep her under lock and key all day."

"I would like that very much, but I think our dear Mara might have something to say about that," Cait said, eye twinkling. Mara resisted the urge to prop her head in her hand despondently. "How about you two go mend the fence in the back paddock? I have been meaning to get to that for ages, and it will get you out of the way for a while."

Mara had no doubt the suggestion was done to appease her, but she gladly leapt at the chance to get out of her grandmother's watchful gaze. As she stood, though, a wave of dizziness swept over her and Mara gasped. Her vision blurred until only the table directly before her was clear. She braced her hands on the table, legs trembling. Vaguely, she recognised the voices of her grandmother and Livingston around her, but making out the words was difficult.

Her heart pounded in her ears and her breath seemed to flow like sludge into her lungs.

"What is happening?" Livingston asked, his voice cutting through the miasma like a knife. Mara tried to reach for him and only ended up swaying. She groaned.

"Her magic," Cait said, all teasing gone from her voice. "It's coming to a head. The manifestation is building inside her and she needs to let it out."

"Why doesn't she?" Livingston asked. Mara thought that it was his hands on her shoulders, keeping her upright, but she wasn't sure.

"Water," she gasped. She couldn't get enough air.

"She's a creature of water!" Cait cried. "She cannot manifest her magic on dry land."

"Will the creek be enough?"

Mara's head was beginning to swim.

"For a time. Long enough to get us to the ocean."

Yes! Take her to the ocean, to the waters that called to her and sang to her, begging her to come and stay where she had been born, where she belonged.

"The ocean? Shouldn't we take her somewhere else? Anywhere else?" Livingston's voice was sharp with worry and Mara wanted to reassure him, to tell him that it was alright, that it was time she face the sea that sang in her blood, but her words had vanished entirely.

"The loch is too far away. The ocean is closer. Can you carry her?" Cait's voice was dark and Mara could feel what little healing magic her grandmother had filling the room. Stabilising her.

She was swept off her feet so swiftly that her head spun. Mara groaned again. The world was turning around her and she couldn't quite keep up. Her head pounded to the beat of her heart and she could feel her grasp on reality slipping away. There, was that sun on her face? The sound of birds or the call of something that would carry her away and into oblivion? She heard the splashing of water and then—blessed relief. Her feet touched down into cool, vibrant water, the life-giving substance that soothed her, guided her, kept her safe.

Her awareness was sharpened then, like she could feel every droplet that touched her feet, soaking through her shoes and stockings. Someone's arms were around her and she clung to them, though she could not entirely remember why.

"Come on, Mara," a voice said, one that she knew. Livingston. Her anchor to the earth so that the sea would not sweep her away. "Walk to the ocean."

"Don't let me drown," Mara breathed.

He squeezed tighter. "Never."

The walk down from the hills was the most perilous that Mara had ever known, with her feet wanting to carry her through the water and her body requiring balance and guidance. She stumbled more than once on ground that should have been sure, with only Livingston's arms to keep her standing. She didn't know how long it took, only that it seemed an instant and also interminable. Every few steps, they walked into the creek, only to emerge and stumble down the hill again. It was agony, and it was ecstasy and it burned her entire being.

Finally, they passed through Tallmadge, full of dull-eyed people who could not see the world that Mara could see. She didn't hear the excuse that Livingston gave for her state, if he gave one at all. All she cared about was the roaring of the ocean that grew louder with each step. The song of the water was particularly eager today, as if it sensed the strength it was gaining from the equinox, the impending solar activity. Or as if it sensed her, and her magic.

Mara felt sand beneath her shoes and kicked off the offending slippers impatiently. She still wore stockings, horrid things that kept her from feeling the sand on her flesh. Scrambling, gasping for breath, Mara pulled those off too. Then, she stepped towards the water.

Something held her back. She turned. A hand held hers, anchoring her, holding her here on the land. She looked at its owner, that dark haired human man, eyes bright with unspoken energy, a scar across his face. Mara reached up and traced the line, feeling the magic that had caused it echoing there, still.

"If I let you go," the man said, his voice deep and twisted with emotion, "will you return to me as I know you?"

Mara smiled, though the movement felt strange. "I do not know."

The man—she loved him, didn't she?—bowed his head and nodded. "Then I will have to hope."

He released her fingers and their hands slid apart. Mara would have to walk these last few steps alone. She turned to the water and at once felt the impossible longing in her heart to go to the place that was always meant to be, that was always denied her. She took a step, the water rushing up onto the shore to meet her. It stopped a scant inch away from her bare toes. Mara shivered.

She was not certain that this was a good thing, this rush of power in her head, power that would be hers as soon as she moved into the water. But nor could she resist it. So she stepped into the water, sucking in a deep breath as the enormity of the ocean hit her all at once. She took another step and heard the song and symphony of the waters that had been denied her for so long. Another step, and she could feel the multitudes of life that called these waters home. Another step, then another, and the water was up to her waist, caressing her, coaxing her. Another step, and she was swimming despite having never done so in her life. A wave came in and surged for her.

Mara did not resist. She did not worry about the air in her lungs or what fate awaited her. She merely closed her eyes and let the wave carry her under, submerging her in the sea.

Welcome home, a presence said, as old as the world and as fresh as the rain.

Mara's eyes snapped open.

CHAPTER 25

The sea was singing to Mara.

It had always sung to her, at least in the sense that she could hear its wants and desires, know what mood it was in, know its movements. She could hear the song in the storms, the waves upon the shore, all the touches of the water against the hulls of boats. It had been Mara's gift for as long as she had known magic, though it had grown in specificity and knowledge over time.

This song was something entirely different.

It resonated through her body, shaking her bones until they nearly ached with potential. It rang through her head, waking thoughts in her head that she didn't know she had. It wooed her and it cursed her in the same note, calling forth the magic that swam in her blood.

And when Mara opened her eyes in the gloom of the salt water, the song rose to a deafening crescendo, in which she could hear the ocean's words.

You have awoken, it said, tone gleeful.

Mara swam easily, her arms barely twitching to hold her in place beneath the waves. In this northern water, the ocean was dark for many leagues in every direction, only a light blue around herself and at the surface to light her way. She felt no need for air, nor for warmth when she knew, rationally, that she should have needed both. No, here, she met the ocean on equal ground.

"Yes," Mara said, surprised at how clear her voice sounded, even muffled by the water. "I have awoken."

Very well, then, child of twain. Choose.

"Choose what?"

The ocean laughed, increasing some of the pressure against her body. Mara pushed back with her own ability and felt the pressure lessen.

The ocean growled, pushing back, testing her. *Siren or selkie. You cannot be both, and your magic must have a shape.*

"I do not want either," Mara said with a surety she had never known about her own heritage, about what she was. She just wanted to be herself.

You do not have a choice, foolish child. The magic within you demands shape, form. Or, and here the ocean swirled around her, trying to spin her in circles and disorient her. Mara refused to be disoriented. *Or, it will burn you up until you drown.*

"I want neither selkie nor siren," Mara insisted. She wasn't even sure she wanted this magic, though it was a part of her so deep that she could not extract it if she wanted to do so.

Choose, the ocean insisted. *You have little time.*

She sensed that the attention of the waters shifted to the world above, at a place so distant that it was an impossible dream, yet affected its very movements and moods. Mara tilted her head towards the surface. The light that had been there, as bright as midday could ever be, was fading fast. An unnatural darkness was starting to descend. The eclipse. She could feel it in the pull on the water, the change in the tides. Her magic rose in anticipation.

With the peripheral senses of her magic, now amplified by the water, she could sense other movement as well. There were vast numbers moving towards her, drawn inexorably by the call of her unformed, unclaimed magic. The battling sides of her family, the sirens and the selkies, exactly the people the ocean demanded she choose between, were approaching to stake their claim.

Choose! The ocean was insistent. Mara sensed something deeper in its distress, something that had more to do with a lack of balance and order than anything. It needed her to choose, she realised, before the war beneath its waves tore its inherent magic apart and left it just a dead husk, a body of water at the mercy of the wind and the currents and nothing more. Just another piece of magic, lost.

That was why the ocean wanted her. Not to kill her, not to subjugate her, to beg her to save it.

Mara felt her power swell further. She closed her eyes again and tilted her head towards the surface, where Livingston waited. Everything was so clear to her now, where before it had been muddied by the unformed nature of her magic, of her mind and her soul.

CHOOSE! the ocean screamed.

Mara spread her hands, magic strong enough to tame the tides at her fingertips. "Very well," she said. "I choose."

Her magic took form as the two armies converged on her spot, reaching for her with arms outstretched and teeth bared. Mara gave a wave of her hands and the currents shifted, pulling them both back, away. Then, she gestured towards the surface and the water obeyed, dragging selkies and sirens both to the air, where they would be on a more equal footing. Mara rose with it, the water supporting her every movement and whim, swirling around her and caressing her.

When she emerged from the water, she was clad no longer in homespun cottons and linen, but in pearls like the one at her neck. They were in a myriad of colours and sizes, ranging from pearlescent white to cream to gold and blue and black with traces of red thrown in. Each one sang with magic that resonated with her own, ready to do her bidding. Her hair was dark with water and plastered to her skin. Her limbs felt enervated, more sure of themselves than they had ever been. And at her fingertips, storms swirled.

"Daughter of song," a siren called, beautiful and enticing, her blonde hair sticking to her head and her smile wide. This was not her mother, Mara knew, but another trying to claim kinship where there had never been any. "You are *magnificent*."

"To you, siren, I am nothing," Mara snapped, lightning snaking over her skin.

"What of us?" a selkie, large and male and definitely not her father, swam closer, his seal's whiskers twitching as he took in her scent. "We have allowed your father to visit you every seven years, surely that must mean something?"

Mara scoffed and flicked her finger, sending streams of water towards the selkie, pressurised enough to have him yelping as he retreated. "You think that deigning to let my father live and visit me once every seven years is a kindness? That I will fall on my knees and ask you to take control over my life?"

The selkies started huddling closer together, barking softly between themselves. The sirens were doing similar things, whispering to one another and eyeing Mara warily. She saw, at last, how few of each there were and felt pity for them. A scant hundred made up the entirety of both sirens and selkies, each already marred with scars of doing battle. They were so desperate to claim control over the waters and its dying magic that they had hunted each other to near extinction. No wonder they sought Mara.

"This is not a battle you can ignore, child," an ageing siren said, swimming closer. Her dark skin was riddled with scars that looked like they had all been made with teeth. Seal teeth, likely. "The ocean is your birthright, and it is at war."

"It is at war because you *choose* to be at war," Mara said. "Do not drag me into your mess!"

The siren surged forwards, arms outstretched,

mouth wide as if preparing to sing. Mara raised an arm and sent a wave of her magic pulsing out in all directions, just so they could feel what she had chosen, what she truly was now. Neither siren nor selkie. She would not take sides.

She felt it when her magic hit the shore, petering out on the wet sand as though it had hit a wall. Some of it rubbed off on the two figures standing there, watching, and Mara felt a shock wave of an entirely different sort of magic answer her own. It slammed into her and rumbled through her bones, making her gasp. It was familiar, deep and ancient, and yet Mara was certain she had never felt its like before. She fell to her knees, the water still supporting her, but barely.

One moment of weakness was all it took for the sirens and selkies to attack, each trying to lay their claim. They raced for her, cutting through the water with ever increasing speed.

Above her, the sky turned nearly black as the eclipse reached its totality.

Sound dulled.

The water seemed subdued.

But the magic surrounding the warring factions, each desperate to erase the other and use Mara to do it? The magic surged upwards.

One arm was snatched by a hand with slight webbing between the fingers. The other was grasped in seal jaws that clamped down tight enough to draw blood and turn the water red. Mara was pulled beneath the waves.

The darkness of the eclipse made the depths almost

impossible to navigate by sight alone. Mara cursed and struggled against the opposing forces, her storms extinguished by the waves. The siren at her left arm was digging her nails in deep, pulling Mara as far down as she could. The selkie, likewise, dragged her down. The ocean floor here was fairly shallow as it was close enough to land that it hadn't yet fallen away into unfathomable depths. But it was deep enough that the surface disappeared entirely from view and the pressure of the water closed in.

Mara was not going to give in so easily. She forced the currents to hold her still. Then, wrenching against the hold of both her captors, she pulled her arms free. There were large gashes on both forearms, bleeding freely in the water. She could sense creatures coming closer, some little more than sharks, others ancient and eager for a taste of magical blood.

With her power heightened by the eclipse, Mara willed her wounds to heal. Then, she reached both arms out and pulled the currents towards her, taking the siren and the selkie with them. Mara finished her dive to the bottom of the ocean and pinned her assailants there.

"You will destroy both your parents," the siren hissed, her expression ugly and her voice twisted with rage. "You will be the end of the magic in the sea."

Mara scoffed. "Your two peoples have already done that. Don't you see? You are fighting each other relentlessly, picking each other off one by one! Generations of this, I imagine, since the magic of the world began to fall away, leaving what little remained for you two to fight over. But it is *you* and not me that will drive your peoples to an end!"

"You were born to this war," the selkie barked, writhing against Mara's hold. "Your power was meant to end this war once and for all, to see the ocean finally at peace!"

Mara bit back a laugh. "The ocean told me, before you came to net me into your schemes of self-destruction, that I had to choose. One side or the other, and yet look at me now." She waved a hand over her dress of pearls, the hem floating gently in the water. "Do I look like a selkie? A siren? I made my choice and it was neither of you! I refuse to take part in this ridiculous war. I will bring balance by being myself, not a pawn in your games. You have hunted me my whole life, making me fear the water which should have been mine to explore. You have threatened to kill me, my family, any humans who get involved. And yet you think I would fight for you?"

The siren hissed, baring her teeth. Her eyes were wild, shifting between Mara, the selkie, and the surface, as if she could sense the eclipse. Mara looked up, also, and laughed.

"The eclipse will not last forever," she said. "You need this war to end now or both of your people will be dead, slowly, painfully. Well, the answer to you and the ocean is, once again, no!"

Another selkie had found them and was swimming around the perimeter of Mara's hold on the first two attackers. It was agitated, swimming back and forth as if it wanted to go to her and could not. The seal she had in her hold hissed at the newcomer.

"Traitor! Your daughter has abandoned us in our time of need!"

Her father. Mara flicked her eyes to him and he stared back, teeth showing in a nervous look.

"Mara, my child, what did you do?" he asked, his voice wavering. Of all the possible futures they had discussed, this had obviously not been one that crossed his mind. For a moment, Mara wondered what he would have done had she chosen the selkie side of her. Would he have been proud?

She did not know, and she found she did not particularly care, either, which saddened her all the more. Her father, who gave her up to save her, had become no father to her at all.

"I picked something other than what everyone else wanted for me. I chose my life. I chose to end this war on *my* terms instead of everyone else's." Mara laughed drily. "I became a being that hasn't been seen in the waters of the ocean for generations. A sister to those who live on land, whose powers have been forgotten or sucked away by those who wished to use them as you wish to use mine. I am the last sea witch, father, just as I am also the first. And this squabble, this battle between you must end now or you will tear the ocean and all its people to pieces, like driftwood against the rocks. And I will not save you."

Her father reared his head and retreated a few feet. Then, softly, "There is no other way, my child, for this war to end but in blood."

"I chose my life amongst the humans, finding my way there though I never belonged to them. I gave them my heart! I can find a way for the ocean, which has always held my soul."

Another blast of magic, much like the one that had struck Mara down earlier, sought her out, and this time, she recognised it, impossible as it was. Livingston. Her resolve wavered, and in that brief moment, she was not fully part of the sea, nor of the land, but something in between. Something that did not belong beneath the waves. She was Mara, a human born of the sea who had lost her heart to a druid and saved the ocean by making her own choices. She lifted her chin and stared down the selkie and the siren she held in her currents.

CHAPTER 26

Watching Mara disappear beneath the waves was enough to stop Livingston's heart. After all his research, his time spent investigating every aspect of magic that he could find, after making himself an expert on the topic, he could do nothing but stand on the shore and watch as Mara vanished.

It was the worst thing he'd ever experienced. It was also completely necessary.

"What do we do now?" he breathed to Cait, who had caught up to him on the beach, her breath coming in sharp gasps after having moved so quickly from the cottage.

"We can do nothing but wait. I don't know of anyone who could help her now, not a witch, not the sirens or the selkies or anyone. Not even the Fae, if they were still around." Cait wrapped her arms around herself, just like Mara was wont to do. Livingston put his arm around her shoulder and held her close. Cait did not cry, but she shuddered as if holding back tears.

The sky darkened as the eclipse started, the moon eating away tiny bites of the sun. Livingston's heart clamped in dread the longer Mara was beneath the waves.

Then, something happened. A shock wave, or something very like it, resonated across the water, creating ripples and stopping the waves in their tracks as they hurtled towards the shore.

"Hold on," Cait gasped, staggering backwards. Livingston did as she told him and braced his weight to hold himself steady, though it did no good. As soon as the wave of whatever it was—Mara or the ocean, for surely nothing else could create a magical echo like that—hit, his legs buckled and his body went lax. He fell to the sand in a heap and his vision went black.

He wasn't unconscious, surely, for he could still hear the roar of the ocean and feel the grit of the sand beneath him, each particle rich with life and history of rocks and creatures that had once been and now were not. Beneath the sand was bedrock, stronger and deeper than any water the ocean could batter it with, though it endured such attacks every moment of every day. And farther afield, towards the hills, the earth teemed with life so numerous it nearly deafened him.

He tried to take a breath, but it was impossible. The pressure on his lungs was too great. Or was it his mind that was under pressure? Thoughts like he'd never experienced before raced, sending out pulses of energy that felt ancient and patterned, yet new and unshaped.

Livingston sucked in a breath, sinking his fingers into the sand, the flecks as numerous as the stars.

The stars.

As if his vision had suddenly cleared, yet the facts of reality had faded away, he stared up at the sky and found it black, speckled with tiny flames. They seemed to whisper to him, their voices soft as the breeze, calling out to him and supplicating.

"I do not understand," he croaked, though he was not sure whether he actually spoke the words out loud. He tried reaching for the stars and only succeeded in moving his thoughts, not his limbs. They flew outwards like wind rippling over grass, and the effect was so strong that it blinded him.

When the spots cleared from his vision, he saw a tree, branches twining together like the roots, ancient and vibrant and full of sparks that could have been nothing but magic.

You have awakened, a multitude of voices whispered, the effect disorienting. They were ancient, numerous, and quiet.

"A-awakened?" Livingston asked, suddenly aware that he could no longer feel the sand beneath his fingers nor the air over his skin. He was alone in this empty place with nothing but himself and the tree, and the voices that echoed all around.

Long has the earth slumbered. Long have the stars been silent. Long has magic withered away. You have awakened, and so the legacy is yours when once the world shakes off this sleep.

Livingston shook his head. "Wait a moment. You are telling me, what, that I'm responsible for waking up magic?"

The voices were silent, but he sensed a general feeling of disapproval, so akin to the looks that professors at the university would give him when he was just a student that he knew he was wrong. They weren't telling him he was responsible for waking up magic. So what where they saying?

"I don't understand," Livingston said, his own voice barely a whisper though he wanted to scream. "Is this to do with my book?"

A compendium on magic? No, for you need no such thing. Magic is in your blood, was in your ancestors' blood. Dormant, waiting. The right moment has come and you are awakened. Do you deny this right?

Understanding dawned on Livingston and he instinctively backed away from the tree. "My druidic ancestry, you mean. My druid blood. That's what's awoken."

He wanted to pace, to reason through this like the scholar that he was, but magic didn't seem to apply to the rules of well-reasoned scholarship. In fact, if anything, he had learned that it was illogical, impractical, hardly ever reliable. Only those who knew how to use it seemed to understand its mechanics, no matter how often it was explained to him. He loathed that disorder, especially as he tried to organise his manuscript into reasonable, logical sections. He had been terrified of magic, then insatiably curious and now...

Well, now there was Mara. And though he had fallen for her long before he knew of her magic, of her own bloodlines, he had known that magic was as inextricably twined with her life, as he longed to be. So he had tried to understand, to let go of his fear. And he had.

Until now, standing before the reality of his own existence. Something Mara had done when her own magic manifested had started something in him, shaking his druid bloodline awake. It was there, in that tree, vast and magnificent and imposing and impossible. Terrifying.

He did not know if he could claim the right that was being offered him.

The voices remained silent, as if they had said all they could and the rest was up to him. If he turned away, his life would likely continue on as before. A scholar searching out research and trying to present it in such a way that people could understand. He was trying to discover that which had been lost, to learn about how it worked, how it interacted with the world around it. He liked to think himself a scientist, but he was also an historian. He could travel around until he grew old, seeking out more material. And he would never likely understand it the way a true mage could.

Then, Livingston thought of Mara. Below the sea, likely battling with her own newly manifested magic as well as the sirens and the selkies. They would try to control her, to capture her and for her to do their bidding. If her magic was strong enough, she could hold them off, but for how long?

Livingston would give up his books, his travelling research, his position at the university for a life with her in it, and he could not do that if she were dead at the bottom of the sea, torn apart by her own people in their desperation.

He reached out and placed his hand against the tree. He had enough time to note that it felt like any other tree, rough and ancient, before the sparks swirling around the trunk rushed towards him. There was no time to pull away. He tried to gasp, but there was no air.

Magic felt like nothing he had imagined. The shock from Cait's spellwork was just a tiny tingle compared to the lightning that coursed through his blood. He was fairly certain he screamed, but there was no way to tell when all his senses were overwhelmed and blinded. Suddenly he could feel every ripple of energy in the earth, just as he could feel the influence of the stars. It was like someone had ripped away a shroud over his vision and he could see for the first time. He was blind, overwrought, and so truly *aware*.

Aware enough, even, that he could feel Mara and her adversaries on the ocean floor. He could never get to them there, so he reached out and called the land to him. It was an impossible request, one that likely never could have been fulfilled had not the eclipse overhead been channelling magic in its own right. Just then, in that moment, everything was more receptive.

The earth obeyed.

The ocean floor, ancient and immovable, rose up as though there were an earthquake splitting the seas. It sent ripples through the ocean, warning all the creatures there of the magic that had awoken once more. Mara, a siren, and two selkies collapsed onto the land spur as it rose through the waters, unable to flee under Livingston's power. The other two armies, few and desperate, separated, screeching their dismay.

With a crash, the spur broke through the waves, a new point off the coast just large enough for two people to walk abreast. Livingston trembled, his hold on the land tenuous at best now that he had burned through the initial surge of magic. He took enough time to smooth out the sea floor from the tumult before collapsing to his knees, thoroughly spent.

Overhead, the light began to change as the moon passed beyond the reach of the sun and the eclipse began to end. The stars—for who else could those voices be—whispered still in his ears, though it was faint.

You will be the first of many, druid. The ones who speak for the earth and the stars. And your tasks will be varied and vast, for you and your sea witch have shaken what little magic remained into a state of waking. It will return, earth-born, and no one can stop it, now.

"Fine," Livingston murmured. He would face the consequences of his actions, of choosing magic over reason and science, of choosing the unknown and untamed over the rigid rules of society, at a later date. Right then, he had just enough energy to stand and walk towards Mara on the new spur of land.

His legs felt wobbly and he was certain he would collapse when someone wrapped an arm through his.

"Lean on me," Cait said, her voice steady even in the middle of this chaos. "I'm strong enough for that."

He smiled. "I would never doubt that."

"Good. Then at least you're not completely foolish, if you are rash in your actions." Cait snorted and shook her head. "A land spur? You pulled up an entire piece of the ocean floor just to, what, protect Mara?"

It did sound rather excessive when she put it like that.

"I'm not sure I have the energy left to put it back," Livingston admitted. They were almost halfway along the spur, now, and getting closer to Mara. Cait tightened her grip on him as he stumbled again.

"We'll deal with the consequences later," she murmured. "Right now, I want Mara safe. I don't think anyone in this fight is going to give her up so easily. The eclipse is over and I can *still* feel her ambient magic in the water."

The water that was now brushing at their shoes, trying to reach over the newly formed land, reclaim what was its right. The tides were high, so it could not take back the earth completely, but the ocean was nothing if not relentless.

"Mara," Livingston called when they were a few feet away. She was still on her knees, still reeling from what he had done, but she looked at him over her shoulder with something akin to relief. He released Cait's arm and went to her, collapsing to the ground rather than even attempting to help her stand.

"Kyle," she murmured, bringing up a hand to brush his face. "What did you do?"

He scoffed. "I am an expert in magic, my love. Surely, you cannot expect me to know what just happened!"

She chuckled, but the sound was weak, weary. Just beyond her, the siren and the selkies were both struggling to regain their composure. The seals gave off sharp barks then flopped towards the water, becoming increasingly graceful as they submerged. The siren pointed a webbed finger at Mara and Livingston, hissing.

"You have made a grave mistake, human. Your interference will not be tolerated!"

Mara rose to her feet, the dress of pearls she wore shimmering in the returning noonday light. Livingston remained where he was, exhausted. Instead, he admired her from the ground, the way the sun caught in her hair, turning it to copper and gold, the reflection of the ocean in her eyes, the storm at her fingers. Magnificent, he thought, that righteous anger pulsating off of her in waves like the relentless sea.

"You are the ones who have made mistakes," Mara snarled, raising a hand. The sky above started turning dark again, this time with storm clouds that crackled with energy. "More than once you have tried to attack me, attack what is mine. I have told you, I *choose no sides*! And if you wish to test me, truly test me, then I wish you would so that I could send your bodies to depths so deep that you will never be seen again, your bones crushed from the pressure of the water and lost forever to the sky. There is nothing to fight over! You want control over the ocean? Well you have *lost it* to me. To the magic that has awoken inside me."

The siren hissed and lurched for Mara, unsteady on legs that were hardly ever used for walking. With an almost careless flick of her hands, Mara sent a spray of water straight for the siren and knocked her down, her head hitting a rock. The other sirens let out a keening sound.

"Truly, do you wish to try again? To battle against a sea witch?" Mara asked, lifting her chin high. She turned to the selkies who were swimming on the other side of the land spur, their movements agitated. "And you? Do you concede to my power?"

A seal that Livingston hoped might be Othed gave a sharp bark and a nod of the head before corralling the others back from where Mara stood. The sirens were trembling—with fury or fear, it was impossible to tell— but they, too, backed away.

Mara nodded. "Good. Because if you cross me even once, I will not be merciful. The ocean is vast enough for the both of you, but not if you choose to incite warfare. From now on, this spur of land is your boundary. Cross it and you will bring my wrath down upon you all."

She clapped her hands just as the last vestiges of the eclipse vanished. Her storm dissipated in a flash of lightning. And from the tip of the spur, an invisible line was drawn as far as the horizon, marking the new borders of the oceanic kingdoms. Livingston could feel the magic in the water like electricity racing up his spine and he shivered.

Mara watched the two peoples, her two peoples, vanish into the waters. Then, without warning, she wavered and collapsed, landing nearly on top of Livingston. He wrapped his arms around her.

"You did it, my love," he said, pressing a kiss to her forehead.

"I have a feeling this is going to be just the beginning," Mara murmured. Livingston chuckled.

"You may be right. Apparently, I'm a full druid, now. Something you did woke up whatever latent abilities lay within my blood and now I can hear the stars talking to me, and apparently communicate with the earth, too." He gave a bark of laughter.

"Yes, well, I'm now the first sea witch in several generations," Mara said, sighing. "It looks as though we may have set something in motion."

"I'm willing to see it through if you are," he said. Mara—his beautiful, marvellous Mara—just smiled up at him and kissed him gently, tasting of the ocean.

"I am more than willing, my love," she said.

CHAPTER 27

Two days. That was how long Mara slept off her magical exhaustion after the events at the ocean. She woke feeling sore in every muscle, but able enough to venture down the stairs to the kitchen. Her body still sang with magic attuned to the sea, but it was nothing like the flood that had overtaken her during the eclipse. She found these levels far more manageable.

Cait was in the kitchen, bustling about as though nothing had changed. She moved between a cauldron of what smelled like a tincture for arthritis, and a pot of soup. It was normal, something Mara had seen nearly every day for most of her life. But what had changed was that Livingston was there, too, dressed in his shirt-sleeves and with his hair mussed, as though he had also just awoken from his exhaustion. He had a cup of tea before him, as well as several pieces of toast and some slices of apple and cheese.

"Ah, you're awake!" Cait said. She dropped a cup of

tea at Mara's usual spot and filled it to the brim. Mara could smell several herbs—lavender, chamomile, some verbena—and assumed that it had been spelled as well. "Your young man had you beat by half-an-hour. Do you know how much trouble it was getting you up the stairs? You fell asleep, the both of you, on the cart ride back to the cottage and I had to bribe the butcher's son with free poultices for sore wrists for a month so he would help me with the two of you. Hmph!"

"Hello," Livingston said with a sheepish wave, ignoring Cait's diatribe entirely, as though he, too, had been doing this his whole life. "Apparently our bodies have to adjust to the new levels of magic. I must say, it's rather different learning about it from this side of things than as a researcher. I haven't quite figured out how to filter out the noise. The earth is surprisingly loud."

Mara chuckled. She shuffled over to him and pressed a gentle kiss to his head. He beamed in return and Mara felt a warmth inside her that had nothing to do with her magic. Happiness, peace, love, she didn't have a proper name for it, but she would happily seek it out every day for the rest of her life. "You have a great deal to learn, I think. As do I."

"Indeed!" Cait put her hands on her hips. "A sea witch? Really Mara, I understand the impulse to not be siren or selkie, but you had to choose a sea witch? All the creatures of the ocean will be clamouring for your attention to tend to petty squabbles. Potions and hurts and wishes and spells. Pah! Not to mention the humans hereabout when they discover your affinity for storms!"

"Storms?" Mara tilted her head. "People don't have an affinity for storms. They have affinities for water and earth and air and fire, and a few other small things besides. But not storms."

"Yes, well, you're hardly most people." Cait sniffed, her nose high. "I've already sent missives out to the other hedgewitches I know to see if any have books on sea witches. You have a great deal of learning to do before I let you anywhere near sea magic! Not to mention you're going to have to learn a whole new set of herblore and medicines. Land plants will hardly be beneficial to you now!"

Mara couldn't help but smile. She had been worried for so long that it was difficult to comprehend living life without the burden of being hunted by the ocean and all its creatures on her shoulders. She hadn't thought this far ahead when facing the sea, nor had she ever considered what life would truly be like if she did not have to worry about being hunted day by day. She never considered exploring the full depths of her magic. She never thought of any of it. And now, she had a whole future ahead of her. She could even learn to swim! It was enough to make her head spin. Well, it would be, if not for Cait's scolding words bringing her back down to earth.

Cait and Livingston, who looked just as over-whelmed as Mara felt. He nibbled at some toast and flashed her a look. Mara laughed.

"You needn't look so contrite, my love," Mara said,

brushing a crumb from his cheek. "I have no doubt that the hedgewitches will be more than happy to educate you as well. Surely some of the ones you haven't spoken with yet will have information about druids. There are some that are quite eccentric indeed and fancy themselves masters of ancient lore. I remember an old hedgewitch named Cedric; he loved telling stories in his letters about druidic ruins. Don't you remember, Grandmother?"

"That's another thing!" Cait exclaimed, glaring at Livingston. "A druid! You *had* to have druidic magic, didn't you? No affinity, thank goodness, given that druidic magic encompasses so much already. You'll have to learn the rituals for the changing of the seasons, the march of the stars, not to mention when things are best planted, what the earth sounds like when it's winter versus summer, the proper ways to question the future, how to cast runes—"

"Mistress Del Sol," Livingston said, reaching out to take Cait's hand. He wrapped it in both of his own and graced her with a gentle smile that had Mara's skin tingling. "I appreciate your concern, and I shall be sure to make a note of everything that you brought up today and shall likely bring up in the future. After all, there are a great many things that will be requiring our attention—magically speaking—from now on. I thank you for your toast, and for taking such good care of me after the eclipse. But, for now, I really must take my leave of you and go speak with my housekeeper."

"Your housekeeper?" Mara's grandmother looked astonished and a little offended. "Whatever for?"

"So that she does not worry over my absence for the last two days. I know you made excuses about a summer fever, but I really must see her for myself. And also to make certain that when I bring home a new bride, she does not over do things and make a fuss."

"Your new bride?" Mara asked, quirking a brow. She was fighting to keep back her smile and had a feeling she was losing that particular battle.

"Provided she'll have me, of course," Livingston said with a gleam in his eyes. "I would very much prefer to learn about the ancient magics we have awoken with you at my side, but if you prefer to stay here in this cottage, then I will not argue. Granted, I'm not sure Alder House is the most comfortable of residences, given it's size. Perhaps your grandmother would be kind enough to let us build a second cottage here. Or on the cliffs, if you prefer being closer to town. I'm sure we can figure something out. Of course, I'll have to sort out my property in town, and then there's the matter of the university—they'll be terribly annoyed at me for giving up my research project, but I'm sure I can come up with something new that will satisfy them and keep my academic standing in good order. Perhaps a study of ancient runes, if I am to learn about the druids. Or—"

Mara leaned in, close enough to press her forehead to his. He stopped talking immediately, eyes widening at her proximity. "You plan on giving up your research?"

He shrugged and ran a hand through his already messy hair. "I think I am the wrong person to tell the world about magic. I so wanted to be the one to rein-troduce magic to the world, but…I understand so little of it. And I have so much to learn about my own magic, now. It…I think…there will be someone better suited to tell that story."

Mara brushed her hand across his cheek, cupping his jaw. "For what it's worth, I think you would have written a *wonderful* book. Especially now, druid mine."

He replied with a weak smile. "Do you really think so?"

Mara nodded. "I do. And if you want to keep researching, keep writing, I will support you whole-heartedly—though I reserve the right to tell you if you are being boorish."

Livingston chuckled. "Stars and stones, I love you."

Mara bit her lip. "I love you, too."

"You *will* marry me, won't you?" he asked, breath barely more than a whisper. Mara realised it was the one question in his tirade she had not answered.

"I will marry you, strange, wonderful man. On one condition," she whispered. "That wherever we go on our honeymoon, we are a stone's throw from the sea."

Livingston laughed, tossing his head back. He leaned in and kissed her once. Twice. Then he smiled against her mouth and kissed her again, just for good measure. "That can be arranged, dear heart. That can most certainly be arranged."

THE END.

ACKNOWLEDGMENTS

As always, I would first like to thank you wonderful readers. I appreciate every one of you and am so thrilled you picked up my book!

Thank you also to my family, who keep putting up with me when I'm in Writer Mode (which is, let's be honest, most of the time) and don't really interact with the world.

Special thanks to the critters in my life, who force me to interact with the world. ;)

And a huge shoutout to my cover designer, Fay Lane, who managed to create the beautiful design from a "it has to look like the first book, but with water!" to something truly spectacular. Thank you!

ABOUT THE AUTHOR

Evelyn Grimald is a romance author who believes wholeheartedly in love, magic, and the power of words. She has been writing since childhood and since then has pursued her passion for words through a study of linguistics, which she applies to her stories. When not writing, she reads voraciously, herds her cats and dog, draws and sews.